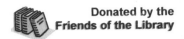

**Donated by the
Friends of the Library**

# MR. MONK IN TROUBLE

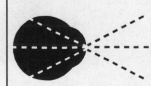

# MR. MONK IN TROUBLE

*A novel by Lee Goldberg*
*Based on the USA Network*
*television series created by*
*Andy Breckman*

**THORNDIKE PRESS**
*A part of Gale, Cengage Learning*

GALE
CENGAGE Learning

Detroit • New York • San Francisco • New Haven, Conn • Waterville, Maine • London

LIBRARY OF CONGRESS CATALOGING-IN-PUBLICATION DATA

Goldberg, Lee, 1962–
    Mr. Monk in trouble / by Lee Goldberg.
        p. cm. — (Thorndike Press large print mystery)
    ISBN-13: 978-1-4104-2486-0 (alk. paper)
    ISBN-10: 1-4104-2486-3 (alk. paper)
    1. Monk, Adrian (Fictitious character)—Fiction. 2. Private investigators—Fiction. 3. Eccentrics and eccentricities—Fiction. 4. Psychics—Fiction. 5. Large type books. I. Monk (Television program) II. Title. III. Title: Mister Monk in trouble.
PS3557.O3577M775 2010
813'.54—dc22                                    2009049409

Published in 2010 by arrangement with NAL Signet, a member of Penguin Group (USA) Inc.

*To Valerie & Madison*

# ACKNOWLEDGMENTS AND AUTHOR'S NOTE

Portions of this book are set in Trouble, a fictional California mining town, in the mid-1850s and I have taken a few historical and geographical liberties to suit my creative needs. I hope you can forgive me.

I am indebted to Dr. D. P. Lyle and Katherine Ramsland for their medical and forensic advice; Richard S. Wheeler, Ken Hodgson, and James L. Reasoner for their wisdom on frontier mining and the Old West; William Rabkin, Grant Logan, and Ripley Hilliard for helping me uncover the legend of the Golden Rail Express; David Breckman for his initial enthusiasm for the idea of this book (and for the contribution of a very funny joke), and finally to my friends and colleagues Andy Breckman, Kristen Weber, Kerry Donovan, and Gina Maccoby for their continued support.

Several reference books were extremely helpful to me in my research: *California Gold and the Highgraders* by F. D. Calhoun, *The Writer's Guide to Everyday Life in the Wild West* by Candy Moulton, *How the West Was Worn* by Chris Enss, *Black Powder and Hand Steel,* and *Western Mining* by Otis E. Young Jr., and two volumes in the Time-Life Old West Series: *The Forty-Niners* by William Weber Johnson and *Miners* by Robert Wallace.

Some continuity notes: The story in this book takes place after the novel *Mr. Monk and the Dirty Cop* and before the events chronicled in the final season of the *Monk* TV series.

For many years on the TV series, and in all of my previous books, Monk only drank Sierra Springs bottled water and nothing else. Recently, however, the producers abruptly changed Monk's favorite water from Sierra Springs, a brand which really exists, to the fictional Summit Creek without any explanation. I have done the same.

While I try very hard to stay true to the continuity of the TV series, it is not always possible given the long lead time between when my books are written and when they are published. During that period, new episodes may air that contradict details or situations referred to in my books. If you come across any such continuity mismatches, your understanding is appreciated.

I look forward to hearing from you at www.leegoldberg.com.

# Prologue

## The Extraordinary Mr. Monk

*(From the journal of Abigail Guthrie)*
*Trouble, California, 1855*

A dream killed my husband, Hank Guthrie, before his twenty-fifth year.

We'd been working this barren patch of dirt in Kansas, trying to make it into a farm and having no luck at it, when he read about all the gold that was sprinkled on the ground out West in California.

The newspapers said the riverbeds there were lined with gold and that anybody with two good arms, a shovel, and a tin pan could earn at least a hundred dollars a day without breaking a sweat. It sounded too good to be true, but that didn't stop every poor farmer from catching gold fever anyway.

My Hank was one of them.

I tried to talk sense to him, but his mind

11

was set on abandoning the farm, packing up what little we had, and heading to California.

I could hardly blame him for wanting to go.

When you're killing yourself trying to grow a crop in a land as ornery, dry, and infertile as my old granny, you want to believe there's an easier way.

I knew California couldn't be the paradise of gold that the newspapers made it out to be, but I figured we couldn't be any worse off than we already were. Besides, I was raised to obey my husband no matter how thickheaded, foolhardy, and stubborn he might act.

So in 1852 we teamed up with four other families and went west. Along the way, we lost nearly all of our cattle and had to toss our stove, our dishes, my momma's candlesticks, and just about every possession we had to lighten our load. Those losses were nothing compared to the human toll. Half of our party died of cholera.

The way west was littered with valuables, graves, and animal carcasses from Kansas to California. More than once during those long, brutal months I wondered what wealth could await us that could match what we'd all lost.

I took it as a bad omen of what was to come. If that wasn't enough of a sign, the first California mining camp we rolled into was named Trouble.

I'd have preferred to stop in a place called Opportunity, Happiness, or Serenity, but I suppose it could have been worse. The place could have been called Futility, Misery, or Death, all of which would have been a more accurate description of what awaited us.

It certainly wasn't a pretty place. The main street was a mire of mud, sawdust, rocks, and horse droppings with an occasional wood plank or two flung atop it to make crossing less of a slog.

Everything looked like it was erected in a hurry by people with little regard for outward appearance, skill in construction, or any thought of permanence.

Most of the structures were one-story, with log walls and sawed-timber storefronts with tall, flat cornices of varying heights. There was also a smattering of shacks, log cabins, and tents of all kinds, some crudely cobbled together out of boughs and old calico shirts. The hotel was a lopsided, two-story building with a sagging veranda. There was a wood-plank sidewalk on each side of the street and plenty of hitching posts.

I didn't see a church, but that didn't mean

13

one of those tents didn't contain a preacher or two. In my experience, preachers and gamblers always showed up where there was whiskey and money around.

The men on the street looked like they'd all just crawled out of their graves. They were covered in dirt. It was caked to their tattered wool shirts and patched britches, it dusted their mangy beards and ragged hats and it clung to their hair, which was slicked back with wagon-wheel grease.

If there were womenfolk around, they were either in hiding or hadn't emerged from their graves yet. Seeing the menfolk, I couldn't blame them for keeping out of sight.

The only evidence of prosperity that I could see was the existence of the camp itself, and as ugly as it was, it was a strong indicator. Trouble wouldn't have been expanding, or even been there at all, if there wasn't gold to support it.

Hank and I might have passed right through, and probably should have, but he couldn't wait to stick his pan in a river. He found some flakes of gold in that first pan of gravel and was so excited about it that he staked himself a claim right away, convinced that we were sitting on our mother lode.

We weren't.

When that patch didn't pan out, we worked our way up and down that river, never straying far from Trouble, staking new claims, hoping we were just one pan away from striking it rich.

We didn't know much about geology but we'd learned that gold was easiest to find in gravel bars where the river widened and bent or where it once did. Gold being heavier than other minerals, the flakes and nuggets would settle in, sometimes near the surface, and sometimes down deep.

The gold wasn't hard to recognize. There was the color, of course, and the soft way it felt when you bit a nugget in your teeth, not that we found many nuggets.

The gold was there — that was for sure — but getting enough of it out of the ground to make a living was backbreaking, soul-bleeding work that was much harder than farming. But gold fever kept men like Hank going in a way that farming never could. There were too many people striking it rich all around us for him to ever stop believing that it could happen to him. The fever blinded him to the pain, futility, poverty, and hardship.

I didn't have the fever. But I had a marriage and a man that I loved. Keeping them both healthy and strong was what kept me going.

We lived in a tent so we could move wherever the gold was. I kept house, cooked our meals, and sometimes patched and sewed up clothes for some of the other prospectors in exchange for necessities while Hank worked our claim.

A man had to pan half an ounce to an ounce of gold a day, about sixteen dollars' worth of color, if he wanted to survive and set a little aside for the lean days.

But we rarely panned more than six dollars a day worth of color, roughly six pinches of gold dust, and with molasses at one dollar a bottle and flour going for fifty cents a pound, we could barely keep ourselves fed.

Most of the time, our bag of flour was worth more than our pouch of gold.

I tried to convince Hank to give up on prospecting and try something else. We argued about it for most of that first year until I finally just gave up and resolved to do my best to support him, no matter how wrongheaded I thought he was. That was what I'd been taught that a good wife was supposed to do.

Two years of panning in the cold river water, day in and day out, bowed his back and swelled his joints. It got so bad that he couldn't stand and could barely breathe. And even then, with all those ailments, his biggest ache was the desire to pan for more gold.

They say it was rheumatic fever that killed him, but I know better.

It was the dream of gold that did him in.

His death left me alone but not without assets. I had our claim, our tent, and his tools, but they weren't worth a sack of potatoes. What I had worth something was my body.

Women were scarce in Trouble, so the instant Hank was buried, I became as rare and valuable a commodity in those parts as gold.

There were a couple of ways I could mine that value.

I could marry a wealthy man, of which there were few, most of whom were living in their San Francisco mansions while others toiled for them in the mines.

Or I could become involved with many less prosperous men, of which there were multitudes, most of whom were willing to pay a pinch or two of gold to enjoy a woman's affection for a short time.

Women who engaged in that sort of barter were called sporting women and lived in rooms behind the saloons. They were generally held in higher regard than such women back East, perhaps because the population in Trouble was mostly made up of lonely men in desperate need of their services. That might also explain why vices that weren't tolerated back home were taken so casually in the mining camps, whether it was drinking, gambling, whoring, or murder.

A few of the sporting women did all right, made enough money to support themselves until they could find a man with plenty of gold — and low moral standards — to marry, and move on. But it seemed to me that most of the women died young, taken by syphilis, abortions, or suicide by laudanum.

I tried to survive instead by sewing and laundering for the miners. But there weren't many men willing to part with their hard-earned gold dust on something as frivolous as clean clothes that were just going to get dirty again the next day. They felt their gold was better spent on whiskey, food, and sporting women.

However, there was one peculiar and extraordinary man who valued cleanliness and order above all else.

I'm talking, of course, about Artemis Monk, Trouble's only assayer.

I've heard it said that assaying — analyzing stones and such and determining the mineral content — is the third oldest profession after doctors and sporting women.

Every prospector and miner came to Monk with their rocks so he could determine how much gold was in them, the quality of the gold, and estimate the potential yield of their claims. That made him easily the second or third most important man in Trouble.

There was either something very unusual about the geology of Trouble, or unique to Monk's calculations, because the various minerals in the samples he analyzed always showed up in even amounts. He attributed it to the "immutable balance of nature," but if that was so, the rest of the world was unbalanced.

As odd as that was, the fact remained that Monk always turned out to be right in his estimates of the worth of a claim and anybody who ever questioned his conclusions eventually found that out for themselves the hard way.

But even if you never had business with Monk, you certainly knew who he was. Monk stood out. He was the only clean-shaven man in the camp, his hair was neatly trimmed and he bathed every day, which in

19

itself was astonishing. He always wore the same thing — a derby hat with a domed crown and a flat, round brim, a long-sleeved white shirt buttoned to the collar, a sleeveless vest with four pockets and four buttons, wool pants, and fine black boots.

His clothes were always clean. I know, because I was the one who cleaned them — not that I ever found a speck of dirt or the tiniest stain. He brought me his clothes neatly folded. They looked as if they'd never been unfolded, much less worn, but I figured if he wanted me to wash clean clothes, so be it. I was in no position to turn down work.

Monk seemed very pleased with my laundering and came back to my tent by the river almost every morning. I never saw him on a horse or even near one. He seemed repulsed by the animals. He got where he was going on foot or by railroad.

One day he showed up at my tent to find me gone and my tent empty, so he searched the town for me. He found me outside one of the saloons with my trunk at my side.

I was trying to swallow down my misgivings and enter the sporting life. It must have been obvious to him what was going through my mind.

"You can't do this," he said.

"I don't have any choice, Mr. Monk. It's the only thing of value that I have to sell."

"You are excellent at laundering," he said. "Nobody here has ever done it better."

"I can't survive doing that."

"But I need you," Monk said.

"And I need food, a warm place to sleep, and a roof over my head."

"Done," he said.

I turned to look at him. "What do you mean?"

"I'll hire you," Monk said. "You can live in the spare room in my office."

I eyed him warily. "What do you expect in return, Mr. Monk?"

"Not what you are prepared to give in there, Mrs. Guthrie," he said, tipping his head towards the saloon. "I need an assistant to keep my life clean and orderly. It's becoming too much for me to handle alone and still do my work."

We settled on a price, one that would sustain me and allow me to set a little aside so that I could someday return to Kansas.

He accepted my terms so quickly that I wondered if I'd set my price too low. But I was grateful for the opportunity and I moved in that day.

It was a purely chaste arrangement though I'm sure nobody believed that.

21

I didn't care what they thought. All that mattered to me was that I wouldn't have to become a sporting woman, at least not yet.

I soon discovered that keeping his life clean and orderly involved far more than simple housekeeping and that his skills, and service to the community, extended beyond detecting minerals in rocks.

Artemis Monk solved crimes.

# CHAPTER ONE:
# MR. MONK AND THE
# TRICK

Adrian Monk dreaded Halloween.

He didn't like people coming to his house, he was afraid of children — whom he called "two-legged rats" and "plague carriers" — and he considered trick-or-treating a form of extortion. So I always tried to be around on Halloween night to keep him out of trouble.

Actually, it's also what I do every day as his full-time assistant. Monk has an obsessive-compulsive disorder and an encyclopedic list of phobias that make day-to-day life a challenge for him, and everybody around him, especially when he's out solving murders as a consultant for the San Francisco Police Department.

But staying with him on Halloween went far beyond the call of duty.

It wasn't as much of an imposition now that my daughter, Julie, was well into her teens and past the age of trick-or-treating herself, but it still wasn't much fun. I would have much preferred to be at a Halloween party somewhere, like Julie was, or even sitting at home answering the door to trick-or-treaters.

Of course, it could have been worse. At least we weren't spending Halloween with Monk's agoraphobic brother, Ambrose, like we did a few years back. That night, Ambrose was nearly murdered by poisoned candy from a deranged killer, but that's another long story.

The point I'm trying to make is that you don't want to spend Halloween with Adrian Monk if you can avoid it. You are guaranteed to face embarrassment or murder, usually both.

I hoped that this Halloween would be different. He wasn't looking forward to it much, either. From the moment it got dark, Monk stood in the entry hall, staring warily at his front door.

"You don't have to stand there like that," I said.

I was curled up on the couch reading trashy magazines that I'd brought along so I could catch up on all the news. There was a big, important feature in the *National Inquirer* on what Hollywood stars look like without their makeup and another in *Star* on who had what done where to their bodies.

"They're coming," Monk said. "I just know they are."

"You don't have to be a detective to know that," I said. "It's Halloween."

"It's a night of unremitting terror," he said.

"That's the general idea," I said.

It would be easy to dress up as Monk on Halloween because his clothing style is so rigid and consistent that it's practically a uniform. His 100 percent cotton shirts were always off-white, with exactly eight buttons and a size sixteen neck, which he buttoned at the collar. He wore a brown sports coat and Hush Puppie shoes tied with perfect bows. His pants were crisply pleated and had eight belt loops around the waist.

Monk lived in a ground-floor, street-front apartment in a Deco-style, two-story apartment building that he admired for its streamlined look and perfect symmetry.

His neighborhood had somehow retained its homey charm, eclectic mix of architectural styles, and middle-class affordability even though it was only a few streets away from Pacific Heights, an old-money neighborhood known for its elaborately ornate Victorian houses, manicured gardens, and extraordinary bay views.

Most of the families on Monk's block knew better than to stop by his door on Halloween but there were always some newcomers each year who didn't get the word.

I hoped that the word would spread fast that night.

"The streets are full of little monsters," he said, peering anxiously through his peephole.

"They're children wearing masks."

"Of course they are," Monk said, looking back at me. "So nobody can identify them."

"They aren't doing anything illegal," I said.

"They're terrorizing me," Monk said. "Terrorism is a crime. This is probably how Osama bin Laden got started."

"Trick-or-treating," I said.

"It's possible," Monk said.

The doorbell rang and he went to answer it. I jumped up and joined him as he opened the door.

Two little kids, around five or six years old, stood on his doorstep dressed as a ghost and a mummy. They were absolutely adorable. Their parents stood behind them, all smiles. The mother held a tiny camcorder.

"Trick or treat," the ghost said and held

out her bag of candy. She had a slight lisp because she was missing some of her teeth.

"I choose treat," Monk said. "But I want you to know that I am doing it under duress."

"You don't have to choose, Mr. Monk," I said, standing behind him.

"They wouldn't make the demand if they didn't expect an answer."

"It's not a demand," I said.

"You're right," Monk said. "It's a threat. You have to perform for them, or pay them off, or you'll have to bolt the door, turn out all the lights, and hide in your closet until they stop tormenting you or the sun finally rises."

I smiled at the parents, who had shell-shocked looks on their faces.

"Your children are adorable," I said. "Cherish it while you can. Pretty soon they'll be surly teenagers who are embarrassed to be seen with you."

I was talking too much. I do that when I am nervous. I should have stopped at *adorable.* Now they were looking at me as if I were as strange as Monk. I stopped myself before I started to explain that I wasn't like him at all, that I was a rational, normal, psychologically stable parent just like them.

Monk picked up a bowl from a side table

and held it out to the kids.

"You can each take two," Monk said.

"What kind of candy is that?" the mummy asked, peering into the bowl.

"It's not candy," Monk said. "It's something much better."

The parents took a step forward and looked suspiciously at what he was offering to their kids.

"You're giving them Wet Ones?" the father said. The bowl was full of packets of moist towelettes.

"Your kids really lucked out this year," Monk said. "I got the party size."

"We like Snickers," the ghost said.

"They will rot your teeth and make you fat," Monk said. "Haven't you lost enough teeth already?"

"It's not from candy," I said. "It's normal for children at her age to lose their teeth."

"What about that flab?" Monk said, gesturing to the little girl's tummy. "Is that normal?"

"That's not flab," the mother said indignantly. "That's baby fat."

"Fat is fat," Monk said. "And she's a fatso."

The mother gasped. So did I.

The father scooped up his daughter protectively and tugged his son away from the door. "C'mon, let's go."

"What about our candy?" the mummy whined.

"The awful man doesn't have any," the mother said.

The mummy started to cry. So did the ghost. Monk immediately closed the door, practically slamming it in their faces. Crying children terrified him — too many tears and too much mucous.

"My God," Monk said. "What is wrong with those people?"

"You called that little girl a fatso."

"She is," he said. "And if she keeps knocking on doors without disinfecting her hands, she'll be a sick little fatso."

"You can't talk to children that way," I said. "You'll traumatize them."

"That makes us even," he said.

"You're not going to endear yourself to them by calling them names and giving out disinfectant wipes."

"I'm stopping the spread of disease," Monk said. "They'll thank me later."

"They'll egg you," I said.

"See?" Monk said. "That's what I've been saying all along. It's extortion."

There was a knock at the door. Monk opened it. Two teenage boys stood outside. One looked like he had an ax in his head,

29

with dried blood all over his face. The other kid had a very convincing alien bursting out of his chest in a spray of internal organs.

I was impressed. Monk was repulsed.

"I choose treat," Monk said before either one could speak. He threw two packets of disinfectant wipes in each of their bags and slammed the door shut, throwing his back against it in case they decided to come in after him.

"You know that's just makeup, right?"

"They're a disgusting mess," Monk said. "How can they go out in public like that? They should be ashamed of themselves."

"It's Halloween," I said.

"It's insanity."

"A little insanity is good sometimes," I said. "It keeps you sane."

"That is the dumbest thing I've ever heard," Monk said.

"Haven't you ever wanted to just let loose and do something wild? It can be exhilarating."

"You mean like drinking water out of the tap?"

"I was thinking of something a bit more reckless than that."

"You mean like putting a loaded gun to my head and playing Russian roulette?"

"There's a big middle ground between

drinking tap water and playing Russian roulette."

"No, there isn't," he said. "They are exactly the same thing."

"One can kill you," I said.

"They both can," he said. "I don't see anything fun about suicidal behavior."

"Who said anything about suicide?"

"You did," he said.

"I didn't say anything about risking your life. I meant doing something wacky and outrageous, just for the fun of it, without caring what anybody might think of you. Haven't you ever wanted to do something like that?"

"No," he said.

"I think that's sad," I said.

"I've never stuck my hand in a blender and switched it on, either," Monk said. "Do you think that's sad, too?"

"I'm talking about dressing up in costumes and having a good time on Halloween."

"You're talking about insanity," he said. "You'd have to be crazy to dress up as a corpse, knock on a stranger's door, and demand a performance or candy. On any other night, we'd arrest people for doing something like that."

"This isn't any other night," I said.

31

"It should be," he said.

I felt the onset of a throbbing Monkache in my head. I decided to stop arguing with him before I had a stroke.

There was another knock at the door. Monk opened it. A young man stood outside. I pegged him to be in his twenties. His white shirt and blue jeans were splattered with blood. He held a bloody knife in one hand and a grocery bag full of candy in the other.

"Trick or treat," he said.

"Aren't you too old to be out trick-or-treating?" I asked.

"It's like Christmas," he said. "You're never too old to act like a kid."

He had a good point.

"I choose trick," Monk said and decked the man with a right hook.

The man dropped like a rock, out cold.

I stared at Monk in shock. "What did you do that for?"

"Call Captain Stottlemeyer," Monk said, taking a disinfectant wipe from the bowl and tearing it open. "Tell him there's been a murder."

"Don't worry," I said. "He's unconscious, not dead."

"I'm not talking about him," Monk said, wiping his hands with the moist towelette.

"I'm referring to the woman that he stabbed to death twenty minutes ago."

# CHAPTER TWO:
# MR. MONK AND THE
# PIRATE

I put on a pair of rubber gloves, rolled the unconscious man over, and bound his hands behind his back with duct tape while Monk laid newspapers down in his entry hall.

I dragged the man inside and onto the newspapers just as a pack of trick-or-treating kids and their parents showed up at our door.

They took one look at what we did to the last trick-or-treater and moved along to the next house.

I kicked the door closed and faced Monk. "I hope you're right about this."

Monk examined the man's bag of candy and bloody knife, which he'd placed on a piece of newspaper on the dining room table.

"It's obvious," he said. "He was covered with blood and carrying a knife."

"It's Halloween, Mr. Monk. There are hundreds of people out there covered in blood and carrying knives."

"That's what he was counting on," Monk said.

"How do you know?" I asked that question a lot in a typical day with Monk.

"Fake blood is red," Monk said.

"So is real blood," I said.

"But it changes color as it dries, becoming a rusty brown," Monk said. "That's real blood on him and on his very real knife."

I turned and looked at the man, who was beginning to moan as he regained consciousness.

"It doesn't mean that the blood came from a murder," I said. "Or that it's even human."

"I don't know many animals that wear perfume, though I wish they would."

Before I could ask him what he meant by that, there was a knock at the door. I opened it expecting the police but instead faced a group of costumed kids. They all looked past me to the bloody body on the floor as they said "trick or treat" in unison.

"Cool corpse," a vampire said.

"You should have a pool of blood underneath him instead of newspapers," a wicked witch said.

"I'm trying not to stain the floor," Monk said as he picked up the bowl and began dropping towelettes in their bags. "Where did you get the Reese's Peanut Butter Cups?"

"The house with tombstones out front," a werewolf said.

"How about the Three Musketeers bar?" Monk asked.

"The house on the corner," the vampire said.

"You should take it back and ask for a Four Musketeers bar," Monk said.

"There's no such thing," the vampire said.

"Then don't eat it," Monk said.

"Why not?" the witch asked.

"It's odd," Monk said.

"Not as odd as getting a Wet One," she said.

Monk closed the door and set down the bowl.

"Why did you hit me?" the man on the floor said with a groan. "Why am I tied up?"

"Because you're a deranged psycho-killer," Monk said.

"It's a costume, you idiot," the man said. "Let me go."

"You're covered in real blood," I said.

"It's chicken blood," he said.

"You butchered a chicken?" I said.

"I strive for authenticity," he said. "Untie me right now."

"The police are on their way," Monk said.

"You better let me go before they get here or I'll have them arrest you both for assault and kidnapping."

"You're saying you don't want to be here when the police arrive," Monk said.

"I'm saying that *you* don't want me to be here," he said. "Think about it."

"I have," Monk said. "I know exactly what happened."

Someone knocked on the door. Monk opened it to reveal a flamboyant pirate brandishing a plastic cutlass above his head. He wore a three-pointed hat, a wig with beaded dreadlocks, a frilly shirt, a skirted frock coat, and harem pants. There were even some beads on the twisted ends of his bushy mustache.

"Yo-ho-ho!" Captain Stottlemeyer said.

"You look great," I said.

"I was on my way to a party when I got your call," he said, sheathing his plastic cutlass. "If we hurry, I can still make it."

"Help!" the man on the floor cried out, squirming towards the door. "These crazy people are holding me hostage."

Stottlemeyer stepped inside and regarded our prisoner on the floor as if it weren't an unusual sight at all. He took most things in stride. I think that was his overall coping mechanism. It certainly helped when dealing with Monk but it was a skill I'd yet to master.

"You missed a 'yo,' " Monk said.

"What?" Stottlemeyer said, shifting his gaze back to Monk.

"The pirate greeting," Monk said. "It's yo-yo-ho-ho or yo-ho, yo-ho."

"No, it's not. It's a classic pirate shanty." Stottlemeyer began to sing and do a little jig, much to my delight. *"Fifteen men on a dead man's chest, yo ho ho and a bottle of rum —"*

"Who cares?" the man on the floor interrupted. "Look at me. I've been attacked. I need help."

"They were clearly drunk from all that rum or they would have said 'yo yo ho ho,' " Monk said. "Everybody knows that."

"I guess that makes me a drunken pirate," Stottlemeyer said.

"Not doing two 'yo's would be like Santa not doing four 'ho's before wishing you a Merry Christmas."

"Santa only does three." Stottlemeyer dug into his pocket and pulled out his badge, which he showed to the man on the floor. "I'm Captain Leland Stottlemeyer, San Francisco Police. Who are you?"

"Clarence Lenihan. Your friend is insane,

as you obviously know. If you'll release me now, I won't press charges and you can get him the help he desperately needs."

Stottlemeyer nodded and turned to Monk. "What have you got to say for yourself?"

"Ho-ho-ho-ho, Merry Christmas."

"About him," Stottlemeyer said, tipping his head towards Lenihan.

"He had dinner tonight with a woman at 178 Pine Street and then stabbed her to death."

"He's out of his mind!" Lenihan said.

Stottlemeyer nodded, took out his cell phone, and called Lieutenant Randy Disher, his eager-to-please underling, and asked him to stop by 178 Pine Street on his way to Monk's apartment.

"You believe this lunatic?" Lenihan said to the captain.

"It can't hurt to check," Stottlemeyer said.

"It's absurd! What he's saying is impossible," Lenihan said. "He only took one look at me, for God's sake."

"You're wearing a confession," Monk said. "The blood covers your clothes in distinct impact spatters that show exactly how you stabbed her."

"I told you, it's chicken blood," Lenihan said.

"There's too much blood for it to be a

chicken," Monk said.

"There was more than one chicken," Lenihan said.

"There would be feathers and down stuck to you."

"I picked them off," he said.

"You can't imitate spatter like this," Monk said.

He explained that stabbing a person is a lot like slapping the water in a bathtub. The water splashes, creating a spray of droplets. The same is true when you stab someone. Even where you stab them, like in a major artery or in the heart, can affect the kind of spatter it creates. And when you continue stabbing, raising your knife up and down, you cast off blood in long streaks.

Monk pointed out the spatter and the streaks on Lenihan's shirt and pants and a partial bloody handprint that the victim left on his sleeve as she tried to defend herself.

"Judging by the spatter patterns, the streaks, and the relative dampness of the blood," Monk said, "I am certain that forty minutes ago, this man fatally stabbed a woman a dozen times."

Stottlemeyer nodded. He was familiar with spatter patterns and how to read them, but he'd also learned long ago not to intrude on Monk's summation of the facts in a case. It was one of the few pleasures Monk had in life and the captain wasn't going to deny him that.

Besides, once Monk showed him the spatter patterns, they were clear to Stottlemeyer, too. But things that were immediately evident to Monk often took others a long time to see for themselves — if they even saw them at all.

I can see how that would make a person feel blind and stupid, though it was easy for me to shrug it off. I wasn't a cop. Monk's brilliance didn't invite comparisons to my own detecting skills.

I believe that most of the time Stottlemeyer's appreciation for Monk's abilities outweighed his feelings of inferiority, especially in situations like this, where there weren't other cops around to make him self-conscious about his relative failings.

"How do you know the victim is a woman?" Stottlemeyer asked.

"He reeks of perfume," Monk said.

"I like to wear a nice floral scent," Lenihan said. "So do a lot of men in San Francisco. That's not a crime."

"How do you know the murder happened after dinner?" I asked.

"He stabbed her with a steak knife that's part of a six-piece dinner set and dribbled salad dressing and butter on his shirt."

Stottlemeyer shook his head in disbelief. "He's covered in blood and you're still able to pick out the food stains."

"That's what I'm saying," Lenihan declared. "It's impossible."

"Maybe for you and me and just about everybody else on earth," Stottlemeyer said. "But not for Monk."

I'd seen Monk solve at least a hundred murders and I never stopped being amazed by his detecting ability, much of which could be attributed to the peculiarities of his obsessive-compulsive disorder. His need to organize everything, and to avoid filth and germs, gave him a keen eye for details.

"How do you know which house it was?" Stottlemeyer asked Monk.

"I backtracked the candy in his bag," Monk said.

"You know what candy everybody in the neighborhood is giving out?"

"Several miscreants have already come by and I saw what they had in their bags," Monk said. "I know where they live and the route they took to get here. The candy I didn't recognize I asked the miscreants about."

"Miscreants," Stottlemeyer said.

"And terrorists," Monk said.

There was a knock at the door. I opened it to find Lieutenant Randy Disher standing there, two uniformed officers behind him. Disher wore his usual off-the-rack jacket and tie, but for some reason he was also wearing sunglasses.

"Monk was right," Disher said as he stepped inside. "There's a dead woman in that house. Her name is Monica Tyler and she lives alone. I found her by the dining room table. She must have been stabbed at least a dozen times."

"Exactly a dozen," Monk said.

Stottlemeyer looked down at Lenihan. "You want to tell us what happened?"

Lenihan just glowered at him.

"I didn't think so," Stottlemeyer said. "Take it away, Monk."

"It wasn't a premeditated murder. Lenihan was at Tyler's house for dinner and they got into an argument," Monk said. "He stabbed her with the steak knife in a fit of rage, then staggered out of the house covered in blood. There were people all over the street. He didn't want to stand out, so he tried to blend into the crowd of bloody trick-or-treaters, to hide in plain sight."

"It might have worked," Stottlemeyer said, "if he hadn't knocked on your door."

Disher sneered at Lenihan. "Do you feel

lucky today? Well, do you, punk?"

Lenihan kept his mouth shut. Stottle-meyer stared at Disher and shook his head.

"What?" Disher said.

"Just read him his rights and get him out of here," Stottlemeyer said.

Disher read Lenihan his rights. Stottle-meyer put the bloody knife in an evidence Baggie and handed it, and the bag of candy, to one of the two uniformed officers. The other officer lifted Lenihan to his feet and led him away.

I was used to the fact that Monk couldn't go anywhere without encountering murder-ers and dead bodies along the way. But now he didn't even have to leave his own home for it to happen. Murderers were literally knocking on his door.

I found it a very unsettling development but the only thing that seemed to disturb Monk about it was the bloody newspapers on the floor.

"I need to clean up," he said and dashed into the kitchen to get his cleaning supplies.

Disher nodded. "A man's got to know his limitations."

"Mr. Monk certainly does," I said.

Stottlemeyer glanced at his watch. "I think we can still make it to the party if we hurry. Do you have your costume with you,

Randy?"

"I'm wearing it," he said in a low grumble.

"Who are you supposed to be?" I asked. I knew, of course, because he'd been quoting lines from the character since he'd walked into Monk's place, but I enjoyed teasing him.

Disher took a step towards me, clenched his teeth, and snarled. "Go ahead, make my day."

"George Bush?"

"No." Disher grimaced.

"Shrek?"

"No." Disher grimaced.

"Elmer Fudd?" Stottlemeyer said.

"Dirty Harry Callahan," Disher said.

Stottlemeyer looked at him dubiously. "You think that all you've got to do is put on a pair of sunglasses and you're Dirty Harry?"

"I've already got the badge, the gun, the attitude, and the intimidating physical presence," Disher said. "All I really need is my own catchphrase and I'm him in real life. I already get mistaken for him all the time."

I gave him a skeptical look. "You do?"

"Tourists always want to have their picture taken with me," Disher said.

"Dirty Randy," Stottlemeyer said and headed for the door. "That's you."

45

"That's what they call me on the street," Disher said, following after him.

"What street?" Stottlemeyer said.

"My street," Disher said.

"I haven't heard that on your street."

"I've heard it," Disher said.

"What your mother says doesn't count." Stottlemeyer turned and winked at me as he closed the door behind him.

# CHAPTER THREE:
## MR. MONK ARRIVES
### IN TROUBLE

Monk had no problem examining a dead body without flinching, but he couldn't live with the thought that there might be a speck of blood on his door or in his apartment. It was one of the many bewildering contradictions in his character.

He spent the next two days scrubbing and disinfecting his entry hall before he gave up and decided that the only reasonable course of action was to replace his front door, refinish his floors, and repaint his walls.

That was actually the compromise that I got him to accept instead of gutting the apartment entirely or moving out and finding a new place to live.

Monk was trying to figure out where to go while the workers remodeled his place, and I was telling him all the reasons why he should stay with his brother, Ambrose, when Stottlemeyer called and said that he wanted to see us at headquarters right away.

On the drive over, I continued to make my case for him to stay with Ambrose.

"It's the home where you both grew up and you can sleep in the familiar, safe, clean surroundings of your old bedroom," I said. "You could even pass the time with your rock shining kit."

"There's only one problem," Monk said.

"What's that?" I asked.

"My brother is crazy," Monk said. "I can't take the stress."

"Now you know how I feel," I said. I regretted the words the instant they were out of my mouth and quickly covered for my gaff. "Living with a teenager is hell. They are so moody and unpredictable. Sometimes it's like Julie has a split-personality disorder."

Monk nodded. Not only had he bought it, but I think it might even have made him reconsider what I knew was coming next. He wanted me to offer to let him stay at my house.

I'd let him spend a few days with me when his building was being fumigated and it was not an experience I wanted to repeat.

"And she makes such a mess," I said, trying to underscore my earlier point. "There's hair all over the bathroom, bras hanging from the curtain rod, and she leaves half-

48

eaten food on the living room couch."

Monk shuddered. I smiled to myself. Mission accomplished.

As we came into the squad room, Disher was walking back to his desk with a cup of coffee. He kept bumping into desks and chairs on his way, fumbling around like a blind man. It wasn't until he sat down at his desk outside of Stottlemeyer's office that I saw why.

He was wearing sunglasses that were so darkly tinted they were practically a blindfold.

"Why are you wearing sunglasses?" I asked him.

"The glare," Disher said.

"There's no glare in here," I said.

"There is on the street," he said. "You'd understand that if you'd ever been out there."

"We just came in from the street," I said.

"I'm not talking about that street."

"What street are you talking about?"

"The mean street, lady, the grimy, blood-stained stretch of asphalt where I enforce the law," Disher said. "Disher's Law."

"Oh," I said. "*That* street."

"At least there wasn't any gum on it," Monk said. "You can wash dirt and blood off the street pretty easily. But gum is a living hell. People who spit out their gum should be put in prison for life."

Disher snarled. "Out there, a cop has to squint straight into the harsh glare of corruption, filth, and despair, and without shades, it'll roast your eyeballs out and incinerate your soul."

Monk looked at me. "I need sunglasses."

I smiled at Disher, though he probably couldn't see it with those sunglasses on. He reminded me of Julie when she was a little girl. It took her a week to stop wearing her Halloween costume everywhere. She hated to give up the fantasy of being the Little Mermaid or a Teletubby.

Stottlemeyer opened the door to his office. "If you two are done chatting with Dirty Randy, I'd like to have a word with you."

"We're done." Disher reached for his coffee cup and grabbed his pencil holder instead. He lifted it up for a drink and spilled pencils on his face as we followed Stottlemeyer into his office.

"Did you find out why Lenihan murdered my neighbor?" Monk asked.

"Yeah. They'd been dating for a couple of months. He killed her because he was tired of her always overcooking his meat."

"You're kidding," I said.

"It was also too salty," Stottlemeyer said. "He likes his steaks a certain way."

"I don't understand how anybody could make a life-or-death issue out of something so insignificant," Monk said.

Stottlemeyer and I both stared at him.

"It's not like she was serving him food on a chipped plate," I said.

"Or letting his vegetables touch his meat," Stottlemeyer said.

"Exactly," Monk said. "His priorities are all out of whack."

Stottlemeyer rubbed his temples and took a seat behind his desk. "Forget about Lenihan. He's not the reason I wanted to see you."

"I know why you asked us to come down here," Monk said.

"You do?" Stottlemeyer said.

"You wanted to apologize to us," Monk said.

"For what?"

"Desecrating Christmas," Monk said.

"How did I do that?"

"You said that Santa only does three 'ho's."

"That's not why I asked you down here," Stottlemeyer said. "I need you to do me a favor."

Monk shook his head. "I won't even

consider it until you apologize."

The captain looked at me. I shrugged. We both knew Monk would never let this go. Stottlemeyer sighed.

"Okay, Monk, I'm sorry I said that Santa Claus goes ho-ho-ho and not ho-ho-ho-ho. Satisfied?"

Monk shook his head again. "What does a pirate say when he greets someone?"

"Yo-yo-ho-ho," Stottlemeyer answered with a pained look on his face.

Monk smiled. "You're forgiven. You may proceed."

"Thank you. This is about a friend of mine, Manny Feikema. You may remember him."

"Wasn't he a beat cop in the Tenderloin for decades?"

Stottlemeyer nodded. "That's the guy."

"The last time I saw him was May 17, 1997. He had a stain on his tie," Monk said. "It was spaghetti sauce."

"He retired about five years ago and moved to Trouble, a tiny old mining town in the California gold country. Manny got bored after only a couple of months, so he signed up as a security guard at the history museum they have there. He was glad just to get out of the house and wear a uniform again."

"I hope he isn't still wearing that tie," Monk said.

"He was killed two nights ago while doing his rounds."

"And the tie?"

"Forget about the tie," Stottlemeyer said. "The man was murdered."

"I suppose if he's cremated with the tie on, that will solve the problem."

"I don't know what he was wearing, Monk. I just know that Manny is dead and that whoever killed him is still out there," Stottlemeyer said. "That's the issue that concerns me."

"Manny was doomed from the start," Monk said.

"Because of his tie?" I said.

"Because of where he lived," Monk said. "The place is called Trouble. It's a warning sign that he blithely ignored at his own peril."

"It was common for Old West towns to have colorful names," I said. "Like Tombstone, Hangtown, Cadaver Gap, Gnaw Bone, Purgatory, or Deadwood. It doesn't mean anything."

"Would you retire to a place called Misery?" Monk asked.

"If it was nice," I said.

"How about a place called Filth?"

"I don't think there's a place called Filth," I said.

"That's because nobody would live there," Monk said, then turned to Stottlemeyer. "How did you hear about Manny's murder?"

"The chief of police out there contacted us about Manny's cases on the off chance someone with a grudge might have come after him to settle a score," the captain said. "I've got Dirty Randy checking to see if anyone Manny put away has been released from prison lately. But what the request tells me is that the local yokels don't have anything to go on."

"What did the thieves take?" Monk asked.

"Nothing. Manny must have spooked them before they got what they were after."

"What do you want me to do?"

"Catch the son of a bitch who did this."

"Can't the local police do that?"

"Trouble only has a three-man police force, not counting the chief. They don't have the experience or the resources to solve a murder," Stottlemeyer said. "Manny may have retired, but he was still a San Francisco cop as far as I'm concerned. We owe him our best. And that's you, Monk. I'd go up there myself but I'm all out of vacation days.

So I'd appreciate it if you'd look into it for me."

"It's perfect timing, Captain," I said. "Mr. Monk needs to be out of the house for a few days anyway."

"I can't do it," Monk said.

"Why not?" I said.

"Tumbleweeds," Monk said. He was terrified of them.

"What do tumbleweeds have to do with anything?" Stottlemeyer said.

"It's an Old West town," Monk said. "The Old West is where tumbleweeds like to tumble."

"I'll protect you," I said.

"How?"

"If any tumbleweeds come along, I'll throw myself in front of them."

"You'd do that for me?" he asked.

"Just like I did when you were nearly hit by that runaway dandelion a few weeks ago."

"It's not the same thing," Monk said. "Tumbleweeds are like dandelions on steroids."

"I'm willing to take that chance if it means catching a cop killer," I said. "Don't you think that's worth the risk?"

Monk sighed and looked at the captain. "All right, I'll do it."

The little I know about the California Gold Rush I learned back in grade school, so you'll have to forgive me if I'm a bit sketchy on the details.

The gist of it is this: In 1849, workers at Sutter's sawmill on the south fork of the American River stumbled on some flakes of gold. The accidental discovery sparked a stampede of hundreds of thousands of people into Central California from every corner of the world to seek their fortune. They became known as the forty-niners.

Whenever someone found a flake of gold in his pan, people would swarm to the same spot like ants. Overnight a mining camp would go up. And so it went, all along the rivers of California's Central Valley and the western slopes of the Sierra Nevadas until there were camps everywhere. If the pickings were good and steady, the camps became boomtowns.

Most of the wealth, though, eventually found its way to San Francisco, where the major mine owners, railroad barons, and titans of industry lived in their Nob Hill mansions.

Ten years later, when the gold became

harder to find and more expensive to dig up, most of the mining camps and towns dried up and were abandoned.

The majority of the towns that survived have become sprawling bedroom communities of housing tracts and shopping centers that retain only a few traces of their frontier pasts.

But there are still a handful of old mining camps, a hundred miles southeast of Sacramento along Highway 49, that have hardly changed over the last one hundred and fifty years.

Driving with Monk on the highway, right down the center of the California gold country, was like passing through one Western movie set after another.

Some of the towns were nothing more than tourist traps, selling T-shirts and Western memorabilia from within the aging, wooden storefronts. Others were meticulously restored and upscaled into pricey antique shops, French cafés, and elegantly quaint B and Bs so the towns looked more like Western-themed shopping malls than the authentic nineteenth-century mining camps that they once were.

We took a turn off the highway and drove for miles up a badly maintained, two-lane road that snaked past farms and abandoned mines, covering the car in a thick layer of dust.

All of a sudden we started getting pelted with what sounded like hail but covered the windshield with what looked like raw eggs without the shells. Yellow goop dripped down the glass.

Monk shrieked. "What is going on?"

"I don't know," I said.

"Is it the end of the world?"

"I doubt it."

I pulled the car over to the side of the road and came to a stop. And that's when I saw what was hitting us.

Butterflies. Tens of thousands of them fluttering across the highway. And they were still hitting the car, only not as many as when I was driving.

"It's only butterflies," I said.

"Is there any way around them?"

"I don't think so," I said. "This is the only way in and out of Trouble."

"Then we'll have to turn around and go home until they are gone."

"We can't do that, Mr. Monk," I said. "You'll just have grit your teeth and get through it."

I looked over my shoulder and drove back onto the highway. Almost immediately butterflies started splatting against the glass.

I tried spraying the windshield with washer fluid and running the wipers, but it only smeared the insect goo and dirt together into a disgusting muck.

"I hope you've got some money saved up," Monk said.

"Not on what you pay me," I said.

"Then I don't know what you're going to do."

"About what?"

"Buying a new car," he said.

"What do I need a new car for?"

"You've totaled this one."

"It's running just fine," I said.

"It's unsafe to drive," Monk said. "It's pestilence on wheels."

"I'll take it to a car wash," I said. "It will be good as new."

"A car wash isn't going to be enough," Monk said.

We might have kept arguing about that, but we made it through the butterflies, rounded a curve in the road, and there was Trouble laid out below us, capturing our attention.

The small town was tucked into a bend of the Stanislaus River and set against a sparse forest and disfigured hills that still bore the ravages of the hydraulic mining that had dissolved them like sugar cubes. It was a striking image. It was as if we'd just driven through a time warp and arrived in the 1850s.

The heart of Trouble was comprised of four intersecting streets that were laid out in a perfect tic-tac-toe pattern, which struck me as curiously well planned for what must have been a wild and unruly mining camp in its day.

The asphalt on our road ran out into the packed gravel of Trouble's main street, which was lined on either side with weather-beaten wooden storefronts and plank side-walks.

The two-story buildings and their painted signs were all faded the same shade of sun-bleached gray. Wild burros wandered lazily on the streets and people walked around them with casual familiarity.

I drove slowly, the uneven and rutted gravel road gently rocking the car. It reminded me of my dad bouncing me on his knees when I was a child. Maybe that's because he used to hum the theme to *Bonanza* when he did it, bouncing me to the beat. I would giggle until I could barely breathe. Just thinking about it brought a smile to my face.

Monk, however, was grimacing, gripping the dashboard as if it were the security bar on a roller coaster.

I glanced down the side streets as we passed them. I saw a railroad station, some stately Victorian homes, a church, and an imposing stone building that looked like a bank.

It wouldn't have surprised me one bit to see a stagecoach rushing into town, pulled by a team of horses.

The only signs of modern life were the telephone poles, the power lines, the street-lights, and at the far end of town, a 1950s-era gas station, diner, and motel. The few dusty cars I saw looked as out of place amidst the nineteenth-century buildings as flying saucers.

It was a miracle that the authentic, Wild West charm of the town had not been spoiled yet by fast-food franchises, neon signs, souvenir shops, or even asphalt roads. Either the town had a very strict planning commission or there was nobody who wanted to open a McDonald's or was willing to pay for a road.

I stopped to let a burro cross in front of us. The animal looked up at us, chewed on something, then ambled slowly to the plank sidewalk and continued on like a window-shopping pedestrian.

We'd only been in Trouble for a few

minutes but I was already utterly charmed by the place.

Monk looked at me. "Turn the car around and floor it."

"Why?" I said.

"Because we're leaving," he said.

"But we just got here."

"And we should escape while we still can," he said.

"We haven't even visited the crime scene yet."

"This entire town is a crime scene," Monk said.

"What are you talking about?"

"Unpaved roads, rabid animals in the streets, dirt everywhere," Monk said. "It's a complete breakdown of civilization."

"It's quaint," I said.

"It's the end of the world," he said. "The whole place should be quarantined. We need to alert the authorities."

"We can alert them after you've found Manny Feikema's killer."

"I already know who his killer was," Monk said.

"You do?" I said.

"I knew it the instant we drove into Trouble," Monk said.

"Whodunit?"

"Trouble done it. It's this town that killed

him, just like it will kill us if we don't get out of here."

"We aren't leaving until you solve the murder," I said. "So you'd better make it quick."

"Pray that I do," Monk said.

And that's exactly what he did, putting his hands together, closing his eyes, and mumbling to God as I drove on.

# CHAPTER FOUR:
# MR. MONK MEETS
# THE CHIEF

The police station occupied the first floor of Trouble's city hall, a two-story building with Doric columns, arched windows, faux turrets, and a cupola on top of the domed roof. The architectural flourishes, which were meant to create a sense of authority and permanence, might have worked on a grander scale but were overpowering on such a small building and conveyed instead a buffoonish pomposity.

I couldn't say the same about the police chief, Harley Kelton, who was rugged, relaxed, and unpretentious in every way. There was stubble on his cheeks and his hair, lightly flecked with gray, was disheveled, like he'd just rolled out of bed. He wore a denim shirt, jeans, and running shoes. I would never have guessed he was a cop, much less the chief, if not for the badge clipped to his belt.

His station was as simple and straightforward as he was. There was a front desk instead of a counter and it was occupied by a secretary who looked old enough to have personally witnessed the Gold Rush. Behind her were three other desks, each occupied by a uniformed officer and equipped with computers, and there were two holding cells, one of which was open and occupied by a man who was snoring.

Kelton's desk was in the far back corner of the room so he had a view of his entire domain. We sat in the stiff wooden chairs facing him.

"I've been expecting you," he said after we made our introductions and took our seats. He leaned back in his creaking chair and put his feet up on the desk. Monk winced.

"Does that mean you're glad to see us," I said, "or that you were dreading our arrival?"

He smiled at me and it felt as intimate as a kiss.

"I can't imagine anyone being unhappy about seeing you, Ms. Teeger, and I am familiar with Mr. Monk's reputation as a detective. But we aren't the inexperienced country bumpkins that Captain Stottlemeyer thinks we are. I was a homicide detective in Boston."

"You shouldn't do that," Monk said.

"Do what?" he asked.

"Put your feet up on the desk," Monk said. "It's unsanitary."

"This isn't a hospital and I don't perform surgery on my desk."

"There are wild animals in the streets and you're putting whatever you've stepped on all over your files and papers that you share with other people. And from the crumbs at the edge of your blotter, I know you eat at your desk, too. Think what might be going into your mouth with each bite."

Monk shivered all over at the thought.

Kelton took his feet off the desk. Monk motioned to me for a wipe.

"Why did you leave the Boston Police?" I asked Kelton as I gave Monk his wipe. But instead of using it on his hands, Monk began to wipe the desk where Kelton's feet had been. Kelton watched him warily for a moment.

"I was fired for being a drunk," he said. His frankness disarmed me almost as much as his smile did. He seemed to realize that. "Acknowledging your failings is part of the recovery process."

"I see," I said. "How's that going?"

He shrugged. "Some days are better than others."

"And today?"

"Much better since you walked in," he said.

He was flirting with me and I liked it. Working with Monk involved a certain degree of social isolation. Sure, I got out when he was investigating things, but most of the people we talked to were cops, grieving relatives, possible suspects, and cold-blooded killers. The investigations didn't create particularly flirtatious circumstances.

Granted, I was still in a police station and talking to a cop, but already I could see that Kelton wasn't like anybody in law enforcement I'd met before.

"Is everyone in this town an alcoholic?" Monk dropped his used wipe into Kelton's trash can.

"No," Kelton said. "Why would you think that?"

"Because then everything would make sense," he said.

"Everything?"

Monk tipped his head back towards the street. "There are dirt roads and savage beasts out there and nobody seems to care."

"They actually care a great deal," Kelton said. "The people here want to maintain the original character of the town. Paving the streets would encourage more vehicular traffic."

"What about the wild animals?"

"The town owes its existence to those burros. Legend has it that a prospector was roaming around these hills when his donkey wandered off with his pack and wouldn't come back. Furious, the prospector picked up a rock to throw at the animal and was about to toss it when he noticed that it was flecked with gold. He struck it rich and Trouble was born. The burros you see in town are descendants of the donkeys used by the prospectors and miners. They were let loose when the gold ran out and the mines closed up. They're a living connection to Trouble's past."

"That doesn't mean they should be allowed to rampage through the streets," Monk said. "They should be fenced in somewhere."

"They're friendly and harmless," Kelton said. "And kind of cute."

"Until one of them bites your arm off or infects everyone with bubonic plague," Monk said. "Speaking of plagues, what is going on with the butterflies?"

"It's their annual migration," Kelton said. "One billion monarch butterflies heading south to Mexico for the winter. They've gorged themselves for the trip. They won't stop until they've burned through the fat or smack into something. That yellow gunk on your car is fat."

"Good to know," I said. "What can you tell us about Manny Feikema?"

"Manny was a cop for thirty years. He'd still be one if he hadn't become too old and fat to chase the bad guys. He was a widower with no kids. A real nice guy. We'd meet for breakfast at Dorothy's Chuckwagon on most mornings and trade war stories from our days as big-city cops. He knew me better than anybody else here, maybe even better than I know myself. I'm really going to miss him."

"Did he have a spaghetti stain on his tie when he was killed?" Monk asked.

"I don't recall one," Kelton said. "Why?"

"He had one on his tie on May 17, 1997."

"What makes you think it would still be there now?" Kelton said. "Or that he was wearing the same tie on the night that he was murdered?"

"Nothing at all," Monk said.

"Then why bring it up?"

"It might be pertinent."

"I don't see how," Kelton said.

"That's why you are a cop in Trouble and not in Boston."

"No," Kelton said evenly. "That's because I'm a drunk."

"Maybe you wouldn't have hit the bottle and become a lush if you'd paid more attention to the stains around you."

"What?" Kelton said. "That doesn't make any sense at all."

"It would if you were sober," Monk said.

There went my plan to prevent Monk from offending the local constabulary. I cleared my throat loudly and then asked him a question.

"Did Manny Feikema have any enemies?"

"Not here," Kelton said.

"Except for whoever killed him," Monk said. "Why did he move from civilization to this godforsaken hellhole?"

"No offense intended," I added quickly.

"None taken," Kelton said. "It was my first impression of this place, too, but I needed a job and these were the only people foolish enough to hire me. Manny moved here because he liked to fish at Jump Off Joe, but you can fish only so much before you need something else to do."

"What's Jump Off Joe?" I said.

"It's a small lake, about a mile outside of town. It got its name from a guy who was driving his wagon when his horse got spooked by a rattler. The horse bolted, dragging the wagon behind him. He jumped off, right into the lake, an instant before the wagon tipped over and broke apart, killing the horse."

"It sounds like there's a story for everything in Trouble," I said.

"I'd like to know the one behind Manny's murder so I could get the hell out of here," Monk said.

"Fair enough." Kelton rose from behind his desk. "Let me take you over to the museum so you can see the crime scene for yourself."

He led us to the door, held it open, and ushered us outside onto the wood-planked sidewalk.

"Is there a scrapyard around here?" Monk asked.

"No," Kelton said. "Why do you ask?"

"For Natalie's car," Monk said, motioning to my dirt-and-insect-caked Buick Lucerne.

"All it needs is a wash," I said.

"Give me your car keys," Kelton said. I did. He stepped back into the station and tossed my keys to one of the deputies. "Billy, if you're not too busy, would you mind washing the patrol cars and the Buick parked out front?"

He stepped out again before he got an answer.

"That's very nice of you," I said, "but I don't want you to go to any trouble on my account."

"I'm not," Kelton said. "Officer Crider is."

The chief led us to the left, placing a guiding hand gently on my lower back. It felt warm and strong. His hand was only there for a polite moment, but I felt myself wishing it had lingered.

I walked beside him and Monk lagged behind us, carefully stepping from one board to the next.

"What's he doing?" Kelton whispered to me.

"My guess is that he's making sure he steps on one board at a time and that each one is level and straight."

We passed a saloon, an ice cream parlor, a pharmacy, and small, unassuming stores selling clothes, hardware, groceries, animal feed, books, and assorted knickknacks. Not a single one of the businesses I saw was part of a chain.

"He's an odd one," Kelton said.

"He's an even one," I said. "He hates anything that's odd."

"Ah, so that's why his pants have eight belt loops instead of the usual seven," Kelton said.

"You're observant," I said. "I'm impressed."

"Like I said, I was a detective once." When he smiled at me his eyes sparkled and I tried not to blush.

"How do you like Trouble?"

"It's slow," he said. "Being a peace officer here really is about keeping the peace. There's not much crime to speak of, mostly minor offenses, some drunk-and-disorderly conduct, a few domestic disputes. Whole weeks go by without us having to make an arrest."

"You don't get bored?"

"It's nothing like the excitement I had in Boston," he said. "That's probably why I'm not drinking anymore."

"Run for your lives," Monk yelled, giving me a hard shove and hurrying past me. My hero.

I turned around and saw a burro trailing slowly behind us.

Monk motioned to Kelton. "Shoot it!"

"I don't have my gun," Kelton said.

"Where is it?"

"I keep it in my desk drawer," he said.

"What good does it do you there?"

"I only carry a weapon when I think I might have to use it," Kelton said. "Besides, I can't shoot the animal. It's illegal in

Trouble to harass or harm a burro."

"But it's okay for them to stampede over people?" Monk said. "Has everyone here lost their minds?"

"Don't worry," Kelton said. "I've got things under control."

"If that were true, there wouldn't be wild animals running rampant in the streets," Monk said. "You won't see that in San Francisco or Boston."

"I'll take a few burros over scores of homeless people, prostitutes, gang members, and drug dealers." Kelton stopped at the corner, reached into his pocket, and pulled out a doggie treat, which he held out in the palm of his hand.

The burro came up to him, took the treat from his hand, and gobbled it up. Kelton stroked the burro's head.

"We're making a left here," Kelton said to us.

We went down Second Street and the burro continued on along Main Street.

"Wipe," Monk said, motioning to me frantically. I reached into my purse, pulled one out, and handed it to him. He pointed at Chief Kelton. "Not for me, for him. Hurry!"

I held the wipe out to Kelton.

"Thanks," he said. "But it's not necessary."

Monk gasped. "Do you have some kind of death wish?"

"No," Kelton said.

"Are you drunk?"

"Not presently," Kelton said.

"Then what is your excuse for not cleaning your hands after an animal drenched them with rabid drool and you ran your fingers through its unwashed, flea-ridden fur?"

Kelton sighed, took the wipe from me, and cleaned his hands with it.

"You'll thank me later," Monk said, walking ahead of us, cautiously choosing his path as if he were crossing a minefield.

I took a Baggie from my purse and held it open for Kelton to drop the wipe into. He did. I closed the Baggie and stuffed it into my purse.

"How many of those wipes do you carry around?" Kelton asked.

"Hundreds," I said.

"How long will that supply last?"

"A day or two," I said.

He shook his head. "How long have you been working for him?"

"Years and years," I said.

"And you aren't an alcoholic?"

"Nope," I said.

"Or a drug addict?"

"Nope," I said.

"Have you attempted suicide since you started working for him?"

"Nope," I said.

"How about murder?"

"Nope," I said.

"It's a miracle," he said.

I nodded.

# CHAPTER FIVE:
## MR. MONK AND THE
## GOLDEN RAIL
## EXPRESS

The Gold Rush Museum occupied the town's former train station. It was stuffed with artifacts from the period, like scales and measuring instruments to weigh the gold, and all kinds of prospecting paraphernalia, from shovels and picks to a wide assortment of pans, rockers, and sluices used to separate gold from the dirt.

The museum's walls were covered with dozens of original daguerreotypes, photographs, sketches, paintings, and documents that illustrated the grubby, hardscrabble frontier life of the forty-niners.

There were a wagon, a carriage, a stagecoach, and a full-sized cross section of a miner's cabin.

And there were several hokey dioramas with mannequins adorned in Western garb and posed in the midst of building a cabin, panning for gold, and digging in the mines.

The only items of any obvious monetary

value were the gold-laced quartz rocks, the gold nuggets, and the glittering pile of gold dust in one of the display cases.

The centerpiece of the museum, however, was the engine of an enormous steam locomotive and one of its passenger cars. It was, according to the information placard in front of the display, the "famous" Golden Rail Express.

"This is where Manny was killed," Kelton said. "The assailant was hiding behind the train and hit him from behind with a pick."

"Did you recover the weapon?" Monk asked.

"It was taken from the prospecting diorama over there." Kelton gestured to the diorama on the far side of the museum.

The diorama depicted a bearded, chubby prospector crouching beside a rock formation, examining the rocks while his recalcitrant donkey tugged at a loose strap on his overalls.

I wasn't an expert in California history, but the diorama didn't strike me as historically accurate. It felt more like history Disney-fied, turning the miner into a lovable cartoon character and anthropomorphizing the donkey to create a humorous vignette out of an isolated moment of dull prospecting.

"We don't have a forensics unit, so I called in the state police crime lab to process the crime scene for me," Kelton said. "The pick was wiped clean, of course, and since this is a museum that thousands of people have walked through, fingerprints and fibers are dead ends."

"Did Manny have a patrol routine?" Monk asked.

Kelton nodded. "He walked the perimeter of the building every hour. Along the way, he had to swipe his security ID into a special reader that logged the time of his patrol. This way the museum director can be sure that he didn't spend his shifts sleeping at the front desk."

"How did the intruder get in without setting off the alarm?"

"I think he came in sometime during the day as a regular visitor and hid somewhere in the museum until after closing. He used Manny's card key to leave at 2:32 a.m. so he wouldn't set off the alarm when he left either. We found the card key outside by the door. No prints on it, of course."

"What do the security cameras show?"

"There aren't any cameras," Kelton said. "The museum staff figured an alarm and a security guard were enough. It's not like we've got the crown jewels or the *Mona Lisa* in here."

"What about the gold?" I gestured to the display with the nuggets and the dust. "It must be valuable."

"It might be worth a few hundred dollars," Kelton said. "It's not worth killing a man for."

"People are killed for a lot less every day," I said.

"In San Francisco or Boston," Kelton said. "But not here."

Monk held his hands out in front of him, framing the scene with his thumbs and index fingers like a director. Then he tilted his head from side to side, did a little pirouette, and began moving around the museum in what looked like a fumbling, slow-motion ballet.

Kelton watched him. "What is he doing?"

"Surveying the crime scene," I said. "I call it Monk Zen."

"Does it work?"

"He hasn't failed yet," I said. "So what do you think happened?"

"I have a few theories that I'm exploring. One is that the murder had nothing to do with an aborted robbery or the museum at all. Killing Manny was the objective."

"Why do it here and not in his house or on his way to or from work?" I asked.

"To make it look like a robbery," Kelton said.

"But the killer didn't steal anything," I said.

"That's one of the problems with that theory." Kelton glanced at Monk again, who was now peering around the train.

"So what's your other theory, Chief?" I asked.

"Maybe the killer was after something here that wasn't worth a lot of money but has priceless sentimental or collectible value to him or whoever he was working for."

"How are you going to figure that out?"

"I've asked the museum director to check into the history of the pieces to see if there's any controversy attached to any of them — besides the train, of course."

"This train?" Monk said, stepping out from behind it.

"That's the Golden Rail Express," Kelton said.

"So?" I said.

"The *famous* Golden Rail Express," Kelton said.

"I've never heard of it."

"Neither have I," Monk said.

"Really?" Kelton said. "The way they talk about it here, I assumed everybody in California knew about it."

"I wish they did," said someone behind us. We turned to see a rotund man in a golf shirt and slacks walking our way. He looked like a peach that had been granted its wish to become human. He was accompanied by a uniformed security guard. "We'd be packed with tourists all the time."

"This is Edward Randisi, the museum director," Kelton said. "And this is Bob Gorman, our local auto mechanic. Well, at least he was."

"Bob has agreed to come on as our new security guard," Randisi said.

"I was real sorry to hear about Manny, but this job was an opportunity I couldn't pass up," Gorman said. He was tall and gangly, with an Adam's apple so large it looked like he was trying to swallow a baseball.

"No worries, Bob. I understand," Kelton said. "This is Adrian Monk, a homicide consultant with the San Francisco Police Department, and his associate, Natalie Teeger. I would appreciate it if you gave them your full cooperation and unrestricted access to the museum."

"Of course, Chief," Randisi said. "I'm here during the day, except for lunch from noon to one at the Chuckwagon, and Bob will be doing the night shift starting to-night."

"I'm gonna bring my uncle's twelve-gauge to work with me," Gorman said. "Any of those drug-crazed devil worshippers comes after me, I'll send 'em to hell with both barrels."

"What makes you think Manny was killed by a 'drug-crazed devil worshipper'?" Kelton asked.

"That's what I heard," Bob said.

"It makes sense to me," Monk said.

We all turned to Monk.

"Based on what?" I said.

"The way these people are living," he said.

I forced a smile. "Mr. Monk is joking."

"I am not," he said.

I elbowed him. "So tell me, Mr. Randisi, what makes this train famous?"

Randisi smiled and rubbed his hands together with pleasure, dismissed Bob Gorman, and then began telling us the story.

"The Golden Rail Express was a private railroad for the wealthy and elite that carried them from their mansions in San Francisco to their gold mines in Central California. Trouble was the last stop on the line," he said. "But the incident that would make the train famous happened almost a hundred years later."

Randisi clearly relished the opportunity to talk about the train, leading us up the steps and through the cab, past the soot-stained furnace where the engineer shoveled in the coal that kept the boiler going.

The Golden Rail Express remained private for another decade or so after the end of the Gold Rush and then was opened to the public. The route was eventually shortened to just the gold country stretch between Sacramento and Trouble. It continued in operation, its ridership steadily declining, until 1962, when its final run was commemorated with a high-stakes poker game with a pot of gold coins, worth over $100,000 at the time, as the prize.

The game was a publicity stunt concocted by a developer to generate attention and investors for a massive housing tract he wanted to build outside of Trouble. The plan was for the entire train to be stripped of its fittings and scrapped after its final run.

Things didn't go as planned.

The Golden Rail Express was robbed midway into the trip by at least three men masquerading as passengers. They covered their faces with masks and robbed everybody in the gambling car of their cash and the entire pot of gold. During the robbery, two men were killed — a security guard, who was shot, and the conductor, who fell from the moving train. Since the train never stopped during the crime, it was assumed that the robbers were among the passengers.

The crew and all the passengers were searched when they got off the train in Trouble. Two of the robbers were caught because they had some of the distinctive gold coins in their pockets. They were tried and sent to prison for fifteen years to life, but they never revealed who their co-conspirators were and what happened to all the cash and gold.

The police investigation was based on the theory that there must have been one or more accomplices who leaped off the moving train with the loot or they tossed the bags to an accomplice already on the ground and that the bags were buried for later retrieval.

There were lots of problems with that theory. Many believed that the jump from the moving train would have badly injured or killed the accomplices and that the heavy sacks would have broken open on impact with the ground, scattering cash and gold coins all over the place. But all they found along the tracks were the robbers' guns and their masks. A fingerprint recovered from one of the guns matched one of the two men who'd been captured.

In the nearly fifty years since then, tens of thousands of people have scoured the route and the surrounding area looking for the treasure. Not one of the coins has ever turned up.

"The train was supposed to be decommissioned after that fateful run, but thanks to the enormous publicity generated by the robbery, the Golden Rail Express continued in operation for two more decades as a tourist attraction before it was finally taken off the tracks," Randisi said. "It was sold off as scrap, but not before the entire train was torn apart and meticulously searched, inch by inch, for hidden compartments. None were found. We managed to save the locomotive as the centerpiece of our museum."

"What happened to the developer and his housing tract?" I asked.

"He went bankrupt before it could be built," Randisi said. "It was his gold that was lost in the robbery."

Monk rolled his shoulders and tipped his head from side to side. "The gold was never found?"

Randisi shook his head and smiled. "Maybe you can find it."

There were no maybes about it. Monk was hooked. We wouldn't be leaving now until we solved both mysteries, even if one of them was nearly fifty years old.

"Where can I learn more about the Golden Rail Express and the two men who robbed it?" Monk asked.

"You'll want to talk with Doris Thurlo, our town historian. Doris runs the historical society and the chamber of commerce out of the Box House at the end of the street," Randisi said. "You can't miss it. The building is perfectly square."

Monk blinked hard. "Perfectly square?"

"Even the windows," Randisi said. "It's been a curiosity in this town for over a hundred and fifty years."

"I've got to see it." Monk started for the door. Kelton stepped in front of him.

"You're going sightseeing?" Kelton said. "I thought you came here to offer your assistance on the murder investigation."

Monk stepped around him and continued walking. Kelton and I followed after him.

"You should have the museum staff do an inventory of the offices and desks, not just the collection," Monk said. "Perhaps what was taken wasn't something on display. It could be a file or some personal item belonging to one of the employees."

"I'll have Ed Randisi get right on it," Kelton said. "Any other thoughts or observations?"

"You said that Manny was killed with a pick from the prospecting diorama and that the murder occurred beside the train."

"There's no mystery there," Kelton said. "It's a fact, at least according to the state police forensic team."

"But the diorama is on the other side of the museum," Monk said, walking out the door.

"What does that have to do with anything?" Kelton said, hurrying after him onto the sidewalk.

"Why did the killer go all the way over there for a weapon when there were other, closer items that he could have used?"

"Maybe he was hiding in the diorama until closing time so he grabbed the pick out of convenience."

"Maybe," Monk said, heading with determination down the street, watching his feet to make sure he stepped on the right boards. "But if the killer came here intending to murder Manny, why not bring a weapon with him?"

"I don't know," Kelton said. "Nothing seems to fit."

"Everything fits," Monk said. "That is the natural order of things. We're just missing a few pieces. I'll find them."

I took Kelton by the arm, slowing him down to allow Monk to get a bit ahead of us and out of earshot.

"You can take that as a guarantee, Chief. Mr. Monk won't be able to go on if he doesn't solve the mystery."

"Go on with what?"

"His life," I said. "Manny Feikema's murder will be all that he can think about until he solves it. He won't give up, even if it means staying in a town full of drunks and drug-crazed devil worshippers."

I didn't see any point in mentioning that Monk would be solving the Golden Rail Express robbery, too. That crime wasn't one of Chief Kelton's priorities.

"That's dedication," Kelton said.

"That's obsession," I said.

He shrugged. "Whatever works. If you will excuse me, I'm going to have a few martinis and sacrifice some goats on my altar to Satan. Afterwards, I'll arrange accommodations for you both at the motel. One room or two?"

"Two, definitely two," I said. "And they need to be even-numbered rooms."

"Of course. I'll catch up with you later," he said and walked away. I watched him for a moment. I hoped he'd catch me soon.

Monk had reached the Box House and stopped to admire it. Randisi was right — it was hard to miss. It was a log cabin with square windows and a wraparound porch that was supported by four posts on each side. Not only that, the cabin was perfectly symmetrical, with two windows on each side and a back end that looked just like the street-facing facade.

I know this because the cabin was surrounded by a parking lot and I followed Monk as he walked all the way around it in admiration. That's also how I know that the property was square, too, each corner marked by a tree.

"It's a work of art," Monk said as we stepped up to the front door.

He stopped to count the logs. There was an even number of them from the ground to the roof. And the square windows were placed so that the top and bottom of the frames touched even-numbered logs.

"Exquisite, isn't it?" he said.

"It's too boxy," I said.

"There's no such thing as too boxy," he said. "That's like saying something is too perfect."

Monk opened the door and I followed him inside. It was like a mini-version of the museum that was filled with prospecting tools and old photographs. There was also a display of brochures, pamphlets, and books about Trouble and the surrounding area.

There was a woman in her sixties sitting at the front desk. She had a beehive hairdo, a Wilma Flintstone necklace, and a pair of glasses hanging on a thin chain around her neck.

Her eyes went wide when she saw us. She stood up slowly and, with shaking hands, put on her glasses.

"Good day," Monk said. "Are you Doris Thurlo?"

She nodded nervously.

"Mr. Monk?" Doris said, her voice quivering. "Is that really you?"

"In the flesh," he said. "And I've come here for you."

She let out a little shriek and fainted.

# Chapter Six:
## Mr. Monk and Mr. Monk

Doris Thurlo crumpled at the knees, but I managed to reach her before she hit the floor and eased her back into her chair.

Her eyes fluttered open. "Abby?"

"Are you okay? Would you like me to get a doctor?"

She looked over my shoulder at Monk, who stood behind me, and she shuddered. "Am I still alive?"

"I think so," I said.

Doris looked into my eyes. "Are *you* alive?"

She seemed pretty disoriented. I was afraid that perhaps she'd had a minor stroke or something.

"Maybe I'd better call an ambulance," I said, reaching into my purse and taking out my cell phone.

"Wait," she said, grabbing my wrist. "If you were Abby, you wouldn't have a cell phone."

"I don't know who Abby is. My name is Natalie Teeger. I work for Adrian Monk."

*"Adrian?"* she said, staring at him.

"Have we met?" Monk asked. "Or do you recognize me because I am a world-famous detective?"

I looked back at him. "When did you become world famous?"

"They know me in France and Germany," he said.

"That's not the entire world," I said.

"Word gets around," he said.

"Mr. Monk is a consultant to the San Francisco Police," I said. "We're helping Chief Kelton investigate the murder of Manny Feikema, the security guard at the Gold Rush Museum."

"Oh my," Doris said, sitting up straight. "You must forgive me. When he walked in and said he was here for me, I thought he'd come to take me to Jesus."

"You thought he was the Grim Reaper?" I said.

Monk's reputation must have preceded him. Corpses seemed to show up wherever he went. That was one of the reasons he never got invited to any parties, weddings, or anything else. I could certainly understand why people, in a town as small as this, would be afraid to see him walk through their door. The pool of potential murder victims was much smaller here than in a big city.

"I thought you were ghosts and that my time had come," Doris said.

"You thought I was a ghost?" I said.

"I've never seen a picture of Abigail," she said, "but he's the spitting image of Artemis."

"I don't spit," Monk said. "Nobody should. I think it's disgusting and wrong."

"So did Artemis," she said. "He hounded the sheriff and saloon keepers to outlaw tobacco spitting. Artemis was fortunate that the town needed an honest assayer or the prospectors would've hung him for it. The prospectors didn't have many pleasures and tobacco chewing was one of them. They weren't about to let Artemis deprive them of it. But they put up with a lot of his other nonsense out of respect and necessity."

"Who is this Artemis you keep talking about?" Monk asked.

"Artemis Monk, of course," she said. "This cabin was his home and office."

I felt a chill of recognition go down my spine. It was no wonder the cabin was a perfect square made up of an even number of logs or that it was built in the center of a square lot or that the streets of Trouble were laid out in a rigid, tic-tac-toe pattern.

It's exactly what Adrian Monk would do if he'd lived in the Old West.

Doris got up and led us over to a photo on the wall. It was a daguerreotype portrait — a monochrome photo on a scratched silver-coated, copper plate — that was about the size of a compact disc sleeve and set in a wooden frame.

"This is Artemis, circa 1855," she said. "He was a very important man in this town."

I studied the picture.

Back when Julie was a baby, before my husband was killed flying a mission in Kosovo, we went to the Monterey County Fair and visited a booth where we dressed up in vintage clothes from the Old West and a photographer took an "old-fashioned" family portrait of us. We used the picture for our Christmas card that year. That was what the photo of Artemis Monk reminded me of. It looked like Adrian Monk had visited one of those booths for a novelty photo. Or one day he'd stepped into a time machine, visited the past, and had his picture taken without telling me.

Monk and the man in the photo could have been identical twins. Their clothing was similar, though Artemis wore clothes distinctly nineteenth century in the cut and materials. Artemis even buttoned his shirt right up to the collar.

"Amazing," I said and turned to Monk. "Did you know you had an ancestor who lived in the Old West?"

"What makes you think I'm a descendant of his?"

I stared at him, hoping my expression would be enough to convey the message. It wasn't. So I spelled it out.

"You both demand that things be even, straight, and symmetrical. You dress the same. He was an assayer and you like to shine rocks —"

"In other words," Monk interrupted, "he was a normal, well-adjusted, rational person, and so am I. That hardly makes us related."

"You have the same name."

"There are a lot of people named Monk that I am not related to," Monk said. "Thelonious Monk comes to mind."

"You look identical."

"You're just seeing what you want to see," Monk said. "If she hadn't told you his name was Artemis Monk, you wouldn't have seen any resemblance at all."

"Didn't you say that you're a detective?" Doris asked.

"A world-famous detective," Monk said.

96

"It must run in the family," she said. "Artemis had a remarkable talent for ferreting out crime and solving mysteries. The sheriff, who was a brave and dedicated lawman but hardly a deductive genius, often called upon Artemis and his assistant, Abigail Guthrie, to aid him in his investigations."

"Artemis Monk had a female assistant?" I said.

"Without her, Artemis would have been lost," she said. "He was the most peculiar man who, despite his brilliance, had trouble dealing with the basics of everyday life."

The similarities between the two Monks were giving me the creeps. "What can you tell me about Abigail Guthrie?"

"I'll let her tell you her own story." Doris went to a display case full of old, leatherbound books, pulled one out, and handed it to me. "Abigail published a journal of their adventures. Only a few copies are known to remain in existence. You might find it interesting."

It was entitled *The Extraordinary Mr. Monk.* I held the book out to Monk for him to see. "Isn't this incredible?"

Monk shook his head. "I'm more interested in the Golden Rail Express robbery and the men who committed it."

"So are most of the people who come to Trouble," Doris said. "They all want to find the gold."

"Mr. Randisi told us you are the town historian," Monk said. "What can you tell me about the robbery?"

Doris told us basically the same story that Edward Randisi did, but she added some details. The two robbers who were caught, George Gilman and Jake Slocum, claimed that they were hired by the conductor, Ralph DeRosso, to pull off the robbery and that they brought the burlap bags of cash and gold to him. They claimed that they didn't know what happened to the loot after that or how DeRosso fell from the moving train. It was Gilman's fingerprint that was recovered from the gun.

"Mr. Randisi didn't mention the conductor's possible involvement in the robbery," Monk said. "He told us that the robbers never revealed who their co-conspirators were."

"Ed was being respectful of the DeRosso family, who are very well liked here in town," she said. "The prevailing opinion at the time was that it was easy for Slocum and Gilman to put the blame on Ralph DeRosso, since he was killed the night of the robbery and wasn't around to defend his good name. Most people felt Gilman and Slocum were lying to cover for someone else."

Doris went on to say that Leonard McElroy and Clifford Adams, the boiler man and the engineer of the train that night, continued to operate the Golden Rail Express in the years that followed the robbery. McElroy died of lung cancer six months before the train was finally scrapped in 1982, but Adams worked until the very last day.

I'd heard too many names in too short a time and I wasn't taking notes. I couldn't keep track of who was who and what was what, but I knew that Monk could, and that was all that counted.

Doris must have read the confusion on my face because she handed me a thin pamphlet entitled *The History of the Golden Rail Express.*

"Most of the story is in here," she said. "We also offer a hiking tour through the forest to the tracks. The guide shares the various theories about what happened to the loot and talks about some of the unsuccessful efforts to find it."

The pamphlet folded out to include a map of the railroad that highlighted the length of the track where it is believed that the robbery occurred.

"Are any of the robbers, witnesses, or railroad employees who were on the train that night still alive?" Monk asked.

She narrowed her eyes. "Are you after the treasure, Mr. Monk?"

"I'm after a resolution. Fifty years is too long for a robbery to remain unsolved. It leaves things unbalanced and that has consequences. All you have to do is look outside at what is going on in this town to see that. I have to set things right."

"You don't live here," she said. "You could just leave it be."

"I wish I could, but I can't." Monk rolled his shoulders. "It's a curse."

She nodded, as if he'd given her the answer she was hoping to hear.

"I don't know anything about the passengers, gamblers, or security guards who were on the train. George Gilman died in prison, but Jake Slocum was paroled in the early nineties. I don't know where he ended up. Clifford Adams still lives out at the old McMurtry mine. Ralph DeRosso's wife died a few years back, but his daughter, Crystal, still lives here in town. She's a waitress at the Chuckwagon."

We thanked Doris for her help and I promised to take good care of the book that she'd let me borrow.

It was dark and a little chilly when we left the Box House and walked towards Main Street. I noticed that it was quiet and still, something I never experienced in San Francisco. The stars were much brighter, too, unobscured by the glare of tens of thousands of city lights. The street was lit by only a few dim lampposts and the glow from a couple of storefront windows.

"I'll watch the way ahead," Monk said. "You keep a lookout behind us."

"What am I looking out for?"

"Burros, coyotes, mountain lions, goats, grizzly bears, rattlesnakes, wild boars," Monk said. "There could be all kinds of vicious creatures stalking us."

"Not to mention dandelions and tumbleweeds."

Monk quickened his pace. "It's a miracle that Manny Feikema is the only one who has been killed here lately."

"How's that investigation going?"

"You've seen and heard the same things I have," he said. "You tell me."

"It looks like we have nothing to go on," I said. "But I always think that. For all I know, you're just one tiny clue short of solving it."

"I'm not," he said sadly.

"So where do we start?"

"We ask Captain Stottlemeyer to find out where Jake Slocum, the surviving train robber, is these days."

"What does he have to do with Manny's murder?"

"Nothing," Monk said.

"So shouldn't you be concentrating first on the murder that was committed a couple of days ago rather than a crime that happened in 1962?"

"The Golden Rail Express robbery isn't solved," he said.

"Two men were caught, tried, and punished for their crimes," I said. "Justice was done. Case closed."

"But there may have been other robbers who got away unpunished with all the cash and gold."

"If there was anybody else involved, they're probably dead and the money long gone. But Manny Feikema's killer is definitely still out there and very much alive."

"I'm going to solve both mysteries," Monk said.

"So why not start with Manny's murder? The other one can wait; it happened nearly fifty years ago."

"Because I don't have anything to go on and you won't let me leave this savage wasteland until we solve the case. So we might as well accomplish something in the meantime."

"This savage wasteland could be your ancestral home."

"Be serious," he said. "The streets aren't paved. The sidewalks are made of wood. They might not even have running water or electricity. Can you imagine a man like me living here?"

"I don't have to," I said, hefting Abigail Guthrie's book. "I've got this."

"Artemis Monk has nothing to do with me."

"How much do you and Ambrose know about your family heritage?"

"Nothing," Monk said.

"So now you've got another mystery you can solve while you're here."

I called Captain Stottlemeyer's office on my cell phone as we walked. He wasn't in, so I left a message on his voice mail asking him if he could track down Jake Slocum, the surviving robber, for us. I didn't mention that this had to do with a crime that happened in 1962. I figured he'd move faster if he assumed that it had something to do with Manny's murder.

We stopped by the police station. My car was parked out front, gleaming in the floodlights as if it had just rolled off the assembly line.

"I told you it was a lost cause," Monk said.

"The car is sparkling, Mr. Monk," I said.

"They only did a superficial wash."

"It was only superficially dirty," I said.

"A cake tainted with poison still looks delicious," Monk said. "That doesn't mean it won't kill you."

"It was the exterior that got dirty, not the interior."

"I'm sure it seeped in," Monk said. "It always seeps. It's a seeping thing."

I didn't bother arguing the point and went inside the station to get my keys while Monk waited outside.

Chief Kelton was away but the receptionist had my keys. She told me that our rooms were ready at the motel down the street and handed me the card keys.

I thanked her for her help and went back outside. Monk was squatting in front of my car, peering into the grill.

"I see a suspicious fleck in there," Monk said, pointing. "I think it's the remains of a dead butterfly."

"So what?"

"It could get sucked into the fan and out an air vent into the car, where I could inhale it and die instantly," Monk said. "Do you want that on your conscience?"

"I certainly don't," I said. "I'm driving up to the motel, but you're welcome to walk. It's only a block or two."

Monk looked warily down the dark, dimly lit street towards the motel. "I could be mauled by a burro on the way."

I opened the driver's side door. "I'm going now."

"Maybe an armed police officer could escort me," he said.

"Couldn't hurt to ask," I said and got in. I was starting the ignition when Monk knocked on my window. I rolled it down. "Yes?"

"Could you go inside the police station and ask for me?"

"No," I said.

"Isn't that what I pay you for?"

"It might be, but my shift just ended. I'm on my own time now. Unless you're paying for overtime."

Monk grimaced, walked around the front of the car and got inside, put on his seat belt, and covered his nose and mouth with his hands as I drove to our motel.

The Trouble Motor Inn was shaped like a staple around a fenced-in pool. It was a flat-roofed, low-slung cinder-block building that looked more like a collection of storage units than a motel. We were booked into rooms two and four. I parked the car in front of room two.

Monk took one look at his simple room, with carpet about as plush as plywood, and asked me if I could get him the maid's cleaning cart. I talked to the unshaven, sallow-faced manager, who insisted that the room was already clean. But I explained that Monk liked his rooms clean enough to perform open-heart surgery in them.

"You aren't planning on drugging some-one and removing one of their kidneys to sell on the black market, are you?" he asked.

From the yellow tinge of his skin, I won-dered if that had happened to him.

"Not on this trip," I said. "Maybe next time."

He gave me a maid's cart, which was stocked with a big laundry sack, a garbage bag, and plenty of assorted cleaning sup-plies, as well as a mop, broom, and vacuum. I wheeled it to Monk's room, where he'd already stripped the bed and dumped the sheets on the floor.

"I knew I should have brought my own mattress," he said.

"I would have had to tie it to the roof of my car," I said. "It would have been covered with dead bugs and dirt when we got here."

"It still would be cleaner than this one,"

Monk said, scowling at the stained mattress. "It's a good thing I brought plastic sheeting with me. You should never leave home without it."

"That's what all the professional assassins and serial killers always say."

Murderers like to spread plastic sheeting over surfaces before they do their killing so they won't leave blood or other trace evidence behind. Monk liked to do it to protect himself from whatever germs might be lurking around, waiting to pounce on him.

We covered the mattress in plastic, tucked it in, then we made the bed with the sheets and blankets that he'd packed for the trip. We removed all the towels, toilet paper, and tissues in the room and replaced them with supplies he'd brought from home.

I stuffed the hotel linens in the laundry bag and Monk began to clean.

There are professional crime-scene cleaners and hazardous material teams who don't do as thorough a job as Monk does. The only way Monk could be more thorough was if he stripped the room to the studs and remodeled it entirely, which wasn't something I'd put past him.

At the very least, I knew he'd be at it for hours and I wasn't going to help, since I was officially off duty and, therefore, could pick and choose what tasks I was willing to do or what I would put up with.

After a long day with Monk, I admit I could get a bit surly and disagreeable. But I figured after all of our years together, he ought to be used to it and make the necessary adjustments in his behavior to lessen the risks for him, which he didn't, either out of ignorance, stubbornness, or spite.

So I settled into one of the chairs and read aloud to Monk, my captive audience, from Abigail Guthrie's book. It was the one way I could be sure that he'd at least give some attention to the story of Artemis Monk.

## THE EXTRAORDINARY MR. MONK
### The Case of Piss-Poor Gold

*(From the journal of Abigail Guthrie)*
*Trouble, California, 1855*
The commerce in Trouble relied almost exclusively on gold dust, which people carried around in leather pokes tied to their belts. A pinch was worth about a dollar and just about everybody, from the clerk at the general store to the sporting women, had a set of scales.

It was usually the seller who did the pinching and it was common for them to engage in some trickery to gain a few extra grains of gold in the transaction.

Most of the bartenders, shopkeepers, barbers, and sporting women in town kept their nails long, the better to capture dust in a pinch, and in their spare time, rolled rough pebbles between their thumbs and index fingers to create indentations in their skin to trap more dust.

The shopkeeper at the general store went a step further. He was known for his abundant, and slickly greased, head of hair, which he smoothed before every transaction and then raked his fingers through afterwards as the customer was leaving. According to Monk, that was because the gold stuck to his greased fingers during the pinch and was wiped off in his hair afterwards. Each night the shopkeeper washed his hair into a gold pan and made more than most prospectors did squatting beside a river.

But I suppose it all evened out in the end, since many prospectors and miners were known to salt their gold with pyrite and brass filings to give their poke a little more volume.

Monk didn't bother himself with those petty crimes but he did catch plenty of more ingenious thieves.

I remember one situation in particular, because it happened in the first few weeks that I was working for him and because it also happened to be the first murder I'd seen him solve.

It was a warm morning in September and I was indexing samples and updating his assay ledgers in the front office of his large, perfectly square cabin.

Monk kept a representative sample of the rocks that were brought in for him to test. He placed the sample in a jar and labeled it with the date it was tested and index numbers that corresponded to entries in a ledger that he kept of the various claims, their locations, and the owners. The ledger also contained the results of his assays. It was part of my job to maintain those records.

The shelves in the front office were neatly organized with sample jars, reference books, maps, and various rock specimens. His prospecting tools were carefully organized according to size, shape, and function. The tools rested on pegs in the wall specifically fitted for the individual implements.

The cabin was divided into four equal sections — the front office, which doubled as our kitchen and communal living area, the laboratory, Monk's room, and my room.

Monk spent most of his time in the laboratory, where he worked at an enormous desk that he somehow managed to keep dust free, even though he regularly worked with rocks and dirt. The shelves were filled with the specialized tools, chemicals, crucibles, microscopes, and balances required for his trade.

The rear of his laboratory was reserved for the crushing of rock samples into dust, which he would then fire in the two-deck, clay furnace in the back as part of some complicated process I don't pretend to understand. All I know is that when it was done, and the pulverized rocks had been melted, poured into cupels, cooled and cleaned and chemicals added, he could separate the gold from everything else and tell you how rich or poor your claim was likely to be.

Monk was in his lab when a young prospector walked into the front office. I immediately stopped him at the door and led him back outside to the porch.

"I need to see Mr. Monk," he said.

"You can't come in here like that," I said.

"Like what?"

I could tell he was a greenhorn, fresh off the boat, train, or trail and eager to make it rich in the gold country. He had the same feverish look in his eye that my Hank, and hundreds of other men, had. But it was more than that.

His wool shirt was still a recognizable shade of red, his trousers weren't patched, but both were covered with dirt. He had the blistered hands and stumbling gait of someone unaccustomed to working with a shovel and pick, or the long hours squatting in the cold river, swishing gravel around in a pan. He was thin from lack of good food and possibly a touch of land scurvy. His whiskers were mangy but not yet obscuring his youthful features and his hair was long but not yet wild and matted.

"You're too dirty," I said. "Mr. Monk only allows people inside who are freshly washed and dressed in their clean Sunday best."

"This ain't no church and I don't want to marry him. I just want him to look at my rocks."

"What is your name, sir?"

"Nate Klebbin," he said.

"You can give me your samples, Mr. Klebbin, and I will take them in to Mr. Monk. You may wait here on the porch if you like," I said, motioning to the guest bench. "Or I can fetch you in the saloon when Mr. Monk is finished."

"I'll wait here." He handed me his sack of rocks and took a seat on the bench.

I went inside and carried the sack to Monk, who greeted me at the doorway of his laboratory.

"You have a new client," I said.

"I know," Monk said. "I could smell him from a hundred yards away."

"You say that about everybody except me."

"Because nobody except you in this town bathes and wears fresh clothes each day," Monk said. "And many of them regularly sit astride filthy beasts."

"You mean horses."

"That's what I said." Monk took the bag from me and retreated to his laboratory, closing the door behind him.

"I'd ride a horse if I could afford one," I said.

Monk never rode horses and believed they should be prohibited from the streets. If he had his way, everybody would have to hitch up their horses in a corral outside of town and clean up after them.

He emerged again a few hours later, a bewildered look on his face.

"Is there an animal being slaughtered on our front porch?"

Monk was referring to Nate Klebbin, who'd fallen asleep the instant after he sat down on the bench and had been snoring loudly ever since.

"That's the fellow who brought in the

sample for you," I said. "He's sleeping on the porch."

"It sounds like he's being murdered and yet it smells like he died two weeks ago."

"I'm sure he'll be flattered to hear that," I said.

Monk opened the door and stepped out onto the porch, where Klebbin was snoring away. "Mr. Klebbin?"

The man was too deep asleep to be stirred by the mere mention of his name. So Monk reached back into the cabin, grabbed the broom, and poked Klebbin in the side with the handle.

Klebbin jerked awake. "What are you poking me for?"

"I'm Artemis Monk, the assayer. I've finished studying your sample."

Klebbin sat up straight, his eyes flashing with excitement. "Did you find color?"

"I did," Monk said.

"A lot of it?"

"Enough to indicate the possibility of much more to be had with hard labor," Monk said.

"Yee-haw!" Klebbin said.

"I wouldn't yee or haw just yet," Monk said. "Where is your claim?"

Klebbin reached into his shirt for a folded sheet of sweat-stained paper, which he held out to Monk. "It's right here."

Monk took a step back as if he were being offered a dead rat. "I mean, where is your parcel located?"

"In a gulch west of Juniper Creek," Klebbin said. "I bought it from Clem Janklow. You know him?"

Monk knew Clem and so did everybody else in town. Clem was a prospector who scraped by but never struck it rich, and what gold he did find he quickly spent at the saloon. He was always broke and perpetually drunk and relieved his prodigious bladder wherever, and whenever, the urge struck him.

This, of course, disgusted and infuriated Monk, who demanded that Sheriff Wheeler lock Clem up or throw him out of town. But Wheeler was reluctant to do either.

"If I lock him up, then he'll just piss all over my jail," Wheeler said. "And if I drive out everybody who pisses in the street, the town would be deserted. Besides, Clem can't help it. He's got a kidney ailment."

"The ailment is whiskey," Monk said.

Clem claimed it was more than that but that he couldn't afford the medicine that would lessen his need for alcohol and relieve his kidney problem. Monk talked to Dr. Sloan, who confirmed Clem's account and recommended an elixir known as Greeley's Cure, which was used to treat syphilis, alcoholism, opium addiction, and digestive troubles.

So Monk had made a deal with Clem. He'd pay for the medicine himself if Clem agreed to stay out of the saloon and not to relieve himself on the streets.

Since then, Clem hadn't relieved himself once in public and stayed away from the saloon. The bottles of Greeley's Cure cost Monk several dollars a day, but he figured it was a small price to pay to save a man's life and keep the community clean.

Now Monk's face was turning beet red with anger.

"Why did Clem sell you his claim if it was still producing gold, Mr. Klebbin?"

"Clem told me he's too sick and feeble to work it anymore, but it ain't played out yet," Klebbin said. "He's got some kind of kidney problem from too much rotgut whiskey. It's got so bad, he's pissing day and night all over the place out there. You wouldn't believe the stink, but I don't mind if there's gold."

Monk shivered. "You've been swindled, Mr. Klebbin, and so have I."

"But you found gold in them rocks, didn't you?" Klebbin said.

"Indeed I did," Monk said. "Stay here while I get the sheriff."

Monk marched away and I hurried after him to Main Street. He kept his head down, watching the planks as he stepped on them.

"I don't understand the trouble, Mr. Monk. Everything Clem told Mr. Klebbin is true."

"That's what makes it so infuriating," Monk said. "The audacity of the crime."

Monk stopped and pointed to a warped plank. I bent down and marked a big "X" on it with a piece of chalk so the wood could be replaced later. I carried the chalk with me at all times for exactly that purpose.

He took another step and pointed to another plank. This one was cracked.

"I thought you were in a hurry," I said.

"I am," Monk said. "But I'm not going to kill myself getting there."

"You can't die from stepping on a warped board," I said.

"You can trip and break your neck. Or you could get a splinter in your toe that becomes infected. Next thing you know, Dr. Sloan is chopping off your leg to prevent gangrene, but he's too late. You're already dead."

I marked the plank and we were hurrying along again when a man rode in, dismounted, and hitched his horse to the post a few yards ahead of us.

He was a cowhand, not a prospector. He wore a wide-brimmed hat, a calico shirt, a beaten-down charro jacket adorned with silver-threaded brocade, and a pair of chaps. His boots were muddy and his clothes were dusty and stained with splotches of tar.

The cowboy spit some tobacco into the street and stepped up to the sidewalk in front of the saloon, slapping dust off of himself with his hat.

"You can sweep that right up again with that hat of yours," Monk said. "We like to keep our town clean."

The cowboy turned to look at Monk. "What did you say to me?"

"And when you're done sweeping up your dust, you can pick up that disgusting gob of tobacco you left in our street."

The cowboy smiled, flashing his yellow teeth, and scratched at some welts on his chest. There was a murderous glint in his eyes. But he was wearing a gun belt and Monk was not, which may have been the only thing that saved Monk from getting gunned down.

"I'm walking into that saloon and having myself a drink, mister. Maybe you and the pretty lady would like to join me."

"Not with those muddy boots on, you're not," Monk said. "People eat and drink in there. Why don't you take them off and leave them by the door?"

"I got to get me some of whatever you've been drinking." The cowboy laughed and went inside.

Monk was about to go in after him when the horse passed gas and let loose some droppings. He screamed and ran back the way we came, careful to step on the same boards that he had before.

I caught up with Monk around the corner on Second Street, out of sight of the horse and the droppings. He was breathing with a handkerchief over his nose and mouth.

"How are we going to get to the sheriff now?" he said.

"Easy," I said. "We walk down the sidewalk to his office."

"We can't with *that* in the street."

"Unless you walk right behind that horse, there's no danger of stepping in the droppings."

"It's still there," Monk said. "You can see it and you can smell it."

"So close your eyes and plug your nose."

"I'll die of asphyxiation," Monk said. "If my skin doesn't rot off first."

"Why would your skin rot off?"

"Did you see what's in the street?" Monk said. "What I need is my own telegraph in my cabin that's connected directly to the sheriff's office."

"I'm sure he'd love that," I said. "But since it may take some time to build a telegraph line, I'd better go fetch Sheriff Wheeler myself."

I started back towards Main Street but, as it turned out, I didn't have to go far. The sheriff was riding by on horseback with his deputy, Parley Weaver. I ran into the street and flagged him down.

The sheriff drew up beside me. He had a bountiful mustache that looked like he'd skinned a raccoon and hung the pelt from his nose. I'd heard he'd been a gunfighter before he settled in Trouble in search of a peaceable life. Most sheriffs had the same story.

Deputy Weaver was reed-thin and lazy, but moved as fast as a jackrabbit when food, drink, or the attentions of a sporting woman were involved.

"What's the problem, Mrs. Guthrie?" Wheeler asked me.

"It's Mr. Monk, Sheriff," I said.

"You need to arrest Clem Janklow," Monk yelled from where he stood, a safe distance away from the sheriff, Deputy Weaver, and

120

their horses.

Wheeler groaned. "I got bigger problems than Clem's pissing, Monk. There's been a murder. Somebody killed Bart Spicer and stole his poke."

"Did it happen at his mine?" Monk asked.

"As a matter of fact, it did," the sheriff said. "I'm on my way out there now."

"Why are you going there when the murderer is right here in town?"

The sheriff raised his eyebrows. "He is?"

"He's having a drink in Bogg's Saloon," Monk said. "Now can we please go find Clem Janklow?"

The sheriff and his deputy looked perplexed and I suppose that I did, too. Wheeler asked the question that the three of us were thinking.

"How can you be sure that Spicer's killer is sitting in Bogg's Saloon when you didn't even know that Spicer was dead until I told you?"

"Was Spicer killed with a mine timber?" Monk asked impatiently.

"Someone dropped a timber on his head while he was sleeping," Deputy Weaver said. "How'd you know that? Did somebody tell you?"

"The murderer did," Monk said.

"He was bragging about what he done?"

Weaver asked.

"He didn't say a word about it," Monk said. "He didn't have to. He was wearing his confession."

"What's this feller's name?" Wheeler asked.

"I don't know," Monk said. "He just rode into town and messed the whole place up."

Wheeler groaned. "How did he do that?"

"He spit tobacco in the street, brushed dirt on the sidewalk, walked into the saloon with muddy boots, and his horse did the rest."

"Because of that, you think he's also got to be a murderer," Wheeler said.

"I can prove it," Monk said.

If it was anybody else but Artemis Monk who'd said that, the sheriff would have ignored him and rode on to Spicer's mine. But Monk wasn't anybody else.

The sheriff turned to his deputy. "Go over to Bogg's and invite the cowboy to join us."

Weaver rode away. Sheriff Wheeler got off his horse and tied him to a hitching post.

"We're wasting time, Sheriff," Monk said. "Clem might be getting away."

"He's not going anywhere, Monk. And even if he was, he wouldn't be hard to track," Wheeler said, then turned to me. "How are you, Mrs. Guthrie?"

"I'm getting along fine, Sheriff."

"Monk hasn't driven you crazy yet?"

"No, sir," I said, mindful of who paid my wages and gave me room and board.

"It's early yet," the sheriff said just as Weaver approached with the cowpoke at his side.

"This here's Bud Lolly," Weaver said.

Lolly smiled when he saw Monk and me. "You again? Is there a law in this town against spitting?"

"Not yet, but I'm working on it," Monk said.

"Believe me, he is," the sheriff said. "But we do have a law here against murder."

"I ain't killed nobody," Lolly said.

Monk took a handkerchief from his pocket, squatted down, and removed some mud from Lolly's boot. We all stared at him as he did it.

"You want to shine my boots, mister, I'll be glad to take 'em off for you," Lolly said.

"This dirt is from Bart Spicer's property," Monk said. "I recognize the hue, which is indicative of the unusually high silica content."

"I ain't never heard of no Bart Spicer," Lolly said. "And even if I did, you can't know where I've been from the mud on my boot."

"Actually, he can," I said. "Mr. Monk is the town assayer. He knows his dirt."

"The geology and metallurgical content of every piece of property is unique and so is the gold that comes out of it," Monk said. "This mud definitely came from Bart's claim. I can match it to the sample I kept of Bart's rocks. I'm sure if I saw the gold dust in your poke, I'd recognize the color of that, too."

"That don't prove nothing," Lolly said. "I might have walked across his land without even knowing it. And there's lots of gold dust being passed around in these parts. I got no idea where my gold was before it ended up in my pouch."

"He's got a point," Wheeler said. "I can't hang a man because he's got mud on his boots and gold in his poke."

Monk looked Lolly in the eye. "Do you swear that you've never been in Bart Spicer's mine?"

"I've never been in nobody's mine," Lolly said. "I'm a cowhand, not a gold digger. I earn an honest wage."

"That's not what your clothes say."

"What are you talking about?" Lolly said.

"Mines are held up with bracing timbers that are covered in bark and splinters. They're prickly as a cactus and coated with coal tar," Monk said. "So if you've never been in a mine, or picked up a bracing timber, maybe you could tell us how you got those splinters in your chest and that tar on your shirt?"

He couldn't. Lolly hesitated for a moment, then went for his gun. But he wasn't as fast as Wheeler, who had his gun out and aimed before Lolly's hand even reached his holster.

"Go ahead, Lolly, it'll save the town the trouble of hanging you," Wheeler said.

Lolly raised his hands and glared hatefully at Monk. "I should've followed my gut and killed you when we met. But I don't shoot unarmed men."

"You just smash in their skulls while they're sleeping and steal their gold," I said. "That's much more noble."

"Parley, take Lolly back to the office and lock him up," the sheriff said.

Deputy Weaver took Lolly's gun and aimed it at him. "Let's go. You walk in front of me. No funny stuff or I'll shoot you full of holes."

"What about the mess his horse made in the street?" Monk asked the sheriff.

"Parley," Wheeler said, getting his deputy's attention. "Have Lolly pick up his horse's droppings on the way."

"Yes, sir," Weaver said. "Where are you gonna be, Sheriff?"

Wheeler glanced at Monk. "Hot on the trail of that rascal Clem Janklow."

We found Clem Janklow a few minutes later sitting on a bench outside of the general store, surrounded by bags of supplies. His bloodshot eyes peeked out from a face full of mangy whiskers and wild hair and he reeked from days of sweating in the hot sun in clothes that hadn't been washed in weeks, if not months. The once-red wool shirt had faded to a ghastly purple and was caked in a fine layer of dirt. His ragged pants hung from his shoulders from frayed suspenders, the leggings tucked into his mud-caked boots.

He was slurping up sardines from a tin with his fingers, bits of fish sticking to his prickly beard. When miners struck it rich, they were quick to spend the gold on canned oysters, olives, turtle soup, and other delicacies and, thus fortified, moved on to champagne, whiskey, and sporting girls.

"You're under arrest, Clem," Monk said.

"You can't arrest anybody, Monk," the sheriff said. "That's my job."

"I haven't done anything wrong," Clem said. "I'm a law-abiding citizen."

"You swindled me out of a hundred dollars and I don't know how much you took from Nate Klebbin."

"I've never taken a plug nickel from you, Mr. Monk, and I sold my claim to Klebbin fair and square."

"Did you see Dr. Sloan for another dose of Greeley's Bichloride Tonic Cure while you were in town today?" Monk asked.

"I don't need it no more," Clem said. "I'm feeling much better and I thank you dearly for it, Mr. Monk."

"Because without me you couldn't have pulled off your fraud," Monk said. "You relieved yourself all over town, knowing that I wouldn't be able to stand it and that Dr. Sloan would prescribe Greeley's Cure for you."

"It cures your taste for whiskey and calms your kidneys; that's why the doc said I had to have it," Clem said. "But I couldn't afford my own salvation, which is why I'm indebted to you for your kindness."

The sheriff sighed. "If there's a crime here, Monk, I don't see it."

"Do you know what Greeley's Bichloride Tonic Cure is made of, Sheriff?" Monk asked.

"Nope," Wheeler said.

I didn't, either.

"It's a mix of sodium chloride, glycerin,

strychnine, cinchona, and gold chloride, among other things," Monk said. "The tonic, paired with injections, is commonly used in the treatment of various addictions. You have to drink a dram of it every two hours for a month."

"I don't see your point," Wheeler said.

I didn't, either.

"The gold in the tonic and the injections passes right through your body," Monk said. "Clem's been out there relieving himself all over his property for weeks, infusing it with gold, so he could sell it to the first greenhorn who came along. And he forced me into bankrolling his crime."

"How did he force you into it?" Wheeler asked.

"If I didn't pay for his medicine, he'd continue his drinking and indiscriminate urinating," Monk said. "He knew I couldn't take that. But it was all a clever scheme to sell his nearly worthless claim."

Now that Monk had explained it, I saw the past events in an entirely different light and knew that he was absolutely right.

Clem licked his oily fingers. "I had no idea my pissing was salting my claim and you can't prove that isn't so."

"He's convinced me," Wheeler said. "You're going to return the supplies you haven't already consumed and give Mr. Klebbin all of his money back and let him keep your claim for nothing if he wants it. And then you're going to repay Monk by getting the hell out of town and never coming back. Because if I see your face in Trouble again, I'll put a bullet in it."

"You can't do that," Clem said.

"I'm the law," Wheeler said. "Maybe you've been too drunk to notice, but we don't have any judges or courts here. So if I was you, Clem, I'd skedaddle before I change my mind and decide to shoot you right now."

Clem gathered up his bags and shuffled back into the general store without another word.

Wheeler turned to Monk. "Satisfied?"

"This all could have been avoided if we had a law against relieving yourself in public," Monk said. "And spitting."

"What does spitting have to do with it?"

"That's how it all starts," Monk said. "You get away with that and, before you know it, you're letting go of your sphincters willynilly, robbing trains and killing old ladies."

"I see," Wheeler said. "So if we outlawed spitting, we could eventually put an end to all the indecent and criminal behavior in the West."

"It couldn't hurt," Monk said. "What have we got to lose by trying?"

"I'd lose plenty," Wheeler said. "I'd be out of a job."

"So you're arguing that we should allow crime to continue so you can earn a living?"

"Not all of it. Maybe just spitting." Wheeler winked at me and walked away.

Monk sighed wearily. "I'm going to spend the rest of the day washing my hands. While I do that, you can rent two rooms for us at the hotel."

"What for?"

"Because after I burn down my cabin we're going to need a place to live while the new one is being built."

"Mr. Monk, be reasonable," I said. "You can't burn down your home just because you brought in some rocks that were pissed on."

Monk stared at me. "Can you think of a better reason?"

# CHAPTER SEVEN:
## MR. MONK AND A
## NIGHT IN TROUBLE

I closed the book, stunned by what I'd read in the first few chapters. I looked up at Monk, who was busy scrubbing the baseboards.

"Isn't that amazing?" I said.

"I thought it was a big cheat."

"What do you mean?"

"Perhaps a reader in the mid-1800s might have had a chance to solve the gold swindle if they were familiar with Greeley's Cure, but not someone today. And there wasn't nearly enough information supplied by the author for a reader in any century to figure out the solution to the murder."

"I'm not talking about its merits as a mystery story. I'm talking about the man. Artemis Monk was way ahead of his time as a detective," I said. "He used scientific analysis of trace evidence and old-fashioned deduction to solve both crimes. He was a pioneer of forensic investigation."

"I'm not impressed," Monk said.

"Aren't you even the slightest bit intrigued?"

"By what?"

"By how remarkably alike you two are. It's uncanny."

Monk stood up and shook his head. "I don't see it."

I wanted to beat him over the head with the book. How could anyone be so willfully obstinate?

"The way Artemis caught the cowboy is the same way you caught Clarence Lenihan on Halloween. It was because of what was on their clothes."

"When someone shows up at your door covered in blood, it's not a big leap to figure out that they've killed someone," Monk said and sprayed disinfectant on the hinges of the bathroom door.

"You told Lenihan that he was wearing his confession and Artemis Monk used almost those same words on the cowboy." My voice was rising and I could feel my face getting hot with anger.

"You're reaching," Monk said, wiping the hinges.

"You're both afraid to step on a warped plank."

"Who wouldn't be?"

"You're both afraid of germs."

"Every sane person is."

"You're both detectives with first names that begin with the letter *A* and the last name *Monk!*"

"It's a coincidence," Monk said.

I would have thrown the book at him if it wasn't such a valuable historical object. I took a deep breath and let it out slowly and made a conscious effort to lower my voice.

"You don't believe in coincidences."

"Then maybe you're related to Abigail Guthrie," Monk said.

That was too creepy to even contemplate. It was *Twilight Zone* creepy.

"Her name isn't Natalie or Teeger," I said.

"But she's a widow and the assistant to a detective named Monk," he said. "Doesn't that automatically make her your ancestor?"

"No," I said.

"Then why do you assume Artemis Monk is mine?"

"Because you have the same name, the same face, the same detecting skills, and the same infuriating personality."

"But other than that," he said, "we're nothing alike."

I think if I'd murdered him at that moment, any jury in America would have understood and let me walk away a free woman. But I managed to control myself. Instead I shouted something profane and stormed out of his room, slamming the door behind me.

I stomped across the parking lot and down the street with no destination in mind. My only goal was to put some distance between myself and Monk.

A few moments later, I found myself standing in front of Dorothy's Chuckwagon and realized it was way past my usual dinnertime and that I was hungry, which explained, at least to some degree, my short temper.

So I tucked Abigail's book into my purse and went inside. I wasn't concerned about what Monk would do for dinner. He'd brought along a box of Wheat Thins and enough Summit Creek bottled water to survive a nuclear winter.

The small restaurant had wood-paneled walls decorated with bad, assembly-line paintings of Western landscapes and yellowed posters for long-past rodeos and county fairs. There was a very low counter, shaped in an elongated U, and just four booths, two on each wall. There were three customers in the place and only one of them was under the age of sixty — and that was Chief Kelton, who could barely fit his knees under the counter. Seeing him there, looking so ungainly and uncomfortable, reminded me of all those events at my daughter's preschool where the parents were forced to sit on chairs made for toddlers. I took a seat beside him without waiting for an invitation.

"Hello, Chief," I said.

"Has Monk solved the murder and found the gold yet, Ms. Teeger?" Kelton asked.

"No, I'm afraid not. He's running a little behind."

"Will he be joining us for dinner?"

"Are we having dinner?" I said, giving it a coy spin that was about as subtle as batting my eyes and blowing him a kiss. I'd gotten rusty at flirting.

"I hope so," he said with a smile. "That's what I've been waiting for."

There was no rust on his flirting skills, which should have given me pause. It didn't.

"You've been waiting?"

"Yes, ma'am," he said.

"Then you can call me Natalie."

He waved the waitress over. She was probably in her late forties and wore a short-sleeved white uniform with a zippered front and a black apron over the flared skirt.

"Could we please get a menu for the lady, Crystal?" Kelton said.

"Are you Ralph DeRosso's daughter?" I asked her.

"Yes," she said, setting a menu down in front of me. "Why?"

"My boss, Adrian Monk, is curious about the Golden Rail Express robbery and I'm sure that he would like to talk with you about your father."

"If I knew where the gold was, do you think I'd still be working here?"

"Take it easy, Crystal," Kelton said. "Adrian Monk is a famous detective from San Francisco who is helping us investigate Manny's murder."

"What's that got to do with the Golden Rail Express and my dad?"

Kelton looked at me. It was a good question and he was as interested in the answer as Crystal DeRosso was.

"Nothing," I said. "But Mr. Monk can't let go of a mystery until he solves it. He's not going to be able to give his full concentration to the investigation of Manny Feikema's homicide while this is still on his mind."

"It happened forty-seven years ago," she said. "I wasn't even two years old. What can I tell him that's going to make any difference?"

"I don't know," I said.

"He's not going to figure out what happened anyway," she said.

"Yes, he will," I said.

"What makes you so sure he's going to succeed where so many others haven't?" she asked.

"Because he's the best," I said. "He never encountered a mystery he couldn't solve."

"I'd consider it a personal favor if you'd indulge his curiosity and answer whatever questions he has," Kelton said.

"I always liked Manny." She sighed in assent and took out her pad. "What'll it be, Chief?"

"The usual."

She glanced at me. "What would you like?"

"A cheeseburger and fries would be great," I said. "With a chocolate milk shake."

"Two usuals, coming up," she said and walked away.

I shared a smile with Kelton. "You eat that every night?"

"I probably shouldn't have a milk shake every night," he said. "But I figure it's got to be better for me than what I used to drink with dinner. Are you sure Monk won't be in tonight to talk with her?"

"I doubt he'll show up," I said. "He's busy cleaning his room."

"The motel didn't give you clean rooms?"

"Oh, they did, just not up to Mr. Monk's standards," I said.

"How clean does it need to be?"

"Totally sterile," I said. "You should be able to lick the floor, which is a strange metaphor for me to use, since if you *did* lick the floor, Mr. Monk would have to start cleaning all over again."

"How did he get this way?"

"I used to think it was his mother's fault," I said.

"That's because you're a mother, Natalie."

"How did you know that?"

"It shows in your warmth and infinite patience with Monk," Kelton said.

"And you checked me out," I said.

"That, too."

"So you know I'm single."

"Why do you think I checked you out?"

"We're getting off topic," I said.

"I like this topic," he said.

"I thought that Monk's mom was responsible for his eccentricities because she was so unbelievably rigid and overprotective. But after what I've learned today, I'm beginning to think that his problems are a genetic predisposition that goes back generations."

"What did you find out today that changed

your mind?"

I took out the book that Doris gave me and set it on the counter.

"I discovered that Mr. Monk had an ancestor who was as smart and unusual as he is and was also a brilliant detective. His name was Artemis Monk and he lived right here in Trouble in 1855."

"Monk didn't know anything about him before?"

"He doesn't want to know anything about him now," I said. "He refuses to accept that they're related."

"What difference does it make whether Monk acknowledges it or not?" Kelton picked up the book and flipped through it. "It is what it is."

"Because if he does, it might give him a new perspective on his life and a better understanding of himself," I said. "It might help him overcome his problems."

"Or not," he said.

"You can't run from your past," I said.

"Now you tell me," Kelton said.

"Is that why you came to Trouble?"

"Let's just say that I needed to put some distance between me and the things that I've done."

"Were they that bad?"

"I'm not proud of them. At least here I

had a chance at a fresh start."

*"Had?"*

The question hung in the air as Crystal came out and set our hamburgers down in front of us. We were silent until she dropped off our milk shakes a moment later. Kelton took a sip of his shake. I followed his lead and tried mine, too. It was the best shake I'd ever had. No wonder he had one every night. But if I did that, in no time I'd need to sit on two stools.

"Manny's murder is the first major case we've had in Trouble since I got here and I'm not exactly impressing the city fathers with my progress."

"It's only been a couple of days," I said. It took enormous willpower not to finish my luscious milk shake before I even took a bite out of my cheeseburger.

"They know I've got no leads and that I'm sitting around, waiting for something to break."

"Why did you tell them that?"

"I didn't. My officers are their eyes and ears."

I bit into my cheeseburger and couldn't believe how good it tasted. I realized in that instant that it had been years, perhaps decades, since I had a genuine hamburger the way God intended hamburgers to be.

140

Juicy, fatty, and salty with a real fire-grilled, meaty flavor. The cheese was thick, extra-sharp smoked cheddar that was hot and gooey. I took another bite before I even swallowed my first one.

I was in hamburger heaven.

Kelton hadn't touched his burger yet. He seemed to have lost his appetite. I was tempted to ask if I could have his burger, too. Instead, I took another big bite of mine and washed it down with a sip of chocolate shake.

"Well, this sure isn't going the way I planned," he said.

"The investigation?"

"Our dinner."

As far as I was concerned, dinner was fabulous. "You planned something?"

"I planned on being upbeat, witty, and charming," Kelton said. "Instead, all I've done is unload all of my problems on you."

"I'm flattered that you did," I said, wiping the juice and drool and cheese from my mouth with a napkin. "I much prefer a real conversation to a performance. I feel that I know you better after one day than I've known some men that I've dated for weeks."

"I could have listened more and talked less."

"There's still time," I said, though the

truth was I was hoping he'd talk some more about anything he wanted so I could keep on eating.

And I wondered if he'd think less of me if I ordered another cheeseburger, not that I intended to let that stop me.

Kelton had revealed so much about himself to me that I told him my life story to even things up a bit, though I suspect he knew most of it already from the digging that he'd done. But he listened intently anyway, probably looking for inconsistencies between what he'd learned and what I was telling. Not that I'd hold that against him. He couldn't help himself. Kelton was a detective, after all. After that, we talked about this and that and nothing in particular.

I liked him. He was honest, warm, and self-deprecating. And there was a tragic undercurrent to his life that made him oddly compelling. He never explained how or why he'd become a drunk, or went into any more details about the shameful things he did in Boston that got him fired, but that only made him more interesting to me.

I'm not sure what that says about my personality, or my taste in men. But I liked that he wasn't perfect, that he knew it, and didn't have a problem admitting it. I've met too many men who try way too hard to convince me how wonderful they are. Harley Kelton didn't do that.

There was a comment he'd made about Monk rejecting the possibility of an ancestor in Trouble — "it is what it is" — and I think that pretty much summed up Kelton's approach to dealing with life. He took things as they came and didn't make excuses for the choices he made, good or bad.

Speaking of choices, I showed incredible self-control and didn't end up ordering a second cheeseburger, but I devoured a big slice of apple pie à la mode instead.

I reached for my purse when the check came, but Kelton insisted on picking up the tab for dinner, which I thought was awfully nice, and then he walked me back to the motel. We walked slowly and I felt sure he was tempted to take my hand or put his arm around me. Or maybe I was just projecting my own desires. We bumped into each other once or twice as we walked, accidentally-on-purpose, but that was it for physical contact.

It was about nine thirty by then. The lights were still on in Monk's room and we could hear the sound of him vacuuming.

Kelton didn't make any moves on me, unless you count the polite kiss he gave me on the cheek, which I don't. I gave him a kiss on the cheek right back, bid him good night, and went into my room.

I'll admit I peeked through my curtains and watched him as he walked slowly back to the center of Trouble. He probably knew I was watching him, too. I found myself wondering where he lived and what his home looked like.

I was too keyed up from the nice date and all that sugar to go right to sleep. So I got into bed and read a little more about Artemis Monk until the excitement gradually wore off, the sugar finally metabolized in my system, and my long, trying day of travel and assisting finally caught up with me.

## THE EXTRAORDINARY MR. MONK
## The Case of the Snake in the Grass

*(From the journal of Abigail Guthrie)*
*Trouble, California, 1856*

It wasn't just his job as assayer or his cleanliness that drew attention to Artemis Monk. He had strong, peculiar opinions about the way things ought to be done and he expressed them at every opportunity.

For instance, he believed it should be illegal for prospectors to eat from the same pans that they used to pan gold.

144

He believed that horses should be prohibited from the streets and tied to hitching posts outside of town so they couldn't make a mess on a public thoroughfare.

He believed that all the planks in the sidewalks should be evenly spaced from one another and kept dirt free.

He believed people should be required to bathe each day and wear clean clothes.

He believed that spittoons, and spitting of any kind, should be outlawed.

He believed that the buildings should all be the same height and perfectly symmetrical or face immediate demolition.

Unfortunately for Monk, nobody else shared those beliefs. But because he was an important man in town, over time some compromises were reluctantly reached between him and the citizenry.

Sheriff Wheeler made everybody clean up after their horses, shoveling the droppings into buckets that had to be emptied in a specified patch outside of town. It was terribly inconvenient, but as much as the townsfolk grumbled about it, the truth was that people, especially the womenfolk with their long skirts, appreciated the clean streets.

Merchants were asked to keep the portion of sidewalk in front of their businesses dirt free and in good repair. If they didn't, Monk would soon be out there doing it himself, which was never good for business, since he tended to shoo away customers who didn't meet his standards of cleanliness.

Tobacco spitting was restricted to the spittoons in the saloons and gambling halls, where Monk was unwelcome anyway, since he abhorred drunkenness and could instantly spot shaved dice, a crooked roulette wheel, or marked cards. Neither the management nor the clientele wanted him around to spoil things for them.

Nobody liked abiding by even those rules, but they were afraid that Monk, the most accurate, honest, and incorruptible assayer they'd ever met, might leave Trouble if he got too annoyed, and that would have been much harder to live with than the compromises they'd struck.

So people in Trouble were well aware of Monk's often-infuriating peculiarities and made accommodations for them. Some people, though, tried to take advantage of them, which brings me to a case in point.

Roger Ewing, a prosperous hotel owner from San Francisco, wanted to invest some of his profits in a gold-mining operation and had his eye on one in Trouble.

The easiest way to get gold is placer mining, which is sifting through a deposit of gravel, dirt, or clay in an old or active streambed for particles of color. All you needed for that was a pan, a strong back, and plenty of luck. It was a poor man's mine.

But once you've scraped up all the easy pickings, then you have to go after the gold that's sunk down through the sediment to the bedrock, where it accumulates to create what prospectors called a pay streak. To get to the pay streak, if it's even there at all, takes some heavy work and, if you need to dam up or divert a stream to do it, considerable financial resources, which is where a well-to-do man like Roger Ewing comes in.

Lute Asper had been working a wide stretch of placer not far from Trouble for a few months. It yielded steady if unspectacular color. The talk was that he'd reached the point where, if he really wanted to exploit the potential of his claim, he'd have to put in far more effort than he already had. Problem was, his gold fever had broken and he was pining for his abandoned law practice and the wife he'd left behind in Philadelphia.

Asper spread the word that he wanted to sell out and soon Ewing came to Trouble to check out the claim for himself.

Ewing was nobody's fool, as he was quick to tell anyone that he met, which told me that his biggest fear was being seen as one.

So he wasn't going to take Asper's word on anything. He decided to show up unannounced to survey Asper's gold claim. Ewing also brought along his own prospectors to sample the placer in random spots to avoid any possibility of Asper engaging in chicanery to artificially inflate the yield.

And he hired Monk to do an on-site assay.

Ewing, prosperously rotund with a handlebar mustache and a top hat, kindly offered us a ride to Asper's claim in his rented buggy, but Monk insisted on walking, which I could see surprised and offended our client.

As smart as Ewing said he was, his research on Monk clearly hadn't extended beyond confirming his reputation for honesty, accuracy, and objectivity or he wouldn't have been taken aback by the refusal. It was common knowledge that Monk didn't ride on, or behind, horses or any other animals. His preferred forms of conveyance were his own two feet and locomotives, which traveled a predetermined and level course. He also loved bicycles, and the perfect balance that was required to ride them, but they were very impractical in most situations.

We stuck to well-worn trails as much as possible on our way out to Asper's claim, so it wasn't a hard trek, just a long one, especially in the dry heat. But despite the discomforts, I was glad to be out in the countryside and away from town for a change.

Monk was miserable. He chose each step carefully and kept his arms close to his body for fear of brushing up against something.

"I hate nature," he grumbled.

"How could anybody hate nature?"

"Because there's too much nature in nature," Monk said. "There's nature everywhere. It's completely out of control."

"God's got his eye on it."

"Then he must be easily distracted," Monk said, pointing to some bushes and trees. "Look over there. The ground is covered with all kinds of leaves mixed together. It's intolerable. Someone should clean that up."

"God does, in his own way," I said. "Eventually the leaves rot and become part of the soil."

"Eventually is a very long time and it involves rotting," Monk said. "Rot is bad."

"What is bad about rot?"

"Rot rots," he said. "Would you eat something that was rotten?"

"No," I said.

"So there you have it: Nature is a rotten mess. But that's only the beginning. If you take your eyes off of it for one second, it will kill you. Thorns, insects, fungus, worms, birds, reptiles, wild animals, raging rivers, bottomless ravines, dry deserts, snow, quicksand, tumbleweeds, sap, and mud. Rot, poison, and death. That's nature."

"It's a wonder you even step outside of your cabin," I said.

"My bravery exceeds my good sense," he said.

"That must be it," I said.

Asper's claim was in a wide wash of what was once a streambed with high banks on either side. There were lots of rocks and patches of dry brush where the ground hadn't already been dug up and scoured for gold. A half dozen prospectors were crouched in a creek that meandered through the property. They were panning the dirt that was shoveled into their pans from various spots on the claim.

Ewing watched them, chewing on a cigar, his face already burned from the sun. It was clear he wasn't used to being outside for long periods. He was an office man.

The same couldn't be said of Lute Asper, who was waiting for us on the trail as we approached, a shotgun cradled in his arm. He had a hard, angular face, flinty eyes, and the dark skin of a man who'd spent more time in the sun than in the shade. His hair and beard were neatly trimmed, probably to make a better impression on Ewing.

Asper touched the brim of his hat and smiled at me as we approached.

" 'Morning, Mrs. Guthrie. You and Mr. Monk watch your step. It's crawling with rattlers out here."

Monk looked at me. He was ashen-faced. "You didn't tell me anything about rattle-snakes."

"Why do you think they call this Rattle-snake Ridge?" Asper said.

"They do?" Monk said.

I knew it, of course, but I had decided it was best not to share that bit of information with Monk before our trek.

"Those colorful names usually don't mean anything," I said. "I thought they were refer-ring to the way the stream snakes through the landscape."

"We're going to die," Monk said.

"Not on my watch," Asper said. "I know you're afraid of snakes and the like, Mr. Monk. That's why I'm carrying this shotgun. I'll keep you safe."

Ewing marched over to us. "I'm glad you're finally here."

"I want to go home," Monk said.

Ewing held out his hand to us to show us a vial that, in my estimation, held about five pinches of gold. "This is all we've come up with so far out of all those pans."

Monk studied the dust. "That's gold and not much of it. Glad to be of service."

He turned and started to go, but I stopped him.

"I'm sure there's more that Mr. Ewing would like us to see," I said.

"Mr. Monk might as well go," Ewing said. "It's not a very promising patch of dirt."

"That's because you're looking in all the wrong places," Asper said.

"These are professional prospectors," Ewing said.

"They're drifters and no-accounts who couldn't find water if they were standing in a stream or they'd be working their own rich claims now instead of working for you," Asper said. "The best pickings are obviously over there."

Asper motioned to the rock and brush to his left.

"An area that I'm sure you've salted liberally in expectation of our arrival," Ewing said and turned to Monk. "You're the expert. What area looks good to you?"

Monk took a few steps forward, cocked his head, held his hands out in front of him, circled here and there, stopping every so often to roll his shoulders, crouch, stand again, and sway from side to side.

"What is he doing?" Ewing asked.

"Studying the landscape for telling geological and metallurgical features," I said.

"I figured that," Ewing said. "But why's he doing some kind of Indian rain dance?"

"He's stretching," I said. It was a bald-faced lie. I didn't know what he was doing. "He's tormented by muscle spasms in his back from all the hours he spends sitting in his laboratory."

"Is that why he walks everywhcre?" Ewing asked.

I nodded. "That's right. It loosens him up."

Monk spun around, squatted, and peered into some dry brush and rocks at the base of the ridge. He turned to us.

"I think this would be a good spot." Monk started towards the brush. "Right here you —"

Asper rushed forward, pushed Monk aside, and fired into the brush, the sound of the gunshot echoing loudly off the bluffs.

"What the hell are you doing?" Ewing said.

Asper shoved his shotgun into the brush and, when he pulled it out again, a dead rattlesnake was draped over his barrel. It was the largest rattler I'd ever seen.

"Saving Mr. Monk from a nasty surprise," he said. "If there were any more rattlers in there, they're gone now."

Ewing called his men over and they began shoveling dirt into their pans in the area Monk had picked out and going back to the stream.

Monk was shaken. He staggered over to Ewing's buggy and climbed up on the rear, as far from the horses as possible.

"Are you going to be all right, Mr. Monk?" I asked.

"I just want to sit here," he said. "Safely away from nature for a while."

Asper admired the dead snake. "That's gonna make a mighty fine belt."

After a time, Ewing came over with a big smile on his face, holding one of the wet pans.

"Look at that," Ewing said, keeping his voice low so Asper, leaning against a tree about ten yards away, couldn't hear him.

Monk peered into the pan and so did I. My Hank had dreamed of coming up with a pan full of color like that. There must have been fifty dollars worth of dust at the bottom of the pan.

"What does this tell you?" Ewing said. "You think there's more where that came from?"

Monk slipped off the buggy, glanced back at the bluff and, after regarding it for a moment, cocked his head and rolled his shoulders. "I'm sure there is."

Ewing nodded with satisfaction, swallowed his smile, and walked over to Asper. We joined them.

"I've been conferring with Mr. Monk. This claim isn't measuring up to your boasting," Ewing said. "But I might take a chance on it if the asking price wasn't so outrageously steep."

Asper grinned and set his shotgun down against the tree. "Are you a poker player, Mr. Ewing?"

"I abstain from liquor and games of chance," he said.

"Good thing you do, because you'd lose your shirt. I can see all your cards on your face," Asper said. "That must have been some pan you took over to Mr. Monk."

"It showed more promise than the others," Ewing said.

"This whole patch is nothing but promise

155

waiting to be fulfilled. If I had your wealth, Mr. Ewing, and didn't dream of Philadelphia every time I closed my eyes, I'd hold on to this claim and not let go until I'd taken every last flake of gold out of it. I'm selling it to you for a price far below what you are going to pull out of the ground once I'm gone just so I can go home. You'd best settle for that or I'll find somebody else who will."

Monk screamed, shoved Asper aside, grabbed his shotgun, and fired at the tree, the three of us scrambling away an instant before we would have been riddled with buckshot ourselves.

Asper, furious, yanked the shotgun out of Monk's hand. "Are you crazy? We could have been killed!"

"That's why I did it," Monk said. "To save you."

"From what?" Asper yelled.

"An ant," Monk said.

"So you shot it?" Asper said.

"It was about to crawl on your head," Monk said.

"Couldn't you have just asked us to move?" Ewing said.

"It might have pounced on someone else."

"Ants don't pounce," Asper said.

"That's like saying that gold doesn't grow

on trees."

"It doesn't," Asper said.

Monk stepped up and squinted at the tree. "Then why is this bark sparkling with gold?"

Ewing and I joined Monk and examined the trunk. Sure enough, the tree glittered with specks of gold.

Asper turned and ran to his horse. But one of Ewing's men tackled him before he could get there and pinned him down. Everybody except Asper, who was facedown in the dirt, turned to look at Monk for an explanation.

"What in blazes is going on here?" Ewing said.

"If you send some men up on the ridge," Monk said, "you'll find a sack full of dead rattlesnakes and one of Asper's men running away."

"You're not making a lick of sense," Ewing said.

"Here's what happened," Monk said. "Lute Asper wasn't carrying the shotgun to protect us from snakes. The buckshot was laced with gold dust. Asper was just waiting for someone to get close to one of the ridges so he could pretend to spot a snake. As soon as he fired his shotgun, one of his men tossed a dead snake over the edge for him to find."

Ewing nodded with a frown. "It was just a scheme to salt his claim, make it appear richer than it actually was, and get a higher price out of me."

"I'm afraid so," Monk said. "The snakes were also meant to unsettle me so I couldn't concentrate."

Ewing frowned and faced his men. "Tie Asper up and throw him in the back of my buggy. We're taking him in to the sheriff. Looks like I wasted a trip here."

"I wouldn't say that," Monk said and led Ewing off to one side for a private chat. I didn't hear what they said, but I could see Ewing nodding.

After a moment, Ewing headed back over to Asper, who was being hog-tied by two men.

"I'm going to give you a choice, Asper, and it's only good for thirty seconds," Ewing said. "You can sell me this claim for the price of passage back to Philadelphia and your promise never to return to California or you can go to jail, where you'll probably be hanged."

"I'll take the ticket," he said.

"I thought you might," Ewing said. "Sign the claim over to me now and let's be done with it."

Monk started to walk away. I hurried after

158

him, more than a little confused.

"What did you say to Mr. Ewing?"

"I told him that Asper didn't need to salt the claim," Monk said. "From what I can tell looking at the burned color of those ridges, they're rich with iron oxide and manganese, which are likely indicators of the presence of gold-laced quartz. I'm certain that the claim is worth everything he says it is and probably more."

"Do you think Asper knows that?"

Monk shook his head. "If he did, he wouldn't have gone to the trouble of concocting this scheme."

"It's poetic justice," I said. "But if Asper's claim is genuinely as rich in gold as he boasted, what tipped you off to the scheme?"

"He shot at the snake before I finished what I was going to say," Monk said.

"Which was?"

"I thought it was a good place to build a cabin because it was the one spot on this claim where you probably *wouldn't* find any gold."

# CHAPTER EIGHT:
# MR. MONK HAS
## BREAKFAST

I knocked on Monk's door at nine a.m. on the button. He was dressed and ready to go, as I expected him to be.

"Good morning," he said.

I looked over his shoulder. The bed was made and nothing in the room seemed to have been disturbed at all.

"Did you sleep last night?"

"Yes," he said. "Very well, thank you."

"In the bed?"

"Where else would I have slept?"

"I don't know, but it looks like the room hasn't been occupied."

"That's how everybody should leave their hotel rooms," Monk said, stepping out and closing the door behind him. "Which reminds me, we should tell the manager not to let the maid into mine."

"Because there's nothing to clean," I said.

He nodded. "And I don't want to have to clean it again."

"Do you think she'd come in and make a mess?"

"Everybody makes a mess."

"Except you," I said.

"It takes a lot of concentration and effort. I seem to be the only one willing to make the investment."

"I know at least one other person," I said as we headed towards the manager's office.

"My brother?"

"Okay, make that two people."

"Certainly you're not thinking about yourself," Monk said.

"No, it's not me."

"Because you're a tornado of filth."

"Thank you," I said. "I'm talking about Artemis Monk."

"A fictional character," he said.

"A real person," I said. "Your ancestor."

"Please, let's not start that silliness again."

"I read more of Abigail Guthrie's book last night. You're obviously a descendant of his. He hated nature and was afraid of tumbleweeds."

"That's like saying I'm related to him because I eat food, drink water, and breathe air."

"He did this," I said and mimicked Monk's Zen dance. I rolled my shoulders, tipped my head, did a few pirouettes, and

161

held my hands in front of me like I was framing a camera shot.

Monk stared at me. "What are you doing?"

"I'm doing you," I said.

"I don't do that."

"Yes, you do," I said. "And so did Artemis Monk."

I went into the office and asked the manager to have the maid skip Monk's room and spend the extra time on mine since I am such a tornado of filth. He eyed me suspiciously.

"Don't worry," I said. "We aren't hiding any blood on the walls or bodily organs on ice in the bathtub."

"I didn't say anything," he said.

"But you thought it."

"I might be thinking a lot of things," he said. "You see it all in this business."

"I don't want to know," I said.

"No," he said. "You don't."

After that creepy conversation, Monk and I walked down to Dorothy's Chuckwagon for breakfast. Two of the four booths were occupied but nobody was at the counter, though there was a plate with the remains of two fried eggs and a stack of hotcakes.

I took a seat at the counter, a few stools away from the dirty plate because I knew it would unsettle Monk to be close to it. Monk remained standing behind me.

"I'd prefer a booth," he said.

"It will be easier for the waitress to talk to us if we're here."

"Why would I want to talk to her?"

"She's Crystal DeRosso, the Golden Rail Express conductor's daughter."

"She can talk to us in a booth," he said.

"But then only three of the booths would be occupied," I said. "The balance of the universe would be totally disrupted."

"You're right," Monk said and immediately took a seat next to me. "What was I thinking?"

"You're hungry," I said.

"That must be it," he said. "Thanks to you, we narrowly averted disaster."

"I bet you're sorry about that tornado of filth remark now."

"No," he said. "Why would I be?"

We heard a toilet flush and then Bob Gorman, the new security guard at the Gold Rush Museum, came out of a side door and took a seat at the counter in front of his unfinished breakfast. He was wearing a sleeveless T-shirt and jeans that showed off his lean physique.

"Hey, it's the detectives," Gorman said. "How's it hanging?"

"What's hanging?" Monk bolted up from the stool and began frantically brushing his clothes. "Where is it? Is it still there?"

"Relax, buddy, nothing is hanging," Gorman said. "It's an expression, like 'hi.' "

Monk sat down and rolled his shoulders. "Right. Of course I knew that. I'm groovy with that jive. But you can never be too careful where things that hang are concerned. You dig?"

"Sure," Gorman said and reached for his fork.

"Stop!" Monk said.

"What?" Gorman said, a bit startled by Monk's outburst.

"Don't pick up that fork," Monk said.

"What's wrong with it?"

"It's your hands," Monk said. "They're disgusting. You didn't wash them."

It was true. There was black stuff worked in deep around his fingernails and on the back of his hands.

Gorman examined his hands. "This? It's nothing. It comes with the job with grease monkeys."

"You were handling monkeys?" Monk said. "Greasy ones?"

"The problem with being a mechanic is that the grease, grime, and oil don't come off no matter how hard you scrub. That's one reason I'm glad to have this new job. I'll have clean hands again someday."

"Make it today," Monk said and motioned to me for wipes. "Try scrubbing with soap, water, and some of these."

I handed Gorman some wipes.

"If that doesn't work," Monk said, "try steel wool."

"Won't that strip off my flesh?" Gorman said.

"At least you'll be clean," Monk said. "You should go now, before the monkey germs spread. Monkeys have Ebola."

I met Gorman's eye. "He won't give you any peace if you don't."

Gorman sighed, gathered up the wipes, and returned to the bathroom.

Monk shook his head in disgust. "Greasy monkeys, wild burros, this place is hell."

Crystal came out, carrying some plates. She acknowledged us with a glance and took the plates to one of the booths, setting eggs, bacon, biscuits, gravy, and pancakes down in front of two couples. Then she came back behind the counter.

"What'll it be?" she asked.

I wanted another cheeseburger and a shake, but I restrained myself. It wasn't easy. "Two pancakes, four strips of bacon, and some coffee, please. And could I have the pancakes and bacon on separate plates?"

I made that last request to score some points with my boss.

"Sure, it just means an extra plate to wash for no good reason," she said and turned to Monk. "And you?"

"Do you have Chex cereal?"

"No," she said.

"How about Cap'n Crunch?"

"No," she said.

"Then I'll have toast with the crusts cut off."

"Will that be all?"

"He also has some questions," I said. "This is Adrian Monk, the detective I mentioned last night."

"How's it hanging?" Monk asked. "As in hello, not as in there are things hanging from you."

She gave him a withering look. "Let me put your order in and I'll be right back."

Crystal returned to the kitchen. Gorman came out of the bathroom. His hands were much cleaner, but not perfect. Monk scowled and turned to me.

"Do you have any steel wool?"

"No, I don't," I said.

"Sandpaper?"

"Sorry, all out."

"What's the matter with you? You

shouldn't venture out into the world without essential supplies. You need to be better prepared. Our survival could depend on it someday."

"Steel wool and sandpaper," I said. "I'll put them on the checklist."

"I'd like to see your checklist."

"I don't have one," I said. "It's also going on the checklist."

"You're putting a checklist on your checklist."

"It will be the first thing on it," I said. "I promise you that."

Gorman picked up his fork, cut into his pancakes, and ran the morsel through the egg yolk. He was about to eat it when Monk yelled out:

"Don't!"

Gorman froze. "What's wrong now?"

"You have yolk on your pancakes," Monk said.

"I like it," Gorman said.

"You can't," Monk said.

"Why not?"

"Because you aren't allowed to mix entrées together," Monk said. "They are separate entities. Think of them as continents. What would happen if North America collided with Europe? The earth would be ripped apart. That's your plate."

"You should let him eat, Mr. Monk."

"I can't stand idly by while a man commits suicide," Monk said.

"Look, buddy, everything gets mixed together in your stomach anyway," Gorman said and ate the morsel off of his fork. "It's like shoveling coal into the boiler of a train. There aren't compartments in there."

"The stomach knows," Monk said.

They might have argued the point further, but that's when Crystal came out and stood in front of us.

"What do you want to know?" she asked Monk.

"How can you serve food to someone who lets yolk touch his pancakes?" Monk said, tipping his head towards the security guard.

Crystal glanced at Gorman, who made a show this time of smearing his piece of pancake through the yolk, butter, and maple syrup before eating it. Monk did a full-body cringe, which made Gorman grin and only encouraged him to continue.

"There's no law against it," she said.

"Would you let him drink and drive?"

"We don't serve alcohol here," Crystal said. "Is that what you wanted to talk to me about?"

"He's curious about your father," I said.

"I don't remember my dad at all," she

168

said. "I only know him through pictures in an album and the stories my mom and people in town have told me over the years. He used to come here and eat breakfast every morning before work."

Monk glared at Gorman. "I bet you take drugs."

"Never touch the stuff," Gorman said. "I don't drink or smoke either."

"But this is how it starts," Monk said. "Yolk and pancakes today, hooch and weed tomorrow. No wonder you think nothing of cavorting with greasy monkeys."

"Mr. Monk," I said. "Don't you have some questions for Crystal about her father?"

Monk looked at her. "Did your mom ever talk about the robbery?"

"Of course she did," Crystal said. "What kind of stupid question is that?"

"A simple one to get you focused on the specific topic that I am interested in," Monk said. "Perhaps I should have been more direct. Was your father one of the robbers of the Golden Rail Express?"

Crystal glowered at him. "That train was his life. He loved trains. Ever since he was a kid he wanted to work on the Golden Rail Express. He started at the bottom and worked his way up to conductor. He wore that uniform with the pride of a four-star general. Working for that railroad was the only job he ever wanted and the only one he ever had. So no, Mr. Monk, he couldn't have robbed that train. He was devoted to it, probably even more than he was to Mom and me."

"If he knew the train so well," Monk said, "how did he fall off of it?"

"He didn't," Crystal said. "He was thrown off. He was murdered just like that poor security guard, for putting up a fight."

"Did anyone see him get pushed?" Monk asked.

"Nobody saw what happened to him," she said. "He wasn't on the train when it arrived in Trouble, so they went looking for him. They found his body along the tracks."

"Maybe he died jumping off with the loot and was left behind by his uninjured accomplices," Monk said.

"They didn't find any coins or money near him," she said. "If the fall was hard enough to kill him, don't you think it would have broken the bags of money and gold? Or at least spilled some of what was inside when he let go of the bags?"

Monk shrugged. "I suppose so. But I can still see why people suspected him of being involved."

"Nobody in town did, only people who didn't know him," Crystal said. "Leonard McElroy and Clifford Adams kept running the Golden Rail Express and gave my mom a portion of their paychecks every week for twenty years. They wouldn't do that if they thought Dad was one of the robbers, would they?"

Gorman spoke up as he cleaned the last of the yolk and maple syrup off his plate with a piece of toast. "What does any of this matter now anyway?"

"It's unsolved. Unfinished. Incomplete," Monk said. "It's a missing piece of history."

"That's all it is, history," Crystal said. "What about the here and now? What about poor Manny?"

"I'm working on that, too," Monk said.

The cook rang a bell in the kitchen and Crystal went back to get the food.

"So why aren't you asking us about him?" Gorman said.

"Do you know something about his murder?"

"No, but a few days before he was killed, a guy came by the garage asking about him," Gorman said.

"Did you tell the chief about it?" I said.

"The chief never asked me," Gorman said. "The guy said he was an old friend just passing through and remembered that Manny lived around here. He asked if I knew him and if I could give him directions out to his place."

"Why did he come to you?" Monk said.

"I worked at the only garage in town," Gorman said. "It's the only place you can go if you need to get your car fixed. So I know everybody and everybody knows me."

"Did you tell him where Manny lived?"

"I didn't see the harm," Gorman said. "I offered to call Manny for him but the guy wanted to surprise him."

"He certainly did," I said. "Did he tell you his name?"

"Nope, but he drove a red 1964 Ford Thunderbird," Gorman said. "I remember it because it was in mint condition. You don't see many of those around here. Did you know the sixty-four had a swing-away steering column? It swung to the center of the car to make it easier for the driver to get in and out. That feature never caught on, though. They have steering wheels that tilt up and down, but not side to side."

"That's really interesting. I could talk steering wheels all day," I said. "But you need to go see Chief Kelton right away and give him a description of the man and his Thunderbird."

"Maybe I'll stop by on my way to work." Gorman picked up his plate and, looking straight at Monk, he licked it clean. "Now I need some sleep. I've been up all night."

"A man is dead," I said.

Gorman set down the plate, wiped his mouth on his bare arm, dropped a few dollars on the table, and got up from his stool.

"Manny isn't going to get any deader if I have a little snooze."

He walked out just as Crystal came out with our breakfast. She set the plates down in front of us. Monk's toast was cut perfectly square and was evenly browned but he didn't notice. He was staring at Gorman's plate.

"Will there be anything else?" she asked.

"I'd like you to take away that plate, please," he said, pointing at it. "And have it destroyed."

# CHAPTER NINE:
# MR. MONK AND THE
# MINE

We walked to the police station after breakfast to alert the chief about the mysterious man who'd asked Gorman about Manny. And we needed directions out to Clifford Adams' place.

Kelton was standing at the front counter going over a stack of files when we came in. He smiled when he saw us, but I wanted to think it was mostly for me.

"Perfect timing," he said. "These files just arrived from Captain Stottlemeyer. They're people Manny sent to prison who might carry a grudge against him and were recently released."

"Maybe we can help you narrow down the list," Monk said. "There was a guy in town asking about Manny a few days before the murder."

Kelton's face got tight. "Nobody told me that. How did you find out?"

"We kind of stumbled on it," I said. "Bob

Gorman told us. The guy stopped by the garage. I don't understand why Gorman never told you about it."

Kelton frowned. "Because we're the only ones who think Manny's murder was personal and not about stealing something from the museum. Even so, Bob should have said something. He's a nice kid, but not too bright."

"That's an understatement," Monk said. "Did you know that he mixes his pancakes with his eggs and that his hands are as black as coal?"

"Shameful," Kelton said. "Did Bob get the guy's name?"

"No," I said. "But he's going to stop in to see you on his way to work and give you a description of the man. All Gorman could tell us was that he was driving a sixty-four Thunderbird."

"That's something, I guess," Kelton said. "We'll see if that matches anything in the files. What's your game plan for the day?"

"We'd like to talk to Clifford Adams, the engineer of the Golden Rail Express," I said. "Can you tell us how to get out to where he lives?"

Kelton drew a map on a piece of paper and gave me the directions.

"The Adams place is about five miles

175

outside of town at the end of an unpaved dirt road," Kelton said.

"Why isn't it paved?" Monk asked.

"Because nobody paved it."

"Roads should be paved," Monk said. "Everything should be flat, smooth, and even."

"Wouldn't that make life pretty bland?" Kelton said.

"Yes," Monk said. "As it should be."

"Paving isn't one of my responsibilities," Kelton said.

"You enforce the law, don't you?"

"There's no law on the books requiring paved roads."

"It's a matter of basic human decency," Monk said.

"That's out of my jurisdiction, too. Don't wander off the road if your car breaks down. The land out there is dotted with abandoned mine shafts and unstable tunnels held up with decaying timbers."

"We'd never leave the road, even an unpaved one," Monk said. "Otherwise we'd run the risk of encountering nature."

"How can you have a problem with nature?" Kelton asked. "It's everywhere."

"Exactly. It's out of control."

"You mean it's out of *your* control," Kelton said. "Welcome to life."

"I don't find life all that welcoming," Monk said.

"I wouldn't have guessed," Kelton said.

The drive out to Clifford Adams' place was slow-going, bumpy, and dusty, and we ran through that superhighway of butterflies again, splattering my windshield with bug goo.

Monk whimpered in misery the whole way.

I turned on the radio to drown him out but the only signal I could get was from an outlaw radio station run by some crackpot who was convinced that the migration of butterflies was the omen of an imminent alien invasion.

Maybe he was right. In fact, it looked like the alien invasion had already come and gone. As we drove across the broad, desolate landscape, I didn't see any indications of life, only the remnants of it. There were a few dilapidated houses, the rusted hulks of abandoned cars, and the weed-choked entrances to a couple of mines dug into the ragged hillsides. It was a bleak, sun-bleached, rocky, and totally uninviting place.

The road ended at a weather-beaten Quonset hut, one of those prefabricated, corrugated metal structures that was mass

177

produced for the military during World War II and later sold as surplus to the public. There were Quonset huts all around Monterey and Salinas when I was growing up. They were cheap, durable, and could be used for anything from warehouses to restaurants.

This particular hut was about twenty feet wide and fifty feet long and looked like an enormous pipe half buried lengthwise in the dirt. It was surrounded by scrapped cars and trucks, oil drums, appliances, sheets of corrugated metal, stacks of railroad ties, and assorted junk.

Underwear and socks and a set of pinstriped, denim overalls dangled from a clothesline strung between the hut and a wooden water tower that was probably as old as Trouble.

On the other side of the water tower was a tangle of pipes, engine parts, duct tape, pulleys, and conveyor belts that ended in a funnel that spilled out over several piles of gravel. The contraption was erected at one end of a set of rail tracks that ran ten yards up a hillside and into a mine opening. A trolley full of rocks was parked at the top of the track.

I expected Monk to leap out of the car

the instant we came to a stop, but he didn't move.

"What's wrong?" I asked.

He looked at me sorrowfully. "Everything."

"Could you be a little more specific?"

"If Trouble is hell," Monk said, "this is hell's hell. The man who lives here must be a Neanderthal. I can't decide what's deadlier, staying in this rolling bucket of pestilence or going out there."

"Let me see if I have this straight," I said. "I'm a tornado of filth and my car is a rolling bucket of pestilence."

"They tend to go hand in hand," Monk said.

"You're not winning any points with me today, Mr. Monk."

"I'm the employer and you are the employee," Monk said. "I'm the one who has all the points and you're the one who is supposed to earn them."

"I'm the one who is supposed to earn money," I said. "Employers pay employees and you still owe me last week's paycheck."

That would have shut him up if we hadn't both been silenced by the snap of a door slamming.

The sound came from a tiny wooden shack set out by itself a good twenty-five yards away from the Quonset hut.

Clifford Adams stood in front of the shack, adjusting the shoulder straps of his faded bib overalls. He took a pin-striped, pleated engineer's cap out of his chest pocket and put it snugly on his head and then walked purposefully towards the hut.

Adams was a trim, tough-looking man in his seventies with a fine layer of dust on his clothes and his leathery skin. His eyes were flinty, his face as craggy as the land he lived on.

"What do you suppose that tiny shack is for?" Monk asked.

It was obvious to me and probably would be to anyone else but Monk. I could never understand how a man who knew so much about so many esoteric subjects had so little common knowledge.

And yet Monk often saw things that nobody else did, obscure details that would turn out to be the key clues to solving a murder.

So I guess in the cosmic scheme of things, it all evened out, which, if you were to ask Monk, was all that mattered. Life for him was the pursuit and maintenance of balance, symmetry, and order.

"It's an outhouse," I said.

"A *what?*"

"A shack for a toilet."

"He put a toilet way out there, far away from where he lives." Monk nodded appreciatively. "That shows a real dedication to sanitary conditions. I may have misjudged him. It must have taken considerable effort to run a water line out that far in this wasteland."

Monk started to open his door.

"He didn't run plumbing to the out-house," I said.

Monk paused, the door open a crack. "That's ridiculous. If he didn't do that, what kind of toilet could he have in there?"

"A seat with a hole in it placed over an open pit."

Monk let out a little horrified squeak and then slammed the door shut and locked it.

"I'm staying in the car," he said.

"How do you intend to talk with him from inside the bucket of pestilence?"

"You can bring him to the window," he said. "But not too close."

I got out and Monk immediately locked my door. I met Adams halfway between the outhouse and his hut.

"Mr. Adams?"

"Are you a bill collector? Because if you are, you'll have to wait here while I go get my rifle."

"I'm not a bill collector," I said. "If I was, would you shoot me?"

"That depends if you're still here when I come back with my rifle and how fast you can drive away. Are you a process server?"

"Do you shoot them, too?"

"I try," he said.

"Do you shoot the police?"

"Are you a cop?"

"I'm not, but my boss is, sort of." I motioned to the car. Monk slunk down a little bit in his seat. "Adrian Monk is an investigative consultant to the San Francisco Police Department."

"I haven't been to San Francisco in ten years," Adams said.

"We're helping the police in Trouble investigate the murder of a guard at the Gold Rush Museum."

Adams squinted at me. "What happened?"

"It was after-hours. The guard was doing his rounds. Somebody jumped out from behind the Golden Rail Express and hit the guard over the head with a pick."

"What was stolen?"

"Nothing," I said.

Adams shook his head. "Makes no damn sense."

"That's why Mr. Monk is here. He specializes in making sense of things that make no

182

sense," I said. "As part of his investigation, Mr. Monk learned about the train robbery and thinks he can solve that case, too."

Adams squinted at Monk. "Why bother with that after all this time?"

"It's what he does," I said. "He can't help himself."

Adams nodded. The explanation seemed to have struck a nerve with him.

"I know what that's like. I've been trying to get gold out of that old mine up there for fifty years even though it's pointless."

"You must have found some gold or you wouldn't have kept at it."

"Just enough to keep me alive and thinking I'm finally close to that big strike," Adams said, looking up wistfully at the mine. "She's a tease, has been since the Gold Rush, but I keep coming back for more. I can't help myself, just like all the men who owned this godforsaken hole before me."

I pointed to the big contraption beside the water tower. "Does that have something to do with mining?"

"That machine grinds up the rocks so I can sort out the gold," he said. "At least, it's supposed to. I spend half my time going through scrapyards for parts to keep it running. If you look closely at that, you'll see mattress springs, an outboard motor, the blades of a combine, and the innards of a Mr. Coffee."

"What does the coffeemaker do?"

"Nothing, that's why I threw the damn thing into the maw," he said.

He trudged to the car, went to the passenger door, and knocked on the window. "What do you want to know?"

Monk waved me over and motioned for a wipe. I took one out of my purse and he pantomimed washing the window with it where Adams had knocked. I shrugged to indicate my helplessness and pointed to my purse on the seat. He grimaced and leaned away from the window, as if the germs from Adams' knuckles could leach through the glass.

"Is he going to get out or what?" Adams asked me.

"I don't think so. Mr. Monk is allergic to dirt and there's a lot of it out here."

Adams shrugged and faced Monk again. "If you've got a question, mister, spit it out. I've got things to do."

"Tell me what happened the night of the robbery," Monk said, his voice muffled by the glass.

"I wish I knew," Adams said.

"You were there, weren't you?" I said.

"The train never stopped from the time

184

we left Sacramento until we arrived in Trouble. I didn't know there'd been a robbery until we got to the station. Lenny McElroy — he was the boiler man — and I were up front, oblivious to the whole thing, just keeping the train chugging along. The passengers had been warned under threat of death by the masked robbers not to say or do anything to slow the train down."

Monk tucked his hand into his sleeve and knocked on the window with his covered arm. "I didn't hear you. Could you speak up and repeat what you just said?"

"No." Adams looked at me. "Is that all?"

"Do you think Ralph DeRosso was in on the robbery?" I asked loudly so Monk could hear me.

Adams shook his head. "I'm not convinced he was killed by those two robbers, either."

"What other explanation could there be for him falling off the train?"

"Sometimes I wonder if he jumped off the train before the robbery even happened."

"Why would he do that?"

"It was the final run of the Golden Rail Express. It was the end of an era that was long overdue. All Ralph ever wanted to be, all he knew how to be, was a conductor. I think he felt his life was over," Adams said. "Of course, the sad irony is that because of

185

the notoriety from the robbery, the train kept on running for another twenty years for tourists. Maybe if it hadn't, Lenny might have lived longer."

"What makes you think so?"

"Lenny spent more than half of his life shoveling coal into that boiler and breathing in the soot," Adams said. "I hear that when he died, his lungs were black. If he'd left in sixty-two, his lungs might've cleaned out some and he'd still be alive. But he considered that boiler his and wouldn't go until the train's last day. The stubborn bastard died a few years before that day came."

"Why did you stay?"

"I was the last of a dying breed. I figured I might as well see it through to the end. Besides, all I had going for me was this hole in the ground and the one that's waiting for me someday. Maybe it's the same one. My luck, that'll be the day I hit my pay streak."

Monk knocked on the window to get Adams' attention and spoke up loudly. "How do you think the robbers got the cash and the gold off the train?"

"People have all kinds of outrageous theories, but the simple explanation makes the most sense to me. They threw the bags to somebody on the ground."

"Without spilling anything?" Monk said.

"What makes you think they didn't spill some of it?"

"Because nothing was ever found," Monk said.

Adams waved off the remark. "So they say. Let me tell you something. The town was dying in sixty-two. There were a lot of people searching for the loot, most of 'em dirt poor. If anybody found cash, I guarantee you that they shoved it in their pockets and spent it and nobody was the wiser. If they found any gold coins, they kept them and didn't say a word about it."

"But you'd think one of the coins would have turned up by now," I said.

"I'm sure they have," he said.

"And nobody recognized them?"

"Because they weren't coins anymore. They were rings, necklaces, or nuggets," Adams said. "Gold is almost indestructible and yet it's easy to pound into something else without losing any of its rarity, allure, or value. Why do you think people want it so damn bad?"

"Because they're crazy," Monk said, practically yelling.

"There's all kinds of crazy, mister," Adams yelled right back, his face so close to the glass that his nose was nearly touching it. "You've got yours and I've got mine."

And with that, Adams took a pair of rubber gloves out of his pocket and trudged up the hill to his mine.

# Chapter Ten:
# Mr. Monk and the
# Permanent Record

The instant we hit the two-lane highway my cell phone rang, and when I saw that the caller ID read "Stottlemeyer," I pulled over to the shoulder to answer it.

"Hello, Captain."

"How's the investigation going?" he asked.

"It's progressing," I said.

"What's that mean?"

I glanced at Monk, who was looking at me. I was pretty sure that the volume on my phone was high enough that he could hear what Stottlemeyer was saying to me.

"It means Mr. Monk hasn't caught the murderer yet," I said. "But he will."

Monk nodded approvingly.

"Before or after he solves a forty-seven-year-old train robbery?" Stottlemeyer asked.

"You've been talking to Chief Kelton," I replied.

"I didn't have to. I tracked down Jake Slocum for you and discovered that he spent

189

thirty years in San Quentin and I found out why," Stottlemeyer said. "And I know Monk."

"Then you know there's nothing you can do about it," I said.

"You could encourage him to prioritize."

"I don't have that kind of influence," I said. "I'm a tornado of filth."

"That again?" Monk said. "It's a common expression. You're obsessing over nothing."

I nearly dropped the phone in disbelief. "*You're* telling *me* not to obsess about something?"

"You'll feel much better if you don't fixate on things."

"You fixate all the time," I said.

"Only on important things," he said. "I don't sweat the small stuff."

"You don't sweat at all," I said.

"Exactly," he said. "Maybe if you could learn not to obsess over every little thing, you wouldn't sweat, either. Which, I might add, many of us would appreciate."

"*Many* of us?" I said. "You mean you."

"Many times over," he said.

"Is this your subtle way of telling me that I stink?"

Monk rolled his shoulders. "I'm sure in this instance it's the car and not you."

"*This* instance?"

"Though being in a car for long periods of time means that we are in pretty close quarters and you do get moist."

*"Moist?"*

"Are you going deaf?" Monk asked. "You keep repeating everything I'm saying."

I could hear Stottlemeyer laughing. I brought the phone back to my ear.

"What are you laughing about?"

"Nothing, I was just clearing my throat," Stottlemeyer said. "Slocum is living in the Cypress Active Senior Suites in Angel's Camp, which is one of those Gold Rush towns north of Trouble. Maybe you should roll down the window on the way."

I hung up on him.

"That was rude," Monk said.

"Says the man who called me a stinking tornado of filth."

"With affection and deep respect," Monk said.

"It's taken me a few years, but I am beginning to understand why Sharona was so surly," I said, referring to his former nurse and assistant.

"Sharona obsessed over nothing, too," Monk said.

I looked over my shoulder to make sure there were no cars coming and I floored it, peeling rubber as I sped onto the highway.

I knew that leaving a stain on the road would haunt Monk forever.

He looked back. "Wait, we left a mark."

"So?"

"We have to go back and clean it off," Monk said.

"Don't sweat the small stuff," I said, smiling to myself.

It was a pyrrhic victory.

He complained about that tread mark for the next thirty minutes, right up until I pulled in front of the Cypress Active Senior Suites, which resembled a budget hotel for business travelers.

Monk took out his notebook and pen, glanced at something on the instrument panel, and made a notation in his pad.

"What are you doing?" I asked.

"Writing down the miles on the odometer so we can backtrack to the exact spot where you scarred the landscape and your immortal soul."

"I didn't scar anything."

"You left a mark on the highway that might never fade," Monk said. "If we can't clean it up ourselves, we might need to get a crew to sandblast it off. And if that doesn't work, I suppose we'll have to demolish that section of highway and lay fresh asphalt."

"The highway is used by thousands of

cars. You are fixating on a streak of rubber among a countless number of streaks, stains, cracks, and imperfections on the road."

"I am trying to clean up a mess and save you from a mistake that will haunt you for the rest of your life," Monk said. "You vandalized a vital part of our national transportation infrastructure. That kind of offense stays in your permanent record."

"I don't have a permanent record," I said.

"Yes, you do," he said.

"Who is keeping it?" I looked at him and saw the answer in the smug expression on his face. "I withdraw the question. I hope you contacted my kindergarten teacher, who made the initial entries, so you'll have the complete document."

"I did," he said.

"You *did?*"

"YES, I DID," he said loudly into my right ear. "I can't believe that you ate Play-doh and plucked holes in your classmate's Nerf ball. Were you raised by cavemen?"

"I can't believe that you hunted down my kindergarten teacher, and that she actually kept a record, and that she gave it to you. It's a violation of my privacy. What were you thinking?"

"I was thinking about entrusting my safety

and well-being to a barmaid who'd just murdered a man in her home," Monk said. "You'll have to forgive me for wanting to know a little bit about you first."

"He was an intruder who attacked me," I said. "I didn't mean to kill him. I was defending myself. You know that. You were the one who proved it."

"Even so, I felt I needed to do a thorough background check."

"All the way back to kindergarten?"

"I would have gone further, but your preschool teacher moved to South America and the doctor who delivered you had passed away."

I got out of the car, slammed the door shut, and walked a short distance away. There was only so much of Monk that any rational person could take, even someone as inured to it as I was.

With my back to the car, I took a deep breath, let it out slowly, and decided to pretend that the conversations we'd had over the past hour or so had never happened.

It didn't matter if I was in the right or not — sometimes I just had to give up the fight for my own mental and physical health. And before I did or said something that would get me fired.

This was one of those times.

I took another deep breath, turned around, and saw that Monk was now standing in front of the building, watching me.

I walked back and joined Monk in front of the lobby. Without saying a word, I opened the door and we went inside.

The first thing I noticed was the long line of identical walkers, each with a ribbon, flag, stuffed animal, or some kind of marker on them so that they'd stand out individually.

The walkers were parked like cars in front of the dining room to our left. The dining room reminded me of a sit-down restaurant in a mall, complete with a cottage-style street-front facade, a shingled roof section with faux dormers, and exterior window treatments looking out onto the lobby. There were about two dozen old folks sitting at large, round tables, eating fried chicken or Jell-O squares topped with swirls of whipped cream.

To our right was a check-in desk, where the bubbly young receptionist, with the smile of a stewardess-in-training, asked us who we were there to see. I told her. She said that Jake Slocum lived in suite 210 but that we could find him in the garden, which was straight ahead, across the great room and out the French doors.

I thanked her and we crossed the great room, which had a grand piano, a coffee bar, and a massive hearth made of imitation, stacked stone veneers. The flames of a gas fire hissed and flickered between cords of fake wood.

Several old folks sat around in the plush couches and easy chairs, reading books and magazines, napping with their heads slumped on their chests, or chatting amongst themselves.

The French doors opened up to a fenced-in concrete patio with some chaise lounges arranged around a small, rock-rimmed goldfish pond with a clay swan in the center that was covered with bird poop.

It wasn't hard to spot Jake Slocum. He was the only person out there, sitting in a wheelchair and smoking a cigarette. His neatly pressed shirt and corduroy pants were oversized and baggy on his thin frame, a style that was popular with the young hip-hop crowd but that made old geezers look sickly. I could see the bones of his hands and the wormlike veins under his almost translucent, age-spotted skin. He had sunken cheeks and alert eyes set in deep sockets that were like furtive creatures peering out from their dark burrows.

"Jake Slocum?" Monk asked.

"Whatever you're selling, I don't want it," Slocum said, his voice raspy. "And even if I did, I couldn't afford it."

"We're not here to sell you anything," Monk said.

"I don't need Jesus, Muhammad, the Buddha, L. Ron Hubbard, or Joel Osteen either," he said.

"My name is Adrian Monk. I'm a detective, and this is my assistant, Natalie Teeger. We're investigating the robbery of the Golden Rail Express and a murder that occurred a few days ago at the museum where the train is now on display."

Slocum took a drag on his cigarette and blew the smoke in Monk's direction. Monk covered his nose and mouth with his hand and ran back inside the building.

"It's just cigarette smoke," Slocum said to me. "It's not gonna kill you."

"Actually, it will," I said.

"Not instantly," he said.

"Mr. Monk is sensitive to smoke," I said. "He's sensitive to just about everything."

Monk stood at the French doors, watching us through the glass.

"You aren't?" Slocum asked.

"He pays me not to be," I said. "Do you know what happened to the gold?"

"Is that what you're after?"

I shook my head. "Mr. Monk is not interested in the gold. All he wants to do is solve the mystery of how the robbery was committed. You can help him do that."

"Why should I?"

"You spent thirty years in prison for your part in the crime. During those long, painful years, you must have wondered a thousand times where the gold was and if there was somebody out there living large on it while you rotted away. You're probably still wondering about it now. Wouldn't you finally like to know the answer?" I gestured to Monk. "He will find it."

"Others have tried," he said.

"None of them was Adrian Monk. He's the best detective on earth," I said. "I'll be blunt, Mr. Slocum. You're old and you don't look well. He may be your last chance to ever know what really happened."

Slocum thought about it for a long moment, then snubbed out his cigarette on the tire of his wheelchair.

"Go ask your boss if he'd like to hear a good story," he said.

# CHAPTER ELEVEN:
## MR. MONK HEARS A STORY

The way Jake Slocum told it, he and George Gilman were itinerant farm workers who supplemented their meager seasonal and sporadic legitimate income with petty thefts, break-ins, and muggings.

The two men were sitting in a bar in Placerville one night, nearly broke and contemplating their next felonious move, when Ralph DeRosso came in, played a little pool, and had a few drinks. Slocum glimpsed a lot of cash in DeRosso's wallet and saw their salvation. When DeRosso left the bar drunk a couple of hours later, Slocum and Gilman followed him outside.

DeRosso staggered into a dark alley to take a piss. Slocum and Gilman crept up behind him and were about to strike when DeRosso suddenly spun around, stone sober and holding a small gun.

But then DeRosso did something amazing. He took out his wallet and tossed it to

Slocum.

"This is what you came out here to take from me, isn't it?" DeRosso said. "Well, you can have it. I want you to take the cash and have a good look at the name and address on the driver's license. I want you to know who I am and where I live. You'll also see a card identifying me as a conductor on the Golden Rail Express."

He also asked them to look at the pictures of his wife and daughter, whom he identified by name.

Slocum was sure that DeRosso was dangerously insane and this was some crazy prelude to their execution.

But DeRosso surprised them again.

"I've been looking for two enterprising, young adventurers like yourselves to help me pull off a robbery that will become legend." DeRosso stuck the gun back in his coat pocket. "If you're interested, buy me a cup of coffee and a slice of pie and I'll tell you all about it."

They did.

DeRosso told them about the final trip of the Golden Rail Express and the high-stakes poker game for a pot of cash and gold that would commemorate it.

He wanted their help to rob the gambling car on that final ride. Their part in the scheme would be simple and relatively straightforward, requiring only the skills that they'd acquired through their previous criminal experiences.

But there was a big catch. They would only know their part in the plan. They wouldn't know anything else and couldn't leave the train with any of the loot, not even a single gold coin.

That scenario didn't make a lot of sense to Slocum or to Gilman. How were they supposed to get paid?

DeRosso explained that he would meet up with them again in six months, once the heat had died down, and give them their share of the loot.

Slocum and Gilman thought it was a joke. What would stop DeRosso and his unknown cronies from running off with everything and leaving the two of them with nothing?

The guarantee, DeRosso said to them, is me and my family. That was why he showed them his driver's license, conductor's card, and the photos of his wife and daughter. He wanted Slocum and Gilman to know exactly who he was and where he lived.

He was putting his own safety, and that of his family, entirely in their hands. Slocum and Gilman could follow them, betray them to the police, or kill them at any time. Why would DeRosso take that risk if he intended to double-cross the two men?

It was a convincing argument and it took some of the edge off of their reservations about his proposal. Besides, it wasn't as if they had a lot of other opportunities being offered to them and they figured that it beat mugging drunks in alleys. Slocum and Gilman were in.

DeRosso drew a sketch of the train on a napkin. The engine was in front, followed by the coal car, a freight car, the gambling car, the dining car, two passenger cars, and the caboose. There would be a party going on in the passenger and dining cars, but the gambling car was restricted to the invited players and VIP guests.

The important thing was that people would be out of their seats, moving freely between the passenger and dining cars, partying. No one would notice if Slocum and Gilman were absent for three minutes.

The lights in the train would flicker out for a second or two every now and then from the start of the journey and throughout the run. It would happen often enough, and for such a short duration, that the passengers would take it in stride.

The entire robbery was on a strict schedule, timed to the second. Slocum and Gilman had to be at the door between the dining car and the gambling car at the precise time of the prearranged blackout that would cover their exit.

Slocum and Gilman would meet outside the passenger car on the tiny platform separating them from the rear of the gambling car. They would cover their faces with ski masks, pull out their guns, and burst into the gambling car, quickly overpowering the surprised security guard inside the door. At the same instant, another robber would enter from the front of the gambling car, carrying burlap sacks.

During the next two minutes, the cash and gold would be stuffed into burlap sacks. Slocum and Gilman would then cover the other robber while he escaped with the loot out the same door that he came in.

The gamblers would be told that the robbers were staying outside the doors and would kill anyone who attempted to stop the train or alert the conductor before they reached Trouble.

Slocum and Gilman would leave the car, toss their masks and guns off the train and, during another prearranged, momentary blackout, slip back into the dining car and rejoin the party.

Simple.

But things didn't go quite as planned.

Instead of overpowering the guard, Gilman shot him in the chest. Gilman thought it was easier that way and removed any chance that the guard might do something heroic.

And somehow DeRosso got killed falling, or jumping, off the train.

"Even so, we never would have been caught if we weren't blinded by the sparkle," Slocum said, concluding his story.

"What sparkle?" Monk asked. By this time, we were both sitting in chairs facing Slocum, our backs to the pond.

"The damn gold," Slocum said. "We couldn't resist taking just one of those cursed coins even though DeRosso warned us not to. We were greedy, stupid fools."

"Most robbers are," Monk said. "You told the police everything that you've told us?"

"I didn't tell them anything. George Gilman did. I'm not a rat. I haven't spoken about the robbery to anyone until today."

"Why did Gilman talk?"

Slocum shrugged. "He probably would have kept his mouth shut if DeRosso hadn't gotten killed. But with DeRosso dead, George probably figured we'd never get our share. We didn't know who the other robbers were, so they had no reason to cut us in."

"Except honor among thieves," I said.

"There's none between honest people," he said. "What makes you think there would be any among the crooks? But I'll admit that for a while after I got out I hoped that one day I'd find a box of money on my doorstep from an anonymous, thankful stranger."

"So what did you do for a living after your release from prison?" My question had nothing to do with the investigation but I was curious.

"I was a custodian at the Arco Arena in Sacramento," he said. "Then I retired and became an inmate again."

"This doesn't look like prison to me," Monk said.

"You don't live here," he said.

I regarded Monk, who looked puzzled. "What's wrong?"

"The whole story. The criminal plot doesn't make any sense."

"It's the truth. I've got no reason to lie to you now," Slocum said. "But I'm not surprised by your reaction. It's the same one that the police had. They didn't believe a word George told them."

I could see why. It was an outlandish tale

and it wasn't even corroborated by Slocum at the time. On top of that, Ralph DeRosso was a respected, well-liked family man who'd dedicated his life to the Golden Rail Express. George Gilman was just some desperate, murdering hoodlum with a tall tale trying to avoid the electric chair.

"If what you say is true," Monk said, "there's a vital part of the plot that's missing."

"What happened to the loot," Slocum said.

Monk shook his head. "The disappearance of the gold is what happened afterwards. We still don't understand the robbery itself."

"I just told you what happened," Slocum said.

"What you did was make clear how much we don't know. Why did DeRosso want to rob the train? Why did he need you two? Why was he willing to put himself and his family at risk by revealing so many details about his life to you? Why did DeRosso want to wait so long before paying you off? Who was the other masked robber?"

"It was DeRosso," I said, turning to Slocum. "Wasn't it?"

"I always figured it was, but he was wearing a mask and didn't say a word," Slocum said. "We did all the talking. I suppose the robber could have been somebody else. Or maybe DeRosso didn't want to take a chance that the fat cats would recognize his voice."

"Whether it was DeRosso or not, the robber entered the gambling car from the front door," Monk said. "Does that mean he was hiding in the freight car until the robbery? If it was DeRosso, how did he get there? Why were the cash and gold placed in burlap bags instead of something sturdier? Where did the robber go with the bags of gold? Did DeRosso jump from the train or was he pushed? If we can answer those questions, the fate of the gold will become obvious."

While we were pondering those questions, someone stepped out of the building and onto the patio behind us.

"Found the gold yet?" the newcomer asked.

We turned and saw Chief Kelton approaching. He was wearing his gun in a holster on his belt. His badge was clipped to his belt, too.

"It's in the clay swan," I said, gesturing to the pond. "We were just about to crack it open and close the case."

"Glad I could be here to see it," he said.

"What *are* you doing here?" Monk asked.

"There's been a break in the murder investigation and I thought you might want to be a part of it," he said and then leaned forward to offer his hand to Slocum. "I'm Harley Kelton, the police chief down in Trouble."

They shook hands, though Slocum didn't look too pleased to be doing it.

"How did you find us?" I asked, getting up from my seat.

"I'm the chief of police," he said.

Monk got up. "Thank you for your help, Mr. Slocum. I appreciate it."

"Do you really think you can figure it all out?"

"I always do," Monk said.

"Will you tell me what happened?"

Monk nodded. "It wouldn't be complete if I didn't. I complete things."

We walked back inside with Kelton, who filled us in as we crossed the great room and the lobby.

"There was an enforcer who collected protection money for the mob from Tenderloin businesses. If people didn't pay, he'd hurt them bad and then firebomb their business. Manny caught him beating an adult bookstore owner over the head with a lead pipe. The enforcer went to jail, but

208

before he was sent up, he put his prized possession into storage."

"A 1964 Thunderbird," I said.

"You ought to be chief of police," Kelton
said. "His name is Gator Dunsen. He was
released eight months ago as part of a
statewide program to alleviate prison over-
crowding."

The state prisons were so stuffed with
felons that a federal court recently ruled
that imprisonment in California constituted
cruel and unusual punishment. The court
ordered the state to improve conditions immediately or face severe fines and criminal
prosecution of prison administrators. Since
the state had no money to build new prisons, and the administrators didn't want to
become residents of their own jails, they had
no choice but to start letting crooks out
early.

"Maybe you should just stop arresting
people," I said.

"I've made a few arrests since I got to
Trouble, but I haven't had a chance to send
anyone on to the state prison population
yet." Kelton looked at Monk. "You've probably filled a whole prison on your own.
Maybe you ought to take a sabbatical for a
while."

"Not today," Monk said.

"In that case, you two can follow me," Kelton said. "Gator is living at his mom's old place in Jackson. We're halfway there already."

# CHAPTER TWELVE:
# MR. MONK HEARS A
# THEORY

Kelton drove way over the speed limit, but I kept up with him, confident that nobody would pull me over for a ticket as long as I was in his official wake.

I thought about Slocum's story and the questions that it raised. After a time, I turned to Monk.

"I've got a theory."

"About what?"

"How the robbery was committed," I said. "Let's assume Slocum was telling the truth. I think DeRosso was the ringleader but not an active participant."

"What does that mean?"

"He knew trains but he had no criminal experience. So he recruited people who did and let them do their thing while he oversaw the operation."

"He was the brains, not the brawn," Monk said.

"Yes," I said.

"Like the situation with us," he said.

I wasn't quite sure how to take that. Was he implying that I wasn't smart? I was pretty sure that he wasn't, but after being called a stinky tornado of filth, I was a little touchy.

"Since he couldn't pay for their help — something else you can relate to — he had to come up with another way to convince them to work for him. So he leveraged the safety of himself and his family. But I believe it wasn't a gamble at all, because he had every intention of honoring the deal."

"So far it makes sense."

"You don't need to sound so surprised," I said. "I'm brainy and brawny. We know the gambling car was sandwiched between the dining car and the freight car. Slocum and Gilman were in the dining car and I believe the third man was in the freight car."

"But you're saying it wasn't DeRosso," Monk said.

I nodded. "DeRosso was somewhere else. I don't know where. Maybe one of the passenger cars. The third man was supposed to return to the freight car and hide the gold in a secret compartment. I believe DeRosso had some clever plan for off-loading the gold at the station right under the noses of the police. But it never got that far. I have two theories about what happened next."

"So you have three theories," Monk said.

"I have one theory with two theoretical outcomes."

"A theory with sub-theories," Monk said.

"Is there a rule against that in the detecting profession?"

"It's frowned upon."

"Is that why you're frowning?"

"I'm not frowning," Monk said. "This is my face in its normal, rested state."

"What does it matter how many theories I have?" I said. "We're just spit-balling."

"We are absolutely not spitting, together or separately," Monk said. "Now or ever."

"So here's theory number one," I said, ignoring his protest. "What went wrong is that the third man decided to double-cross the others and take the gold for himself. When DeRosso showed up in the freight car —"

"How did DeRosso get there without going through the dining car first?" Monk interrupted.

"He went over it," I said. "He climbed up and walked along the top."

"While the train was moving?" Monk asked incredulously.

"He was an experienced train man," I said. "They do it all the time."

"They do?"

"Haven't you ever seen Westerns or thrillers about train robberies?"

"Those are movies," he said.

"The writers get their ideas from real life and go from there."

"Then explain *The Wizard of Oz* to me," Monk said. "Where in real life can you find flying monkeys, singing scarecrows, and munchkins?"

I pressed on, ignoring his question. "So DeRosso shows up in the freight car, discovers what the third man is doing, and there's a struggle. The third man ends up throwing DeRosso off the train."

"What happened to the gold?"

"The third man jumped off with it," I said.

"In two burlap sacks?"

"Maybe he put the gold into something else and then jumped. Maybe he carefully planned ahead and had a car stashed in the woods and was long gone before people started searching for the gold."

"Let me get this straight," Monk said. "DeRosso is pushed off the train and dies. The third man jumped off the train with two bags of gold and survived."

"Maybe the third man planned his jump for a curve or something where the train had to slow down," I said. "I don't know. I'm not an expert on trains."

"Except you're certain that people can just stroll across the top of a dining car while a train is speeding down the tracks."

"I've seen people have kung fu fights on top of moving trains," I said. "I think Steven Segal did it."

"Oh, then it must be possible," Monk said. "Who is Steven Segal?"

"Nobody," I said.

"What's your second theory on how the plan went wrong?"

"Actually, I have three theories about that."

"You said you had two."

"Well, I just thought of another one. Anyway, my second theory is that DeRosso fell while walking across the top of the dining car and never made it to the freight car," I said. "The third man didn't know what the rest of the plan was, or who the two other robbers were, so he made the best of a bad situation by jumping off the train with the gold."

"And survived," Monk said.

"Obviously," I said. "If he was killed and the gold spilled all over the place, we wouldn't be having this discussion."

"What's your third theory?"

"It's the second theory with a twist," I said. "The third man hid the gold in the secret compartment in the freight car as planned and managed to get it off the train before the police realized what was going on."

"The police searched the train for secret compartments and didn't find any," Monk said.

"Maybe the third man emptied the gold and then dismantled the secret compartment."

"And he did all that without anybody noticing?"

"He must have," I said. "Because he got away with it."

"That's a terrible theory."

"Do you have a better one?"

"No," Monk said. "Because I don't come up with theories. I come up with solutions."

"So let's hear your solution."

"I don't have one yet."

"Then my theory could be correct."

"Which one?" he said. "You have four of them."

"I have one with three possible outcomes," I said. "The solution could be one of them, or a combination, or a fourth outcome I haven't come up with yet."

"In other words, it could be something else entirely," he said.

"Yes," I said.

"I think you're right," he said.

"About what?"

"It's something else entirely."

By that point, we'd followed Kelton into a residential community that dated back to the 1950s with homes that looked like space-age, drive-in restaurants. The homes had sharp angles, flat roofs, lava-rock facades, floor-to-ceiling windows, and carports instead of garages. Gator Dunsen's house was easy to spot because of the 1964 Thunderbird parked under the carport.

From a distance, it looked like Gator's house and property were covered with snow. But as we got closer, I saw that it was white rocks, gleaming bits of shaved dolomite spread on the ground, driveway, and roof. There were some dry, prickly shrubs poking through the rocks here and there, but otherwise it was like the house was built in the middle of a marble quarry.

Kelton parked his cruiser on the gravel driveway behind the Thunderbird, presumably to stop anyone from making an escape with the car.

I parked on the street at the curb. There was a concrete front walk leading to the front steps, which was lucky for me, because otherwise Monk might have asked me to carry him across the rocks to the door. He doesn't like uneven and unstable surfaces.

"Let me take the lead here," Kelton said. "Gator has a long history of violence."

"I guess that's why they call him Gator and not Cuddles," I said.

I was trying to be clever and flirty but it fell disastrously flat. Kelton was unamused and all business.

"We have to assume that he's armed and dangerous, so I'm going to do this according to procedure. Understood? I want you two to stand back out of the line of potential fire until I determine that there's no danger."

Kelton climbed the steps and then stood to the right of the front door.

I followed his example and stepped onto the rocks and out of the firing line of the front door. Monk remained on the concrete walkway but leaned towards me as far as he could without tipping over.

Kelton reached out his left hand and knocked on the door. He kept his right hand on the butt of his gun. I motioned to Monk to come beside me. He shook his head. You'd think I was asking him to walk barefoot across hot coals.

"Who is it?" a gruff voice yelled from inside the house.

"Gator Dunsen?" Kelton asked.

"Who wants to know?"

"The chief of police of Trouble." It was an honest reply and yet it sounded like the kind of cocky, smart-ass remark that Walker, Texas Ranger or Dirty Harry might say.

Gator replied in kind. He blasted a hole through the front door, the stray bullet shattering the right, rear passenger window of my car and my five-hundred-dollar deductible.

I bolted for cover behind the Thunderbird. Monk started to follow me, then hesitated, one foot suspended over the rocks, the other still planted on the front walk. He looked like he was demonstrating a martial arts stance.

Gator fired again.

Monk's fear of getting shot overcame his fear of uneven surfaces. He ducked and ran over to the car, hunkering down next to me.

Kelton called over to us. "Stay where you are."

He crouched low, spun into a firing stance in front of the door, fired twice, then scrambled inside the house.

We heard more gunfire. One of the windows on the side of the house blew out, spraying shards of glass into the rocks. From the sound of things, the gunfight seemed to be moving towards the rear of the house.

Monk plucked a piece of rock out of the tread of the Thunderbird's right front tire, then peered around to examine the shiny chrome grill. I yanked Monk back behind the car.

There was another gunshot, followed by two more in rapid succession, and then a disturbing silence. The only sound I heard was the ringing in my ears from the gunfire.

We both stood up slowly and peeked out at the house. Up and down the block, people were beginning to cautiously emerge from their homes to see what was going on. I could hear sirens in the distance.

Kelton emerged from the house, his gun held at his side. He was bleeding from some tiny cuts on his face and arms from flying shards of wood and glass.

"He's dead," Kelton said.

I hurried across the rocks to him as he sat down on the stoop. Monk went back to the sidewalk, then up the front walk to join us.

"Are you okay?" I asked.

"Could I have one of those wipes?"

I reached into my purse and gave him one. He opened the packet and gently dabbed at the wounds on his face.

Monk walked past us into the house. I handed Kelton some more wipes and hurried after Monk. I didn't particularly want to see what was inside, but it was part of my job.

The house had an open floor plan with very few walls dividing rooms. Instead, low counters, bookcases, and furniture were used to delineate the various spaces.

The living room opened onto the kitchen and a hallway. There was a contemporary-style couch, a leather La-Z-Boy recliner, a huge flat-screen TV, and an overturned coffee table riddled with bullet holes. A big bowl of chips, some dip, a bag of pork rinds, and several bottles of beer were spilled on the floor. There were two bullet holes in the recliner.

Monk held his hands out in front of him, palms out, as if he could feel the heat radiating from the embers of the recent violence. I could smell the onion dip, the sulfur of discharged weapons, and the slightly metallic scent of blood.

"It would have been nice if they'd cleaned up as they went along," Monk said, stepping carefully to avoid the food on the floor.

"I think it's difficult to shoot at each other if you're holding a broom and dustpan at the same time."

"Gator was sitting on the couch eating chips when the chief knocked on the door. He grabbed his gun, flipped over the table for cover, and fired those first two shots," Monk said. "He could have cleared the table before he flipped it over. It would only have taken a moment."

"He must have been deranged," I said.

Monk nodded. "Gator was already moving to his second position when Kelton needlessly shot the recliner."

He headed to the kitchen and the low counter/bar combination that separated it from the living room. I could see that the window over the kitchen sink was shattered.

"Gator took cover behind the counter and opened fire again," Monk said. "Kelton returned fire and hit the window. Gator fired back and Kelton dove to the floor. Gator went down the hall."

I was visualizing the action as Monk described it. I could almost see it playing out in front of me like ghosts.

Monk went down the hall and peeked into the bedroom. He stopped in the doorway and cocked his head from side to side.

I stood behind him and peered over his shoulder into the room.

There was a big man, easily six feet tall and almost half as wide, lying on his back on the floor, his arms flung out at his sides. He was bald with an alligator tattoo that ran around his neck and over his head. He wore a tank top, long shorts, and flip-flops. There was a bullet hole right between his eyes and blood spatter all over the wall behind him.

I was glad that we'd missed lunch or I might have seen mine again at that moment.

Monk crouched beside the body. Once again, I was struck by conflicts in his behavior. He was repulsed by smashed butterflies on my windshield but he didn't flinch while scrutinizing a man who had the back of his skull blown off. It made absolutely no sense to me. But I was self-conscious enough to know that I was only thinking about this familiar contradiction for the thousandth time to distract myself from the gore.

It wasn't working.

"He has chapped lips," Monk said. "They're bleeding."

"There's a bullet hole in his head and his brains are on the wall, and you're concerned about his chapped lips?"

"Was he chewing on them or picking at them during the gunfight?"

"People do that when they are under stress," I said. "Gunfights are stressful situations."

Monk glanced under the bed. "There's

his gun. It must have slid under there when he fell."

"Do we really need to be here, Mr. Monk? It's not like there's any mystery about how Gator Dunsen was killed. We were right outside when it happened."

"And that's where you should be right now," a voice said. We turned to see two uniformed police officers standing behind us, their guns drawn. It seemed like overkill to me.

"You can put those guns away — the shooting is over," I said. "Didn't Chief Kelton tell you that?"

"Outside," the officer said firmly. "Now."

"With pleasure," I said and hurried out.

Monk followed after me, in no hurry at all.

# Chapter Thirteen:
# Mr. Monk and
# What He Doesn't
# See

Within minutes, the property was crawling with Jackson detectives, forensic investigators, and people from the Amador County medical examiner's office.

The investigation was being led by Detective Lydia Wilder, who appeared to be suffering from a bad case of indigestion. She couldn't stop grimacing as she walked the scene and as she questioned Kelton, who sat shirtless in the back of an ambulance as paramedics treated his cuts.

I tried not to stare but couldn't help noticing that he had a nice body and just enough chest hair to suggest a healthy masculinity but not so much that I wanted to offer him a banana. I'd recently read in *Cosmopolitan* that hairy chests were back in style. They'd never fallen out as far as I was concerned.

She didn't seem to notice his chest. Her grimace got tighter the longer she spoke to him. We hadn't talked to her yet. Another detective took our statements and told us that we couldn't go anywhere until Wilder released us.

So I leaned against one of the police cars and watched the activity going on.

Monk made sure that the crime-scene tech who was collecting the bullet from the backseat of my car collected all the broken glass.

After a few minutes, Monk came over to me.

"I'm afraid the car is a total loss."

"You thought it was before the window got shot out," I said.

"But now it's totally totaled," Monk said. "There's no way we can possibly ride in it."

"We'll have to make do," I said.

"But there's a window missing," Monk said. "And the car is caked with dirt and butterfly goo."

"I'll patch the hole with cardboard and duct tape until I can get it replaced."

"That's unthinkable," he said.

"I can't afford a new car and neither can you," I said. "We'll just have to make do."

"Then we'll need a brick," Monk said. "Or a baseball bat."

"What for?"

"To remove the other rear passenger window," Monk said. "Maybe I could borrow a baton from one of the police officers."

He started to head towards an officer, but I grabbed his arm and yanked him back.

"If you do anything to that other window, I won't wash my hands for the rest of this trip," I said. "And the first thing I will do when I get back to your apartment is touch everything."

"You wouldn't dare," Monk said.

I met his eye. "Try me."

"Be reasonable," he said, but it came out more as a whine.

"You first, Mr. Monk."

"I'm trying to be," he said. "But you won't let me."

Kelton put on his shirt and came over to us. Wilder was heading our way, too, a large evidence bag under her arm.

"Are you in trouble?" I asked Kelton. "I don't mean the town. I know where we are. I mean —"

"I know what you mean," Kelton interrupted. "I've been in worse, though not while sober."

Wilder faced us. "This is a hell of a mess."

"I know," Monk said. "Maybe you can talk some sense into her before it gets any worse."

"What are you talking about?" Wilder asked.

Monk tipped his head towards the car. "Natalie won't let me break the other window."

"I thought Gator Dunsen shot the window," Wilder said.

"He did," Monk said. "So now it's imperative that someone break the other one. You could order her to do it as a matter of public safety."

"Are you on drugs or off your meds?"

"Ask her yourself," Monk said, gesturing to me. "Because I had the same question."

Wilder looked at Kelton. "This just gets worse with every passing minute."

"I agree," Monk said.

"You came here to question a suspect without jurisdiction and without notifying local law enforcement," she said to Kelton, ignoring Monk. "You approached a violent suspect without backup and exchanged gunfire with him. You killed the suspect and then sat outside while two civilians, one of them mentally unstable, trampled the unsecured crime scene."

"We aren't civilians," Monk said. "And Natalie seemed stable at the time."

"You aren't police officers," Wilder snapped at Monk.

"I was one," Monk said. "Now I consult for the San Francisco Police."

"But you don't consult for *this* police department," she said.

"I'd be glad to," Monk said.

"I'll send you a rate card," I said.

"We aren't interested." She turned back to Kelton. "The irresponsibility you've shown today is staggering. How did you ever become the chief of police?"

"I drank my way into the job," Kelton said.

"This isn't a joke," she said. "A man is dead."

"A cop killer," Kelton said. "He murdered Manny Feikema, the retired San Francisco cop who put him in prison. Any police officer who showed up at Gator's door was facing a bullet."

"All the more reason you should have contacted my office before coming here," she said.

"I might have been a bit overzealous," he conceded.

"You were dangerously reckless. You're lucky that Dunsen is the only one dead today and that no one else was seriously injured." She took the evidence bag from under her arm and held it up for us to see. "Do you have any idea what these are?"

The three of us drew close and looked at the pictures.

"These are photos of the interior of the Gold Rush Museum in Trouble," Monk said.

Most of the pictures were taken from various angles of the prospecting diorama.

"It's where Manny Feikema worked as a security guard," Kelton said. "Our theory is that Gator came into the museum during the day, hid somewhere, and attacked Manny during his rounds that night. It looks to me like Gator was casing the museum for a hiding place and chose the cabin in the diorama."

Monk rolled his shoulders but didn't say anything.

Wilder stuck the evidence bag back under her shoulder and looked at Monk and me.

"You two are free to go." She glanced at Kelton. "But I'm not done with you yet. We have a lot more to talk about."

She made it sound like a threat.

On our way out of Jackson, I stopped by an office supply store, bought a cardboard box, a box cutter, and two rolls of duct tape. I cut out a piece of cardboard from the box and taped it over the broken window. And, as a courtesy to my aggrieved employer, I taped a piece of cardboard over the intact, left rear passenger window as well. It was a compromise, and a peace offering, that Monk accepted with a grateful nod.

We'd skipped lunch and I was starving, so I stopped at a 7-Eleven and got us both our own boxes of Wheat Thins and bottles of Summit Creek water for a snack. I'm not a big Wheat Thins fan, but I knew they were square and if I got something as unpredictable in size and shape as potato chips, he'd have a fit.

Monk was quiet as we headed back to Trouble. The only sound in the car was the snap of the crackers as we ate them and the whistling of the air buffeting the cardboard in the right, rear window.

I'd been expecting Monk to demand that we return to the spot where I'd scarred the highway with my tires. But he didn't. Which meant something was wrong, something so wrong that it was distracting him from the wrong that I'd committed.

"What's bothering you, Mr. Monk?"

"Something Chief Kelton said to Detective Wilder."

"He said lots of things," I said. "Could you be more specific?"

"Chief Kelton told Detective Wilder that Gator Dunsen killed Manny Feikema."

"Gator did," I said. "Didn't he?"

"No," Monk said. "He didn't."

"I don't usually argue with you about this kind of thing, but the evidence against Gator is pretty compelling. Manny sent Gator to prison. Gator was in Trouble before the killing, asking around about Manny. He took pictures of the prospecting diorama in the Gold Rush Museum. He shot it out to the bloody end with Chief Kelton rather than face arrest. All of that screams killer to me."

"He wasn't in Trouble," Monk said.

"Bob Gorman saw him," I said. "Gorman talked to him."

"Bob Gorman lied to us."

"How do you know?"

"You can't get in or out of Trouble without driving through the migrating butterflies," he said. "But Gator's Thunderbird is perfectly clean."

I gave Monk a look.

"I can't believe that the same man who wanted me to abandon my car because it was a little bit dirty is now criticizing someone for keeping his car sparkling clean. That Thunderbird was Gator Dunsen's most prized possession. He probably washed and waxed it every day. That's why there are no signs of obliterated butterflies on the car. Besides, the museum photos that Detective Wilder found in Gator's house prove that he was in Trouble and casing the museum."

"They prove that Gator is innocent," Monk said.

"I don't see how," I said.

"Because you didn't see what I didn't see."

"You mean what you *did* see," I said.

"No, what I *didn't* see."

"How could I not see something you didn't see?" I said. "That makes no sense at all."

"I didn't see the prospector's pick that Manny was killed with in the photos of the diorama," Monk said. "If the pictures were taken before he was killed, the pick should have been there. It wasn't."

"Oh," I said. "I didn't see that."

"I didn't see it, either."

"You saw it," I said. "But what you saw was what you didn't see. I didn't see what you saw, which is what wasn't there and what I should have seen if I was paying attention to what I saw."

"That's what I said. Do you think you've just stated it more clearly?"

"No," I said, rubbing my forehead with one hand. "I think I'm having a stroke."

"That would certainly explain your behavior today."

"Why didn't you tell Kelton about this

while we were still at Gator's place?"

"Because he was in enough hot water with the Jackson Police as it was," Monk said. "I didn't want to humiliate him and make the situation worse."

I smiled at him. "I'm impressed, Mr. Monk. That was very sensitive of you."

"I'm a very sensitive guy," he said.

It was true that he was sensitive about a lot of things — an endless number, in fact — but other people's feelings weren't ordinarily among them. I didn't say that, of course, because I was actually sensitive to his feelings and to the fact that insulting your employer isn't the best way to stay employed.

"So if Gator Dunsen was innocent, why did he shoot at us?"

"He was innocent of Manny Feikema's murder but that doesn't make him an innocent person. As you pointed out, his name was Gator and he had a tattoo. He had to be guilty of something terrible."

"What are you going to tell Chief Kelton?"

"Nothing until I have more evidence," he said. "But this is our first real break in the case."

"How do you figure that?"

"Someone planted that file of photos in

Gator's house and Gorman lied to us," Monk said. "Not that I'm surprised by Gorman's dishonesty. I knew he couldn't be trusted, and was most likely a communist, the instant I saw him pick up that fork with his dirty hands and dip his pancakes into his egg yolk."

"Are you going to confront Gorman with what you know?"

"I'm not sure that's the best move right now. We might learn more by playing dumb and seeing what happens."

"Do you think you can play dumb?"

"I'm a genius and people know it," Monk said. "But someone out there is underestimating me. I'm hoping that whoever it is will keep on doing it if I stay quiet."

"That's not going to be easy for you," I said. I knew how much Monk liked touting his brilliance.

"I'll just have to draw on my reserves of fortitude," he said, "assuming that I have any left after we drive through those butterflies again in this death car."

# CHAPTER FOURTEEN:
# MR. MONK GETS A
# PHONE CALL

It was getting dark as we arrived in Trouble and I had to stop for a burro crossing the road at the corner of Main and Second streets.

The burro took his time, stopping directly in front of our car to chew on something and stare at Monk.

I happened to glance to my left, towards the Gold Rush Museum, and saw someone I recognized leaving the building.

"Mr. Monk," I said. "Isn't that Clifford Adams?"

Monk followed my gaze as Adams climbed into a rusted old pickup truck that made my car look like a new Mercedes by comparison.

"Yes, it is," Monk said. "I wonder why he decided to visit the museum today."

"Maybe his conversation with us made him nostalgic," I said.

When the pickup crossed the beam of our

headlights, the angry scowl on his face was illuminated in the brief flash of light as he passed by us.

Monk rolled his shoulders. "Maybe."

Once Adams' truck left the intersection, I noticed Bob Gorman standing on the corner. He watched Adams drive off and then his gaze settled on us.

I forced a smile and waved at the liar. He smiled, waved back, and continued on towards the museum.

Monk watched him as warily as he did the burro. "There's a good reason they call this town Trouble."

The burro finally moved on and we drove the few blocks down to our motel. I dropped Monk off and continued on to the gas station, where I filled up the tank and did my best to clean the bugs and dirt off the windshield with a wet, soapy squeegee. It took some real scrubbing to get the goop off. It was like I'd driven through a rainstorm of slime.

I found a hose behind the station and sprayed water on the rest of the car, but it was a superficial rinse at best. It would have to do until the broken window was replaced.

I drove back to the motel and knocked on Monk's door to see if he was interested in grabbing some dinner with me at the

Chuckwagon.

"I'm fine with my box of Wheat Thins," Monk said.

"What are you going to do for the rest of night?"

"Shine my shoes," he said.

"That sounds exciting," I said.

"I dodged blazing bullets, kamikaze butterflies, and rampaging burros today," Monk said. "I need to unwind."

"I understand," I said. "Have a good night, Mr. Monk."

"You, too, Natalie," he said and closed the door.

I went back to my room and called Julie to see how she was doing. I was glad to catch her at home on a school night, studying for a history test. At least that's what she told me she was doing. She could have been doing anything.

Julie was too old now to be treated like a child but too young to be treated as an adult. It was a tricky time to be a mom, especially as a single parent. But I trusted her. She'd never given me a reason not to.

"How are you enjoying your vacation with Mr. Monk?" she asked mischievously.

"It's not a vacation," I said. "It's a business trip."

"That's what you said about Germany

and France."

"Those trips became investigations," I said. "This started as one. But now it's become two."

"I'm not surprised," Julie said. "Mr. Monk is like the Angel of Death. He's so not coming to my high school graduation."

"You have to invite him," I said. "But we'll think of a way to make him decide on his own to politely decline."

"You can tell him that some of the students have chicken pox," she said. "Or that they are purposely wearing mismatched socks."

"Either would work," I said.

"Then we'll do both, just to be on the safe side."

"Okay," I said and then I filled her in on everything that had happened since we'd arrived in Trouble, especially the discovery that Monk had a crime-solving ancestor with all the same brilliance and personality quirks.

"Wouldn't it be cool if Abigail Guthrie turned out to be related to you? You ought to look into it."

"I don't want to know," I said.

"Now you sound like Mr. Monk," she said.

"I do not," I said. "I am nothing like him."

"He doesn't want to know that he's related

to Artemis Monk and you don't want to know if you're related to Abigail Guthrie."

"But he *is* related to Artemis Monk," I said. "I wouldn't mind being related to Abigail Guthrie if she had nothing to do with a Monk. But if I am related to her, the coincidence would just be too terrifying to contemplate."

"What would be so scary about it?"

"It would mean that I've never really had any control over my life. I've always been doomed to this fate."

"Even if you aren't related to Abigail Guthrie, what makes you think that you weren't destined to be working for Mr. Monk?"

"I like to think that I have free will," I said. "Don't you?"

"Yes," she said. "But my mom won't let me have it."

"You're on your own right now, aren't you?" I said. "For all I know, you're naked with three guys and snorting coke."

She gasped. "Oh my God, how did you find out?"

"Very funny," I said.

"Why do you think Mr. Monk won't admit that Artemis Monk is his ancestor?"

"Maybe he's afraid that if his problems

are hereditary, there's no way he'll ever get better."

"Mr. Monk doesn't think he has problems," she said. "He thinks it's everybody else who is screwed up."

"He knows he has problems. That's why he sees a shrink."

"Mom, he sees a shrink because he likes it. He enjoys whining and being the center of attention."

"You're forgetting that he had a complete mental breakdown after his wife was killed. He was booted off the police force because he was psychologically unfit for duty and for years he needed a full-time nurse at his side just to be able to function."

"That was the past. He's changed," Julie said. "If he still needed a professional nurse, you wouldn't have a job. Dr. Kroger and Captain Stottlemeyer hired Sharona, but Mr. Monk hired you on his own. Because the job wasn't about his mental health anymore. Mr. Monk doesn't think he has problems, but I'm sure that he thinks that you do."

She had a good point. It had been years since I'd last heard Monk talk about how he wanted to be reinstated to the force. He seemed content doing exactly what he was doing. And he was always criticizing me for

241

engaging in unhealthy behavior, like wearing a wrinkled blouse, eating tossed salads, petting dogs, and not rinsing my toothbrush with boiling water before and after using it.

I came to the frightening realization that maybe Monk and I were more alike than I thought. Nobody cherished the notion of controlling himself and his environment more than Adrian Monk did. Perhaps acknowledging his relation to Artemis Monk, a man so startlingly similar to himself, meant accepting the inevitability of fate and that he was powerless to shape the direction of his own life.

I wasn't ready for that, either, and I wasn't nearly as uptight as he was.

I'd become so attuned to the differences between us that I'd become blind to all the things that we shared, common aspects of our personalities that might draw us closer together rather than further apart.

Monk was partly to blame for it. He was the one who made lists of his phobias and his rules and made it my job to make his immediate environment as comfortable for him as possible. I'd been encouraged — no, *trained* — to watch out for the things he would find irritating or out of place, most of which wouldn't bother me at all, and mitigate them before they caused him trouble. I'd become attuned to our differ-ences as a way of spotting things he needed to be protected from.

A few moments earlier, I'd told Julie that I was nothing like Monk. But maybe, deep down, Monk and I were much more alike than I ever thought before.

If that was true, perhaps he wasn't so complicated to understand after all. Or maybe I was as messed up as he was, only in my own way.

Now *that* was a frightening thought.

I made a promise to myself to start paying more attention to the important things that we shared rather than the ten thousand insignificant things that we didn't. It might just make me a little more understanding and my job less stressful, too.

"When did you get so smart?" I asked Ju-lie.

"I always have been," she said. "It's just taken you seventeen years to notice."

"I love you," I said. "I've always noticed that."

"I know you have," she said. "I love you, too. Promise me you'll be careful."

"I will be," I said. "But if that isn't enough, I'm with the most careful man on earth."

"He's weird," she said. "But sometimes it's a good weird."

I hung up, stuck the phone in my purse, and wandered down to Dorothy's Chuckwagon for dinner.

Crystal DeRosso wasn't working that night and there was nobody I knew in the place, so I was able to wolf down two cheeseburgers and a shake in complete anonymity and without feeling the least bit self-conscious about it.

I went back to my room, got into bed, and opened up Abigail Guthrie's journal to read more about Artemis Monk before going to sleep.

## THE EXTRAORDINARY MR. MONK
### The Case of the Cutthroat Trail

*(From the journal of Abigail Guthrie)*
*Trouble, California, 1856*
I was hanging a sign that read "No Rock Licking Allowed" from a nail on the front porch of Artemis Monk's newly built, perfectly square cabin when Sheriff Wheeler ambled up. It was the sheriff's first visit since we'd moved into the cabin, which also served as Monk's assay office and was in the exact center of the perfectly square lot, each corner of the property marked with a freshly planted sapling.

"Good morning, Mrs. Guthrie," he said,

taking off his hat as a courtesy to me.

"Good morning to you, too, Sheriff."

He tipped his head towards my freshly painted sign. "I'm afraid to ask what that means."

"A lot of prospectors gather here on the porch awaiting Mr. Monk's assays," I said.

He frowned. "I still don't get it."

"Then you haven't spent much time around prospectors."

"It's true. I try to stay clear of them," he said. "They don't bathe but once or twice a year."

"Now you sound like Mr. Monk," I said.

"It's one of the few subjects we agree on."

"Well, if you'd seen them gather and parley, you'd know that it's customary for prospectors to offer their rocks for inspection by way of greeting."

Wheeler raised an eyebrow. "Say what?"

"The first thing a prospector will do is lick a rock to remove the dust and make the color sparkle before holding it up to his eye for scrutiny. Not only does Mr. Monk find it a disgusting custom, but he won't handle any rocks that have been drooled upon."

"Monk's got a lot of rules," Sheriff Wheeler said. "I don't know how you remember them all."

"He gave me a list," I said. "It's up to fifty pages."

"How nice for you," he said.

"You'll be getting one of your own," I said. "I'm making you a copy now, but I'm slow with my penmanship."

"Take your time," he said. "Take years, if you want to."

I smiled. "What brings you by today?"

"I need Monk's help," he said.

"You have a rock that needs an assay?"

I led the sheriff inside.

Monk was sitting at my desk in the midst of writing another one of his letters to Samuel Colt, inventor of the six-shooter. I didn't have to read the letter to know what it said:

> Your latest firearm is good, sir. An exemplary weapon. But it needs refining. I can't help feeling that in its present form you are still little more than halfway there.

His last four, identical missives imploring Mr. Colt to hurry the manufacture of a ten-shooter had gone unanswered. But Monk was sure that the lack of response had to do with a failure of the postal system and other vagaries and was not a reflection of any disrespect from Mr. Colt. So Monk just kept writing the same letter and sending it off. He was nothing if not persistent, bordering on obsessed.

Monk looked up at the sheriff and set his quill aside. "I'm glad to see you. We have an urgent matter to discuss."

"Your matter will have to wait —"

"It's the scourge of three-card monte," Monk interrupted. "It must be stopped."

"I've told you before, Monk, I can't stop gambling. People don't care that they are getting swindled. They enjoy it."

"If they want to be swindled, that's their own problem," Monk said. "But playing a game with only three cards is a violation of all that is holy and undermines the foundations of human civilization. It can't be tolerated."

"We can talk about that later," Sheriff Wheeler said. "A man has been brutally murdered and a lot of gold has been stolen. I have no idea who is responsible for the crime."

"What does that have to do with me?" Monk said.

"You solved Bart Spicer's murder without even seeing the body or going out to his mine," he said. "I figure you might be able to solve this one, too."

"Why should I?"

"For the good of the community and your

fellow man," the sheriff said.

"That's why we need to stop three-card games of chance in this town," Monk said. "It's a matter of basic human decency."

Wheeler sighed. "I'll make you a deal, Monk. If you solve the murder, four-card monte will be the only monte played in Trouble."

Monk smiled and stood up. "Then let's get this over with and bring civilization to this godforsaken town."

The murder took place at a claim shared by four prospectors on Cripple Creek, about two miles outside of Trouble. Sheriff Wheeler filled us in on the particulars of the case as we walked out there.

Once a month, three of the prospectors went into town for a night of fun while the fourth man stayed at the cabin to guard their gold. They each took turns being the man on guard duty.

When the three prospectors returned to their camp this morning, they discovered their partner dead and all their gold gone.

They immediately sent a man back to town for the sheriff, who went out to investigate with Deputy Weaver.

"Anybody could have done the killing and whoever it was is probably long gone by now," Wheeler said. "I've got no way of knowing. I'm a lawman, not a detective. Keeping the peace is my specialty because it doesn't involve much thinking."

"You're being too hard on yourself, Sheriff," I said. "Establishing authority, earning the respect of the community, mediating disputes, and enforcing the law isn't easy. Few men are capable of it."

"All it takes are quick fists, a fast draw, and a short temper," he said. "I'm best when I've got no time to think."

"But you can track a man," Monk said.

Wheeler nodded. "I can follow a trail that's laid out in front of me."

"That's detecting," Monk said. "There's an order to everything. You know the way things are supposed to be. You can see what's missing, what's been left behind, and what's been disturbed. You can see the mess. That's the trail."

"A murder doesn't leave a trail," Wheeler said.

"Everything leaves a trail, Sheriff," Monk said. "People can't do anything without leaving behind a mess. That's what will tell us who the murderer is and where we can find him."

I could see why Monk liked rocks. There's an order to the natural elements that doesn't change. They're solid, dependable, and organized. Gold is gold, coal is coal. He could find comfort in their immutability when everything else around him was in chaos.

Rocks had never ridiculed him, failed his expectations, or broken his heart. I had a feeling that his experiences with people were a different story and a tragic one at that.

I didn't know much about prospecting, and knew even less about the claim at Cripple Creek. But I could reckon how prosperous a man's claim was, and how willing he was to stay and work it, by his lodgings.

Most prospectors started with a bedroll, then a dugout, a lean-to, or a tent. From there it was on to huts, log cabins, and milled-wood houses with gables, glass windows, and such. And then, if you really struck it rich, you moved to mansions in San Francisco to count your money while others did your digging, and maybe went out to visit your mine now and then on the Golden Rail Express.

The three prospectors were moping around outside their log cabin. Judging by that sturdy dwelling, their elaborate network of sluices and rockers, the massive pile of gravel leavings, and the deep trenches they'd dug to channel the water away from the creek bed, they'd been working their claim hard and getting well rewarded for their labors.

But now that reward was gone, along with one of their partners.

Two of the three men could've been brothers. They both had big, bushy beards, hair like prairie grass, and shirts that might've been red once but were now a washed-out purple, their pants held up with frayed cotton suspenders. The only thing that really told the two men apart were the holes in their hats and their colorful scarves. They certainly weren't spending their gold on clothes. My guess was that most of their earnings were going to the saloons. They had the bloodshot eyes and sickly pallor of men who'd only just sobered up. I suppose there isn't anything much more sobering than finding a bloody corpse and going broke all at once.

Their partner, on the other hand, was all feathered up, squatting underneath the shade tree. His clothes were just as ratty as theirs were but his hair and beard were neatly trimmed and he smelled of lilac water. He must have doused himself with it since I was a few feet downwind of him and the scent was still quite strong. Despite his floral scent, he looked as sickly as his partners, but I think his was a malady of disposition due to the grim situation and not rotgut whiskey.

Deputy Weaver was with them and looked just as miserable, even though he hadn't lost a friend or a fortune. He got up off of the stump he was sitting on and approached the sheriff.

"I sure am glad to see you," Weaver said. "That body smells something awful. I don't understand why you didn't let us give him a decent burial before he became rank."

"I wanted Monk to see everything as we found it," Wheeler said.

"Pete isn't a pile of rocks," the feathered-up prospector said, rising to his feet. "What good is Monk going to do? We should be organizing a posse."

"Who am I supposed to go after with this posse, Pug?" Wheeler asked. "The only trail I see here is from the three of you. Whoever did this crept in without leaving a trace."

"Maybe it was Injuns," one of the other prospectors said. "They creep and they're good with knives. They can scalp a man whilst he's blinking."

"There aren't any Indians around here, Elmore," his look-alike replied. "There are plenty of them Mexicans, though, and them shifty Chinese. I never met an honest Chinaman."

"I saw a Chinaman in town," Elmore said. "It could've been him that done it. Arrest the Chinaman, Sheriff."

"I'm not arresting anybody, Alvie, until I've got some evidence," Wheeler said.

"I still don't see what we need an assayer for," Pug said.

"To assay the situation," Wheeler said and then glanced at Monk. "These men here are Pug Purdum, Elmore Portis, and Alvie Bartell. The dead man in the cabin is Pete Cooley."

The sheriff pointed the men out to Monk as he spoke.

"Somebody cut Pete's throat and took all our dust," Alvie said. "Pete never got a shot off."

"Where was your dust hidden?" Monk asked.

"Wasn't in no hidey-hole," Elmore said. "We kept it in cans on the shelf."

"Right out in the open?" I said.

"No reason not to," Pug said, leaning against the tree. "All of us are usually here working the claim. And if we need to go somewhere, we always leave a man or two behind. We're watchful."

"Did the three of you leave camp together

last night?" Monk asked. They all nodded. "Did you come back together, too?"

"I was the first one back," Alvie said. "Then Pug and Elmore."

"I met up with Elmore on Main Street this morning," Pug said. "We weren't half-way back before we ran into Alvie, who was pitching a fit."

"I was on my way into town to fetch them and the sheriff," Alvie explained.

"What did you do last night?" Monk asked him.

"I drank my weight in whiskey," Alvie said with a lopsided grin. "And yours, too. I played some cards and drank some more until my poke was empty."

"Where did you sleep?"

"On my barstool," he said. "Until I fell off of it; then I slept on the floor."

Monk nodded, frowning with disapproval and then shifted his gaze to Elmore. "And you?"

"About the same, except I paid my last pinch of dust to sleep in Lippy's stable," Elmore said. "I was too drunk to make it back to camp."

Monk looked at Pug. "What did you do for fun last night?"

"What I do every month," Pug said. "I went to the barber for a hot bath, a haircut, and a trim, then I went to the hotel for a good meal."

"Where did you spend the night?"

Pug shifted his weight uncomfortably between his feet and tried not to look in my direction. "With a lady friend."

"Of the sporting variety?" Sheriff Wheeler asked.

"Ain't but two or three grown, unmarried women in town that aren't," Pug said, then faced Monk. "And a man's got his manly needs, you know what I mean?"

If Monk did, he never showed any indication of it to me. He was the one man in town who'd never glanced at me with lustful eyes. Even Sheriff Wheeler had given me that look a time or two, but I didn't hold it against him. It wasn't his fault he had yearnings. He was flesh and blood like everybody else.

Except Monk. He was almost priestlike in his ability to avoid vice and temptation. By that I don't mean he was a cold man. He needed companionship, which was probably the big reason why he'd hired me. He was lonely.

And he was hungry for affection, but for him it wasn't expressed with physical intimacy. I believe that he felt it in the behavior of others, in how attentive and accepting they were of his peculiarities and protective of his feelings. And in that regard, I would say that Sheriff Wheeler and I showed our genuine affection for him every day.

"I would've saved the bath for last," Deputy Weaver said. "Some of those sporting women are uglier than a hog."

"We aren't interested in what you would have done," Sheriff Wheeler said.

"I would've skipped the bath and bought another drink," Alvie said. "I can wash in the river."

"You can drink in one, too," Pug said.

"Water doesn't have the same kick," Elmore said. "You don't know how to have fun, Pug."

"I've still got dust in my poke," Pug said. "How about you?"

Elmore shrugged. "There's always more where that came from. The ground is full of it. No point in working if you can't do some living."

I knew that Monk was probably in agreement with Pug. Any man who bathed regularly had Monk's respect. And I'm sure the woman Pug was with for the night appreciated having a clean, flowery-smelling customer for a change.

Monk took a deep breath and headed over to the cabin. I followed him.

I wasn't sure what I was supposed to do. I didn't want to see a dead man, particularly a brutally murdered one, but I was Monk's assistant and he might need assisting.

But that's not the real reason I went along with him to the cabin. I was curious to see how he would solve the crime, assuming it was even possible.

Monk opened the door to the cabin and stepped inside. I stood in the doorway, repulsed by the smell and what I saw.

Pete Cooley was on his side on the dirt floor in a puddle of dried blood. There was also blood on the wall in front of him. His neck mawed opened like a second mouth in a gruesome mockery of an ear-to-ear grin.

He was a sallow-faced man with sunken, sad eyes. Or maybe it was just death, or the horrid manner of his, that gave Pete that look. Maybe in life he was rosy-cheeked and jolly, but I'd never know now.

There was a sheathed knife on Pete's belt and a broken whiskey bottle on the floor by his outstretched hand.

Monk squatted beside the body. I expected him to be squeamish around so much blood, but he was quite the contrary. He studied the corpse the way he would a rock sample. He even sniffed the man's hair.

Sheriff Wheeler stood at my side and

together we silently observed Monk as he moved through the cabin, doing that odd dance of his.

Monk held his hands out in front of him, palms out, framing what he was seeing. In that way, I was able to tell when his attentions moved from the iron stove to the empty tin cans on the floor, from the prospecting tools in the corner to the benches around the table, and from the rifles on peg racks to the four bunks where the men slept.

He lowered his hands, rolled his shoulders, and shifted his head from side to side, then looked over his shoulder out the window, which was just an opening cut in the wood. He could see the shade tree and the men waiting outside for him to come out.

There were some rocks on the table. Monk picked two of them up, examined them, and came to us at the door. There was a peaceful, contented look on his face the likes of which I'd only seen once before, on the one morning when we didn't find a single warped, cracked, or missing plank on the sidewalks of Main Street.

And in that instant, I knew with absolute certainty that Artemis Monk had solved the murder.

"I'll be damned," Wheeler muttered, his words practically muffled under his enormous mustache.

We stepped aside and let Monk walk between us out to face Deputy Weaver and the three prospectors.

"I was just examining these rocks on your table," Monk said, and tossed one to Alvie, who caught it with his right hand and the other to Pug, who caught it with his left. "Are they from your latest dig?"

"Yes," Alvie said, licking the rock and holding it up to his eye. "We're getting closer and closer to the big pay streak."

"Arrest that man," Monk said to Sheriff Wheeler.

"Alvie killed Pete Cooley?" Wheeler said.

"No, but did you see him lick that rock?" Monk said. "He's disgusting. God only knows what else he licks. Locking him up will serve as a warning to everybody to keep their tongues in their mouths where they belong."

"I'm more interested in locking up the murderers," Wheeler said.

"Rock licking is how it starts," Monk said. "Just ask Pug Purdum."

"What would I know about it?" Pug asked.

"You murdered Pete Cooley," Monk said.

"You're crazy," Pug said. "I didn't kill him."

"I knew it was one of the three of you

when Sheriff Wheeler said he didn't see any other tracks here but yours," Monk said. "And if I didn't know it then, I would have known it as soon as I went inside the cabin. It was obvious."

"Not to me," Sheriff Wheeler said.

"Pete never went for his knife or for a gun," Monk said. "That's because the person who came in was someone Pete trusted. Pete wouldn't have turned his back on him otherwise. The killer grabbed him by the hair with his right hand and slit his throat with his left."

"How do you know which hand the killer used?" Sheriff Wheeler asked.

"I followed the trail, in this case the wound across Pete Cooley's throat. The wound begins high and shallow on the right side of the neck and deepens as it angles slightly to the left. It's got to do with how the arm works." Monk picked up a stick and came up behind me, simulating a knife attack. "May I?"

I nodded. He gently grabbed me by the hair, pulled back my head, and ran the stick slowly across my exposed throat. "It's very difficult to slit a person's throat from behind without the cut ending lower and deeper than where it started, regardless of which hand you use. It's possible, but it would be uncomfortable, awkward, and unlikely, since a killer wants to move fast and not give his victim the opportunity to overpower him."

Monk let go of me. It was the first time that he'd really touched me and it was to demonstrate a brutal murder. It might have been unsettling to me if I hadn't stopped to think that I was the only person there, besides Pug, who had clean hair.

I was also the only person there, with the possible exception of Sheriff Wheeler, whom Monk would have felt safe touching at all.

When I thought of it that way, the demonstration showed two things — how the murder was committed and how comfortable Monk felt with me.

It was a turning point for us, though if Monk realized it, he wasn't showing it.

"Pug is left-handed," Monk said, pointing at him with the stick. "Alvie and Elmore are not."

"How do you know Elmore isn't left-handed?" Deputy Weaver asked.

Monk threw his stick at Elmore, who instinctively swatted it aside with his right hand.

"The odds were in my favor," Monk said. "Besides, I already knew it was Pug. He was the only one who wasn't too drunk to overpower Pete. Here's what happened . . ."

261

Monk explained that the three prospectors went into town and left Pete behind with a couple bottles of whiskey to occupy himself. The three men went their separate ways. Pug waited until he'd had his bath and eaten before returning to the cabin to give Pete plenty of time to get good and drunk. That way, Pete would be easier to overpower.

Pug came back to the cabin, killed Pete, then returned to town and spent the rest of the night in the company of a sporting woman.

"I know the sequence of events because Pete smells faintly of lilac water," Monk said. "That's because Pug was fresh from his bath and slathered in fragrance when he murdered Pete."

"If Pete smells like lilac, that's because I rolled him over when I got here this morning," Pug said. "I wanted to see what had happened to him."

"That's true," Elmore said. "I saw him do it."

"Of course you did," Monk said. "He wanted you to, just in case anybody picked up that scent."

"Your story doesn't make any sense at all," Alvie said. "If Pug stole the gold, how come he didn't run off with it?"

"Because there's a lot more gold still to be made from this claim," Monk said.

"He's loco, everybody knows that," Pug said, leaning back against the tree to show how relaxed and unconcerned he was about Monk's argument. "Five minutes ago he wanted you arrested for licking a rock, Alvie. How crazy is that? He won't let two horses drink out of the same trough. He changed the name of Third Street to Second Second Street. This is just more of his crazy talk."

Elmore tugged at his beard as he considered what he'd heard. "If Pug stole the gold, where is it?"

Monk smiled. "You can tell from the mess in the cabin."

"You can?" Sheriff Wheeler said.

"Any other killer would have wanted to be in and out of the cabin as quickly as possible. He would have taken the gold as it was in the cans and not wasted time emptying the dust into some other container," Monk said, then turned to the three prospectors. "But Pug couldn't take the gold back with him into town in the tins or in anything else. He couldn't risk being caught with that much gold on him. So he had to hide it, somewhere neither his partners nor anybody else would stumble on it, somewhere it would be safe for months, somewhere he could keep his eye on it at all times, day or night."

"I don't see how that thinking tells you where it is," Alvie said.

"It had to be someplace Pug could keep an eye on while he was working or even while he was in his bunk," Monk said. "So I looked out the window and what did I see? The tree, the one you can see from anywhere you're working on the claim, the one Pug has been glued to since we got here."

"I'm telling you, Monk is crazy," Pug said. "You're listening to a man who is afraid of milk."

Monk stepped up to Pug. "It's easy enough to check. I'd start with the knothole above his head."

Alvie shoved Pug aside, shimmied up the tree, and reached into the knothole. He came out with a bulging sack full of gold dust.

Elmore launched himself at Pug, knocking him to the ground and pummeling him with his fists. Wheeler pulled Elmore off of Pug and Weaver lifted the killer to his feet.

"Why'd you do it?" Elmore yelled. "Why'd you take our gold?"

"Better me than the faro dealers and saloons," Pug said, blood streaming from his nose. "You're throwing it all away. We'll never get rich that way."

"You had your share," Alvie said, jumping down from the tree and leaving the gold in its hiding place for the time being. "What did it matter to you what we did with ours?"

"Capital," Pug said. "You need money to make money."

"Money don't do you no good in your poke," Elmore said.

"That's the attitude that would have kept us digging forever and never getting ahead," Pug said. "It was only a matter of time before you three losers got so deep into debt that you'd have to sell out and with just my share, I wouldn't have enough gold to be the buyer. Not unless I did something to protect myself. That's what the gold was for. You brought this on yourselves."

"You're gonna hang, Pug," Alvie said. "And if I have my say, it's gonna be from *this* tree."

"Sounds like justice to me," Wheeler said and then turned to Monk. "And the end of three-card monte in Trouble."

Monk sighed with contentment as we started walking back to Trouble.

# CHAPTER FIFTEEN:
# MR. MONK NEEDS A
# HAND

I was awakened from a deep sleep by the shrill, annoying ring of my telephone. In my drowsy haze, I reached for my cell before I realized that it wasn't my ringtone that I was hearing but the blare of the old telephone on my nightstand.

I grabbed the receiver. "Hello?"

"It's Clifford Adams," he said across a very scratchy line. I could barely make out his words. "I need to see you right away."

I blinked hard and glanced at the clock radio. It was almost six a.m. "What's the hurry?"

"I know who killed the museum guard."

That cleared my head fast. I sat up in bed. "Come on over."

"No, you two come to me, alone. I want to live."

And on that ominous note, he hung up.

If my life had a sound track, and in my mind it often did, that was the perfect moment for an ominous, heavy-handed, music sting.

I heard one and it sounded like distant thunder.

Monk was already awake when I knocked on his door at 6:10 that morning. He'd gone to bed promptly at 9:50 p.m., so he'd fall asleep no later than ten, and set his alarm for 6:00 a.m., giving him an even eight hours of sleep.

But he wouldn't come out when I knocked. He said he needed at least another twenty minutes to boil a pot of water in the electric coffeepot, disinfect his toothbrush, brush his teeth, and disinfect his toothbrush again. And then he'd need another two hours to bathe himself and then clean up the bathroom afterwards.

"And that's if I rush," he said.

"You have twenty minutes," I said. "And then I'm coming in."

"You don't have a key," he said.

"Actually, I do," I said. "I had the manager give me one when I registered us."

"Why?"

"For emergencies," I said. "This could be one."

Monk came out twenty minutes later, but he wasn't happy about it. He spent most of the drive wiping his hands, neck, and face with Wet Ones to avoid, as he put it, "catastrophic organ failure and death from septic shock."

I made a sharp, fast turn onto the dirt road to Adams' place. I did it so Monk wouldn't notice the skid marks that I'd left the day before on the highway and ask me to stop and clean them up.

The look he gave me, though, made it clear he wasn't fooled.

I was going so fast that I didn't see a pothole in the road ahead of us and hit it so hard that we would've slammed our heads into the roof if we hadn't been buckled in.

Even so, we were rattled pretty hard and I'd probably knocked my tires out of alignment.

Monk took a wipe in each hand and pressed his palms against the dashboard.

"Do you have some kind of death wish?" he asked.

"I'm worried about Mr. Adams," I replied. "I didn't like the way he said 'I want to live.'"

"I'd like to live, too," Monk said. "Could you please show the same concern for me?"

We bumped and rattled our way down the dirt road until we finally reached the compound. Much to my surprise, Monk practically leaped out of the car this time.

I got out and joined Monk as he marched to the door of the Quonset hut. "How come you're not locking yourself inside my car today?"

"It's safer out here."

I knocked on the door. "Mr. Adams? It's Natalie Teeger and Mr. Monk."

There was no answer. I knocked again. All was quiet. The only sound was the rusty creak of the windmill blades wobbling slightly in the breeze. Monk shifted his weight.

"Mr. Adams?" I called out. "Are you there? Arc you all right?"

I tried to open the door, but it was locked.

I looked over my shoulder at the outhouse, then back at Monk.

"Don't look at me," he said. "I'm not going out there."

I sighed and trudged out to the outhouse. I was downwind from it and when the breeze kicked up, the acrid stench was so strong that I had to fight the instinctive urge to turn back.

How could Adams go in there every day?

I covered my nose and breathed through my mouth, but I could still taste the odor, which was even worse than smelling it.

I reached the outhouse and knocked on

the door. The last thing I wanted was to surprise Adams in there.

"Mr. Adams?"

When he didn't answer, I slowly opened the door. The smell slapped me in the face and I was assaulted by flies. I glanced inside only long enough to be sure Adams wasn't in there before slamming the door shut.

I practically ran back to Monk, who hadn't moved from where he was standing.

"Maybe he's gone," Monk said.

"His pickup truck is parked here," I said. "He might be working inside the mine."

"I'm not going in there," he said.

"I know that," I said. "But maybe if we go up to the entrance and call his name, he'll hear us."

We started walking up the hill to the mine when Monk stopped, turned to the left, and cocked his head. Something had caught his eye.

"What is it?" I asked.

"Is that Adams?" He pointed to a collection of boulders and scrub grass about fifty years away. A man was sitting with his back against one of the boulders. But he was slumped forward, as if he'd fallen asleep.

"I don't know whether it's him or not," I said and headed out towards the rocks, walking fast, nearly running. Monk followed after me, hurrying to keep up.

"What would he be doing way out there?"

"I don't know," I said. "But he might need our help. He looks unconscious from here."

"Maybe he's just napping."

"At seven thirty in the morning?" I said. "What if he's hurt himself? What if he's been bitten by a snake or stung by a scorpion?"

I immediately wished I could take back what I said.

Monk stopped. "Then we should run back to the car and lock the doors."

I turned around to face him. "You want us to leave without checking if Mr. Adams is all right?"

"We can go back to town and get help. They can look him over."

"By then it could be too late," I said. "He might need our help right now."

"But if he has been bitten or stung or both, the snake and the scorpion could be lurking out there, waiting for us to show up."

"So what do you suggest we do?"

Monk cupped his hands around his mouth and yelled, "MR. ADAMS? IS THAT YOU? ARE YOU ALL RIGHT?" There was no answer. We were still too far away for me to see if it was Adams or not. Whoever it was didn't move.

"I'm going out there," I said. "You can do whatever you want."

I rushed out towards the boulders.

"Wait," Monk said, chasing after me. "If you get bitten, what happens to me?"

As I got closer, I could see that the man sitting on the ground was Clifford Adams — his head was down, his legs splayed out awkwardly in front of him.

I had a bad, bad feeling about this.

And that's when I heard the crack behind me. I whirled around just in time to see Monk dropping into the earth as if a trapdoor had opened underneath him.

One second he was there and the next there was only a puff of dirt in the air where he'd been standing.

"Mr. Monk!" I yelled. "Mr. Monk!"

I ran back to where he had fallen and saw a huge pit still partially covered with the remains of a rotted piece of plywood and dirt.

I dropped to my knees, pushed the board away, and leaned over the edge of the pit, staring into the blackness. The pit seemed bottomless.

"Natalie," Monk whined.

He was about ten feet below me and flush against the side of the pit, holding on to the jutting rock.

But he was trying to find a toehold and the combination of his movement and his weight was jogging the rock loose. I could see it moving, particles of dirt falling onto Monk's shoulder like sand in an hourglass.

"Don't move," I said to him. "Stay still."

"I'm going to fall," he whined.

"No, you're not." I lay down on my stomach, slipped over the edge as far as I could without falling in myself, and reached my right hand down to him. "Take my hand."

He reached up to me with his left hand, but there were still a few feet separating us.

"I'm going to die," he said, lowering his left arm.

"You always say that," I said, trying to keep things light as I sat up and looked desperately for something, anything, I could use to quickly bridge the distance between us.

"But now I'm facing certain death," he said.

"Oh, come on, Mr. Monk." I couldn't find anything. I wanted to cry. "You think that you're facing certain death every time you step out of your house."

"This proves that I'm right!"

I looked back at the Quonset hut, trying to decide if I had the time to run back there to find a rope, a hose, anything. There wasn't time. The rock wouldn't hold much longer under Monk's weight.

"So you should be feeling good," I said. "You love being right."

"For once it would be nice to be wrong," he said. "What are you doing?"

"Looking for something to reach you with," I said.

What could I use? I instinctively patted my pockets, as if there might be six feet of rope in there that I'd overlooked.

*My belt.*

I unbuckled the belt, and yanked it out of the loops of my jeans. I looped the belt through the buckle around my wrist so it would tighten under Monk's weight, grabbed the leather in my fist, and lay down again.

I reached for Monk again, dropping the belt to him. "Hold my belt."

But even as I said it, I could see that it wasn't going to be long enough.

He probably knew it, too, although he tried to grab the belt anyway, but it didn't reach.

There were still about ten or twelve inches between the end of the belt and Monk's free hand, which was grasping at air.

"Oh my God," Monk shrieked, yanking

his free hand back and once again scrambling for a foothold.

"What is it? What's wrong?"

"Spider," Monk said. "I can see a spider."

"If you don't calm down, you're going to fall."

"But at least I won't be bitten by a poisonous spider."

I sat up and stared at my useless belt.

What would MacGyver do in a situation like this? He'd be able to fashion a rope out of whatever he had in the pockets of his jeans, even if it was just lint and a breath mint.

*The jeans.*

Denim could take a beating. They might hold Monk's weight.

"I've got an idea," I said. "Don't move."

"Tell that to the poisonous spider," Monk said.

I stood up, kicked off my shoes, and stripped off my jeans. I tossed the belt to the ground, wrapped the end of one pant leg firmly around my wrist, grabbed the denim tight in my fist, and got back down on my stomach.

I reached over the edge and dropped my jeans down to him.

"What do you expect me to do with that?" he said.

"Grab it," I said.

"Those are someone's dirty pants."

"They are *my* pants and they were clean when I put them on this morning."

"But then you put them on," Monk said. "Against your body. Did you shower before we left?"

"Yes," I said.

"You're lying," he said.

"It doesn't matter whether I showered or not," I said. "You're holding on to a loose rock for dear life."

"Your body is caked in dried sweat and layers of dirt," Monk said. "And now it's infected your pants. What if I have an open wound on my hand? I could get a horrible infection."

"At least you'll still be alive," I said.

"Only to die a slow, hideous, drooling death from a pants infection."

I could see that the rock he was holding was coming loose. It would pop out in seconds and Monk would fall to his death.

"Grab my pants now," I said.

"Couldn't you use something else?" Monk asked imploringly. "Like a rope, a chain, or a ladder?"

"If I had one of those, do you think I'd be using my pants?"

"I'll wait," he said.

276

"Take the jeans, Mr. Monk."

"I'd rather die," he said.

*"You will!"* I yelled.

"But at least the poisonous spider won't get me and I won't get an infection from your pants, have my gangrenous limbs amputated, and die a limbless, pitiful wretch covered in open sores."

"If you die in this pit today, I swear to God that I'll bury you in mismatched socks, an untucked shirt, and a jacket with a missing button."

"You wouldn't," he said.

"You'll be a mess," I said. "For eternity."

Monk gritted his teeth, closed his eyes, and grabbed my pants with his left hand. At the same instant, the rock he was holding gave way and he dangled over the abyss, clutching my pants. His deadweight was pulling me over the edge.

I screamed in pain and fury, digging my free hand and bare knees into the hard dirt to prevent my slide.

*"Climb!"* I yelled.

Monk used my pants like a rope, pulling himself up, hand over hand.

My outstretched arm was burning with pain and I could feel myself sliding over the edge, the gravel scratching my bare legs and tearing at my fingernails.

And then I felt a pop in my arm and a searing pain that made me scream again. Through the agony, I felt my fingers going numb. I willed myself not to let go, to maintain my grip.

Monk grabbed my left shoulder and nearly pulled my hand out of the ground.

"Let go of me!" I said. "You're breaking my hold!"

He swung up one of his legs, got a knee over the edge, and lifted himself out of the pit, landing almost face-first against my butt.

I lay there, tears stinging my eyes, my arm blazing with pain and still draped over the side of the pit.

I struggled to sit up with my good hand, which was covered with blood. I'd torn a couple of my fingernails clawing at the earth. My knees were scraped raw. My dislocated right arm hung uselessly at my side. I must have looked like the heroine at the end of a bad slasher movie.

Monk was sitting up, breathing hard, his eyes closed.

"You can open your eyes, Mr. Monk. It's over."

"Are you wearing pants?"

"Not at the moment," I said.

"Then it's not over."

# CHAPTER SIXTEEN:
# MR. MONK ON THE
# ROAD

He was right, it wasn't over. We were alive, but our struggles were just beginning.

"I can't put on my pants," I said. "My right arm is dislocated and my left hand is covered with blood."

Monk opened his eyes and looked at me.

"Oh, Natalie . . ."

He said it with such tenderness, and with such an expression of sadness on his face, that I couldn't stop the tears. But that seemed to horrify him even more than my nakedness or my injuries.

"Relax, Mr. Monk," I said. "The tears will stop in a minute or two. It's nothing to worry about."

Monk picked up my pants, shook off the dirt, and then carefully fitted my feet into each pant leg, looking away as he did it. He slowly worked the pants over my legs, but he was having a hard time.

"Why did you have to get such tight

pants?" he asked.

I was asking myself the same question but wasn't going to give him the satisfaction of knowing it.

"I didn't anticipate a situation like this coming up," I said.

"I've been telling you that you need to be better prepared for emergencies."

"I'll keep that in mind next time I buy pants," I said.

I swung my left arm over his shoulder so that I could lift myself up a few inches off the ground and he could tug the pants over my hips. It wasn't an easy operation for either of us. I would have found it funny if I weren't in such pain. There was probably a better way to do it, but my head wasn't very clear.

He whimpered, keeping his eyes closed and his teeth gritted, as he zipped my pants up and buttoned the fly.

"I should have just let go of that rock," he said. "Or let the vicious spider get me."

"You would have preferred death over putting my pants on me?"

"And to see you hurt," he said.

"Your eyes are closed, Mr. Monk."

Monk opened them. He looked at my tear-streaked cheeks, my limp arm, and my bloody hand and shook his head.

"You need a wipe," he said.

"I know," I said. "What about Clifford Adams? Can we do anything for him? How is he?"

Monk looked over his shoulder in Adams' direction and winced. "He's dead."

"How can you tell from here?"

"Because there are vultures picking at him," Monk said.

I looked back. Sure enough, two large vultures were stabbing at him with their beaks. That was usually a pretty definitive sign of death. I turned away before I saw something gross, though what I'd seen wasn't so pleasant either.

Monk put my shoes on my feet, making sure the laces were tied in neat, even bows. Then, careful not to touch my bloody hand, he put one arm around my waist, draped my left arm around his neck, and gently lifted me to my feet.

I immediately felt woozy and nauseous and had to clutch Monk for support. I'm sure I got blood on his jacket and that it would probably have to be incinerated as a result, but there was no way around it.

It took a moment for me to regain my balance and for the nausea to pass, then we started walking slowly, and cautiously, towards my car.

"What do you think happened here?"

"It was a trap," Monk said. "Clifford Adams didn't call you. His killer did. Adams was placed out there to lure us across this field. The killer wanted us to fall in one of the mine shafts. There are probably other holes hidden under a thin sheet of plywood and covered with dirt."

"So Adams must have known something," I said.

"Or the murderer thought he did," Monk said.

"Have you figured out who it is?"

Monk shook his head. "I'm too dirty to think."

We reached the car. Monk opened the driver's door, rooted around in my purse, and took out a wipe.

"Sit down," he said.

I sat down on a bench in front of the Quonset hut.

Monk tore open the wipe and softly cleaned the dirt from my face. My right arm was throbbing with pain, my fingers were numb, and my skin tingled, but the disinfectant wipe on my cheeks somehow made it feel a little better.

"You're going to have to drive us back," I said.

"You can drive," he said.

"My right arm is dislocated and my left hand is a bloody mess."

"We can call for help."

He stuck the dirty wipe in a plastic bag and pulled out my phone.

"There's not going to be any reception out here," I said.

A quick look at the screen on my phone proved I was right. Monk grimaced and took out another wipe.

"Let me see your hand," he said.

I raised my left hand and he took it tenderly in his own. He gently dabbed away the blood from my fingertips. The disinfectant stung, but compared to the agony in my right arm, I hardly felt it.

"We could wait for help to arrive," he said.

"Nobody knows we're out here," I said. "I need a doctor and lots of very strong drugs."

"We have wipes," Monk said.

"That's not going to be enough," I said.

Monk nodded, then glanced at Adams' huge machine. "Does that crush rocks?"

"And coffeemakers," I said.

Monk went over to the machine, studied it for a moment, then took off his jacket and tossed it inside. He hit a button, the machine shook, and a few seconds later, shreds of fabric sprayed from the funnel onto the pile of gravel.

He turned the machine off, rolled his shoulders, and sighed.

"Okay," he said. "Let's do this."

Monk drove slowly and cautiously, gripping the steering wheel with both hands (a wipe in each of them) and leaning as close as he could get to the goop-streaked windshield.

His lethargic driving was both good and bad for me.

The good side was that each bump caused me pain and he was driving so slowly that the car wasn't being jarred too much.

The bad side was that it was taking us forever to get anywhere and my pain was getting worse with each passing second. We'd been driving for fifteen minutes and we were barely a quarter of a mile from the compound.

I was beginning to think that it would be faster to walk back to the highway on my own and wait for Monk there.

"You can go a little faster," I said.

"It's an unpaved road and I can barely see through the windshield," Monk said. "We can't be too careful."

"I'm in pain here," I said.

"So am I," he said.

"Mine is different," I said.

"Yes, yours will end," Monk said. "You

have hope. I have no hope."

I gritted my teeth and braced myself for the long journey. After what seemed like days, we finally reached the junction of the unpaved road and the highway.

"Stop," I said.

"Good idea," Monk said, stopping the car. "We should clean up that skid mark while we're here."

"That's not why I asked you to stop. I can get cellular reception here. I can call for help."

"We can do both," he said. "You don't want the authorities showing up and seeing your vandalism."

While I called 911 to report a murder to the police and request medical assistance for myself, Monk went out and examined the skid mark. But he stopped first at the pothole that I'd hit before. He was probably trying to decide whether or not he should fill it. He crouched, picked up a rock from the pothole, and stuck it in his pocket before continuing on.

That was a strange thing for him to do, but I didn't really care. When I finished talking to the operator, I leaned back, closed my eyes, and waited for help to arrive.

Monk found his spare cleaning supplies in

the trunk and was busy scrubbing off the skid mark with a soapy sponge when the phalanx of official vehicles arrived covered in dust and butterfly goop, sirens wailing. Kelton's squad car was in the lead, followed by another squad car, a paramedic truck, and an ambulance.

The chief skidded to a stop, much to Monk's obvious dismay, and bolted from his car, running right over to me. He yanked open the door of my car and grimaced when he saw how I looked.

"What happened to you?"

"Mr. Monk fell in a mine shaft and I pulled him out," I said.

Kelton glanced at Monk. "What is he doing?"

"Cleaning the highway," I said. "Adams was dead when we got there. We were going out to his body when Monk fell in the pit."

"This is getting worse with each passing day," he said.

"Tell me about it," I said.

Two pale and callow paramedics ran up to me and gave me a quick once-over.

"We're going to have to reduce your dislocation," the palest of the paramedics said.

"What does that mean?"

"We've got to pop the ball of your humerus back into your shoulder socket," he said.

"That doesn't sound very funny to me," I said. The paramedic stared blankly at me. "It's a joke. How bad is it going to hurt?"

"Bad," Kelton said. "But you'll feel better right away. At least until tomorrow morning, when you'll be thanking the Lord for the invention of painkillers."

"How do you know?"

"I've dislocated my shoulder nine times," he said. "Mostly playing football. I once did it twice in one day."

Monk ambled over to us, his hands in rubber gloves.

"So how do you pop it back in?" I asked.

"I can do it if you like," Kelton said.

I figured if he'd been through this nine times himself that he probably had more experience than those two paramedics did. Plus I felt safe with him.

"Okay," I said.

The paramedics spread a blanket down on the ground and then they helped me lie down on my back on top of it.

Kelton stood on my right side, put his foot in my armpit, held my right wrist, and told me to scream as loud and as hard as I could.

I did.

And in that same instant, he yanked my

arm straight out to the side. I felt a stab of pain and a popping sensation as the ball of my arm snapped back into the socket.

The pain I'd been feeling eased almost immediately.

"Nice job, Chief," the paramedic said, nodding appreciatively.

Kelton helped me to my feet. "The ambulance will take you to the hospital in town. Monk can follow you in your car."

"I can't," Monk said. "I don't drive."

"I'll drive your car for you," the other paramedic said. "We have to go back to the hospital anyway."

"I'll ride in the ambulance with Natalie," Monk said, then handed the car keys to the paramedic. "Be sure to thoroughly disinfect yourself when you get there. Her car is pestilence on wheels."

I wondered whether he wanted to accompany me because he was concerned for my well-being or because the ambulance was cleaner than my car. It didn't really matter what his reasons were. I wanted him with me.

"Are you sure you wouldn't prefer to stay out here with me and help with the investigation?" Kelton asked Monk. "I could use your insights."

"I've only got one," Monk said. "Be careful where you step."

"Wasn't that the advice I gave you?"

"People don't always follow their own advice," Monk said. "And the next thing you know, you're facing doom."

I spent the next few hours in the hospital emergency room. A nurse helped me change into a gown, then she cleaned up my wounds and bandaged my fingers. They took a lot of X-rays and gave me a bunch of shots in my good shoulder that hurt almost as much as dislocating the other one.

While I was going through all of that, my employer filled out all of my forms. I was glad that Monk was doing that. I wanted him to see for himself how much money I was on the hook for. I had lousy medical insurance, so I knew I'd have a big deductible bill to look forward to and a nasty fight with Monk to get him to pay it.

I dozed for a few minutes on the bed until the doctor came back with my X-rays. He had a warm smile, lots of white hair, and wrinkles that suggested wisdom rather than age.

He told me that the rays showed no signs of fractures and that I'd suffered a simple dislocation. He helped me put my arm in a sling, gave me some prescriptions for painkillers, and told me I could expect the muscles and tendons to complain painfully for the next twenty hours over what had been done to them, especially if I tried moving my arm. The doctor said that it would be about six weeks before my arm was back to normal again, so I could cancel any plans I had to participate in arm wrestling tournaments for a while.

The doctor left and a few moments later Monk came in wearing blue surgical scrubs and disposable white slippers. My purse was over his shoulder and he was carrying another folded set of scrubs in his hands.

"Where are your clothes and your shoes?" I asked him.

"The same place yours are, in the hazardous waste bin." He handed me the scrubs. "The nurse will come in and help you put these on. While you do that, I'll get your prescriptions filled and then a police officer will drive us back to the motel."

He walked out before I could protest, not that I had any intention to. The nurse helped me dress, eased me into a wheelchair, and wheeled me out to the waiting squad car, which drove us the two blocks to our motel.

Monk led me into his room, insisting that it was more sanitary than mine, and got me into bed. He handed me a bottle of Summit Creek water and pulled up a chair beside me.

"Are you hungry?" he asked.

"Not right now," I said.

"You're supposed to take those pills with some food," he said.

"I've got a few more hours until then," I said. "We can order a pizza. Uncut, of course."

"I've got my tape measure, but I forgot to bring string, a compass, a T square, and a level."

"You'll manage to cut the pizza without all of that," I said.

"It's going to be dicey," he said.

"We've been in dicier situations," I said.

"Speaking of which," he said, "you'll be glad to know that I don't have a pants infection."

"That's a big relief," I said. "You have no idea how much that was weighing on my mind."

I knew that the sarcasm was completely wasted on him, of course, and that he was taking my words straight, but there's no harm in amusing yourself when you feel like crap.

"But I insisted on getting a tetanus shot just in case," he said.

"Good thinking," I said.

We were quiet for a long moment.

"Thank you for saving my life," Monk said. "You do it every day, but today you did it especially well."

I didn't know what to say, so I didn't say anything. I just nodded.

"Is there anything I can do for you?" he asked.

"Yes," I said. "You can read me a story."

## THE EXTRAORDINARY MR. MONK
### The Case of the Golden Rail Express

*(From the journal of Abigail Guthrie)*
*Trouble, California, 1856*

Mrs. Cromartie, who ran a boardinghouse in Trouble, showed up at the door of Artemis Monk's assay office one morning asking for help, but it wasn't for his expert opinion on some rocks.

She came to him because Sheriff Wheeler, his deputy, and Dr. Sloan were all several long miles away, dealing with the aftermath of the robbery of the Golden Rail Express, which had occurred the previous night.

Although Monk was the town assayer, he'd developed a reputation in Trouble as a man capable of solving vexing mysteries, yet another reason people tolerated his many eccentricities.

Mrs. Cromartie was pretty eccentric herself. The widow was a large woman with a mustache nearly as full as those of the miners she rented rooms to. She wore a gun belt to ward off unwanted male attention, though from what I'd heard, for a pinch of gold and a bottle of whiskey, she'd gladly drop her gun belt and lift her skirt.

She'd come to Monk because there were two dead men in one of her rooms. She couldn't tell whether they'd died of natural causes, murder, or some horrible plague.

Monk was eager to help, which surprised me. We almost had to run to keep up with him as he bolted out the door into the street.

"What if it's plague?" I asked.

"We'll have to burn the boardinghouse down," he said with a smile. "Perhaps the entire block."

Mrs. Cromartie gasped. "God, no. The boardinghouse is all I've got."

"You're hoping it's plague," I said to Monk. "Aren't you?"

"All the buildings on that street are different heights, some aren't even symmetrical," Monk said. "It's already a serious health hazard."

"So they aren't identical," I said. "How is that unhealthy?"

"It strains the eyes and the sensibility," Monk said. "It could drive a person with a weak constitution into total madness."

I was tempted to ask if that was what happened to him, but I bit my tongue.

"Maybe that's what happened to them," she said.

I turned to her, startled that she'd practically read my mind, though she referred to her tenants and not Monk.

"You're not serious," I said.

"Last night Mr. Durphy, one of the two dead miners, was drooling and dancing naked outside of my room doing birdcalls," she said. "I nearly shot him."

"What do you know about the men?" Monk asked as we hurried along.

"They worked in the mill room of the Big Rock mine," she said.

The Big Rock was one of the biggest mine operations in Trouble. Their tunnels went deep underground to dig up the gold-laced ore, which was pulverized into dust, then mixed with mercury in the mill room. The mercury drew out the gold from the ore into a malleable amalgam. The amalgam could be heated, or simply squeezed with a cheese cloth, to separate out the gold.

The mining company made every employee change their clothes before their shifts, then shower and change clothes again at the end.

Monk admired the Big Rock mine owners for that practice alone, but it wasn't done in the interests of cleanliness. The owners wanted to make sure none of the valuable amalgam was being snuck out.

The owners even made the miners leap naked over a stack of logs before showering to make sure no amalgam was secreted away in body cavities. They also searched the miner's lunchboxes, tobacco pouches, and any other containers they brought to the mine.

"Besides the naked birdcalls, have the men been acting strangely?" Monk asked.

"The other guy stayed in his room all the time. He only came out at night because the light hurt his eyes," Mrs. Cromartie said. "I guess that's what happens when you spend all day in a hole in the ground."

"But he wasn't in the mine," I said. "He was in the mill."

Mrs. Cromartie shrugged. "Then maybe it was the buildings on the street that made them mad as a hatter, like Monk was saying."

Monk rolled his shoulders and tipped his head from side to side like he was trying to loosen a stiff neck. But I'd seen him do that before, right before he solved a murder.

We reached her boardinghouse, a long, simple structure that was, essentially, several one-room shacks lined up in a row and sharing thin walls.

"Which one are they in?" Monk asked.

"Number seven," she said, pointing to the very last room.

"No wonder they were ill," he said. "You should be ashamed of yourself, Mrs. Cromartie."

"What did I do?" she asked.

"You put an odd number on the door," Monk said.

"It's the seventh room," she said. "There's nothing I can do about that."

"You could build another room so you have eight of them," Monk said.

"There would still be odd-numbered rooms, Mr. Monk," I said in her defense.

"She could give them all even numbers," Monk said. "Instead of rooms one through seven, you should have rooms two, four, six, eight, ten, twelve, and fourteen."

"Don't you think people would find that confusing?" Mrs. Cromartie said.

"You wouldn't have as many dead tenants," Monk said.

"You think *that's* what killed them?" she asked.

"I'm sure it was a contributing factor, no matter what happened." Monk stepped up to the door of room seven and, using a handkerchief, pushed open the door.

There was one bunk, a table, a bench, and two shelves. On the table was a large prospecting pan full of cigarette butts.

The two men were lying on their backs on the floor. One of them was, indeed, buck naked. I noticed their pink cheeks and fingertips.

"They're miners," I said. "But they've got shopkeeper's fingernails."

Their nails were long, the better to snag an extra few granules of gold dust with each pinch from a customer's poke.

Monk turned to me and smiled. "Very observant, Abby."

*Abby.*

It was the first time he hadn't called me Mrs. Guthrie. I felt my face flushing and I didn't know why.

Monk crouched beside the dead miner who was dressed, reached into the pocket of his pants, and pulled out a tiny shingle nail, which he held up to his eyes. He nodded to himself, then turned to Mrs. Cromartie.

"These men were gold thieves," he said. "And so are you. If you pay for their proper burials and build an eighth room with the gold you stole from these two, your transgression will be our secret."

Her face became as red as a tomato. I was afraid she might pull her gun and shoot him.

"They hadn't paid me rent this week," she said between gritted teeth. "I only took what I was owed."

"You took far more than that," Monk said.

"Wait a minute," I said. "How did you know they were thieves?"

"It's stealing the gold that killed them," Monk said. "It was Mrs. Cromartie who solved the mystery before I even got here."

"I did?" she said, totally perplexed.

"You said they were 'mad as hatters,' " Monk said. "Indeed they were. These two miners died of mercury poisoning, just like the Huguenot craftsmen who went slowly insane making hats. Intolerance of sunlight, excessive drooling, pink extremities, and profuse sweating are just a few of the many other symptoms as the poisoning progresses."

Monk explained that the two men probably dragged their long nails over the mercury tables at the mine every time they passed them, scooping up valuable flakes of amalgam. They stuck their hands in their pockets and worked the amalgam out from under their fingers with the shingle nails.

"Wouldn't they have been caught with the amalgam in their pockets when they changed clothes?" I asked.

"They put the little balls of amalgam into their tobacco and rolled them into the butts of their cigarettes," Monk said. "During their breaks, they smoked their cigarettes and tossed the butts in the trash. They collected the butts later, outside the mine, when the trash was hauled away and dumped."

He reached into the bowl of butts and unpeeled one of them. Sure enough, there was a tiny bead of gold inside.

"What happened to the mercury?" I asked.

"They smoked the cigarettes too short," Monk said. "The heat vaporized the mercury and they inhaled it with the cigarette smoke."

"So them dying had nothing to do with the odd-numbered room," Mrs. Cromartie said, sighing with relief.

"Their scheme was insane," Monk said. "What do you think drove them to it?"

"An odd number on the door?" she replied incredulously.

"Undoubtedly. I hope you can sleep at night," Monk said and, oddly contented, walked away.

It seemed to me that nothing made him

happier than solving these little mysteries. Perhaps that was his true calling.

Unfortunately, he had no luck helping the sheriff figure out who'd robbed the Golden Rail Express. We learned later that day from the sheriff that the train robbers had killed three men, shot two others, and made off with thousands of dollars in gold coins from the wealthy mine owners from San Francisco who traveled on the private railroad.

Wheeler tracked the robbers back into town, where he lost their trail.

Since hardly anybody ever used gold coins in Trouble, Wheeler figured the robbers probably hightailed it to San Francisco with their loot. Nobody there would look twice at someone spending gold coins. That's where the mint was and where most of the gold that was mined in Trouble and everywhere else in California was eventually sent.

After a week or two, nobody gave the robbery much more thought and everything went back to the way it was.

Except that Monk was still calling me Abby.

Of course, that was his prerogative as my employer, but it meant much more to me. I wondered what would happen if I started to address him as Artemis.

We were living under the same roof, after

all. I washed and mended his clothes, I made his meals, and kept his records, but he never treated me like his servant.

I'd been saving my pay for a ticket back home to Kansas. But as my time with Monk went on, I felt less desire to leave. His home was beginning to feel more and more like mine, too.

One morning I was helping Monk with his elaborate sketches for an underground sewer system in Trouble — modeled after the one in Paris, France — when a man in a fancy suit and hat came in. Two men in decidedly less grand, and far dustier, attire stood behind him carrying some large rocks in their arms.

"Mr. Monk?" the dapper man asked, but he didn't wait for a reply. "My name is Jonas Dehner from San Francisco. I have a sample I'd like you to assay swiftly and at your earliest convenience."

"Now is fine," Monk said.

I pulled out our ledger, dipped a quill into the inkwell, and started to ask Dehner the usual questions.

"Where is your claim, Mr. Dehner?"

"It doesn't belong to me. It's the Jump Off Joe mine, which is presently owned by Mr. Ed Barkley and his associates."

We knew Ed. He came to Trouble about

the same time as Hank and I. He didn't have any money, so Zeb Graves, the owner of the general store, grub-staked him as he had so many others, in return for a share of any profits from the claim.

So far, Ed and his partners had done modestly well. But it was common knowledge that he didn't have the means to fully exploit the mine's possible potential.

It was a unique problem.

Because Ed and his partners were itinerant prospectors with no business background and no local roots, there was no bank willing to loan them the money to finance the digging of deep tunnels, the purchase of a stamping mill to crush the ore, and the hiring of additional labor.

So they either had to do it all themselves, slowly and laboriously over years, or sell out to someone with deeper pockets and move on.

It seemed prospectors got the short end even when they got lucky and found a solid claim.

"I know the mine," Monk said. "Are they looking to sell?"

"Indeed they are," Dehner said. "But don't worry, Mr. Monk. I'm not some rube. I brought my own powder to the mine, drilled my own holes in front of my eyes, and blasted my own drift to expose virgin stone, which I have with me here now."

"You're a cautious man," Monk said.

"I didn't get where I am by being stupid," Dehner said. "How long will the assay take?"

"A few hours," Monk said.

Dehner nodded. "Your reputation for integrity is well known, Mr. Monk. I mean no offense, but I'd like to post my men around your office to make sure no one can enter and, through some clever form of chicanery, tamper with your results. I would be glad, of course, to compensate you for any lost business."

"That won't be necessary," Monk said. "I admire your precautions."

Monk took the samples and retreated to his laboratory. I busied myself with various chores and the hours passed quickly. He emerged in the late afternoon and sent one of Dehner's men to find his employer. In the meantime, Monk refreshed himself with a hot cup of coffee and a pastry.

Dehner returned with Ed Barkley in tow. Ed looked more presentable than I'd ever seen him before. But with his new clothes and fresh-shaved face, he seemed gaunt and uncomfortable.

"I have good news, Mr. Dehner," Monk

said. "Your sample contains eighty ounces of gold per ton with some small copper and silver content. It's very rich ore."

Dehner beamed and so did Barkley, who almost seemed relieved.

"That's marvelous," Dehner said, clapping Barkley on the back.

"But since you are a man who values caution," Monk said, "I suggest that you do one more blast under my supervision to confirm the result."

"I don't see the point," Barkley said to Monk. "Unless you're looking to fatten yourself with another fee."

"There's no additional charge," Monk said. "I'm offering my counsel as a courtesy to a man who may soon become a valued member of our community."

"I would be indebted to you, sir," Dehner said to Monk and then looked to Barkley. "Unless you have an objection, Mr. Barkley."

"Of course not, Mr. Dehner," Barkley said. "You can blast the whole mountain if you like. I was just trying to save you from being cheated, that's all."

"I appreciate your concern," Dehner said, "but Mr. Monk has my complete trust."

"Where did you get your blasting powder?" Monk asked.

"From the general store," Dehner said.

"Then let's go there at once and get this over with," Monk said. The men started towards the door. As soon as their backs were turned to me, Monk whispered in my ear, "Bring the sheriff."

While Monk and the other men went to the general store, I dashed in the opposite direction to the sheriff's office.

I had no idea why Monk wanted to see the sheriff, but my heart was racing and it wasn't from the running.

Sheriff Wheeler was leaning back in a chair outside of the jail, his feet crossed on the hitching post. His hat was low over his closed eyes and he was snoring, making his bushy mustache wiggle like an enormous caterpillar. I was careful to make a lot of noise as I approached so as not to startle him.

"Sheriff?" I said.

"Good afternoon, Mrs. Guthrie," he said. "I wasn't napping. It's just mighty dusty in the street and I didn't want to get any of it in my eyes in case I need to shoot somebody."

"I understand," I said. "Mr. Monk needs to see you."

Wheeler sighed. "Let me guess. He saw two men share a drink from the same glass

305

and wants them both arrested and the glass destroyed."

"I think it's more serious than that," I said.

"A dog crapped in the street," Wheeler said. "He wants the dog arrested and the street destroyed."

I shook my head. "I don't know what it is, but he'd like you to meet him over at the general store. He's there with Ed Barkley and Jonas Dehner, a fellow from San Francisco who is interested in buying the Jump Off Joe dig."

"I'm always glad to meet another rich man from San Francisco."

The sheriff stood up, adjusted his hat, and we headed for the store.

We got there just as Zeb Graves and his boys were loading Dehner's wagon with the boxes of blasting rounds — black powder wrapped in paper cartridges — and a spool of Bickford slow match fuses.

Zeb wore a white shirt, a bow tie, and suspenders. His mustache was waxed thicker than a candle. His hair was always greased and his hands were sticky. I couldn't help but wonder what it felt like for his wife to lay beside him. Their bed must be as slick as a frying pan after cooking up a slab of bacon.

Monk smiled when he saw us approach.

"Perfect timing. Mr. Dehner, this is Sheriff Wheeler."

"Pleased to meet you, Sheriff," Dehner said and shook hands with the sheriff.

"Likewise," Wheeler said.

"Sheriff, you might want to draw your gun and keep it aimed on Ed Barkley and Zeb Graves," Monk said. "Mr. Dehner, your men should probably do the same."

"Why's that, Monk?" Sheriff Wheeler asked.

"Because Ed and Zeb robbed the Golden Rail Express," Monk said. "And I'm about to prove it."

Sheriff Wheeler drew his gun so fast it was as if it had appeared in his hand by magic. Dehner's men followed suit.

Ed and Zeb appeared startled by the sudden turn of events.

"That's just preposterous, Monk," Zeb blustered. "You've gone too far this time."

Monk went to the wagon and opened the box of blasting cartridges. "The Jump Off Joe mine has true potential, but you couldn't stand the thought of a buyer getting it for cheaper than you knew it was ultimately worth." Monk took out one of the blasting cartridges, cut the paper with a pocket knife, and poured the black powder onto the wagon bed. It sparkled with flakes of gold. "So you came up with a clever plan to salt it. What you didn't have was the gold to pull it off. You stole it from the Golden Rail Express."

"Everybody does a little salting," Ed said. "That's just business."

"It's chicanery," Dehner said.

"It's the way things are in the West," Zeb said to Dehner. "You didn't get rich without cheating somebody."

"You did more than that," Monk said to Zeb. "You held up the train, killed three people, and hammered the stolen gold into flakes to mix with the black powder."

"We didn't kill anybody and that gold didn't come from the Golden Rail Express," Zeb said. "It's dust I earned in my store."

Monk shook his head. "I was suspicious of the large flakes of gold in the assay sample, so I did a fineness test on them alone. They were 916.66 parts fine. I'm sure the gold in this powder will have the same results."

"So what?" Ed said.

"It's exactly the same gold and metal content as the coins produced by the U.S. Mint in San Francisco."

"I'll be damned," Wheeler said.

"The copper is used to harden the gold for coinage," Monk said.

Ed spit out an expletive and grimaced, his hands balling into fists. Zeb simply lowered his head and stared at his feet. They were hung and they knew it. The only questions that remained for them were when it would happen and whether it would be from gallows or a tree limb.

"It's devilish what gold does to a person's character." Dehner shook his head in disgust. "Isn't there a single honest man in this wretched country?"

"There's Artemis," I said, smiling at Monk and meeting his eye.

To my surprise, he didn't look away and returned my smile. "You've forgotten the sheriff, Abby."

"Oh my," I said. "That's true."

"I don't count," Wheeler said. "I'm paid to be honest."

"It's reassuring to know that somewhere honesty actually pays," Dehner said.

"It's not much," Wheeler said. "But at least I don't have to worry about getting hanged."

Adrian Monk shut the book.

I could barely keep my eyes open. But even in my painkiller-induced drowsiness, I couldn't mistake the expression on Monk's face. He was at peace.

"Artemis Monk is a genius," he said. "We must be related."

"What did you solve?" I asked, but my tongue was so thick, I'm afraid it came out sounding like this: *"Wffdddgliddddusoffflllllv?"*

But Monk must have understood me, because he smiled and said just one word that I carried with me into sleep . . .

"Everything."

# CHAPTER SEVENTEEN: MR. MONK'S ENDGAME

It was the pain that woke me up.

I was only vaguely aware of the discomfort at first, but it crept up on me, getting stronger and more difficult to ignore as the Vicodin wore off.

I tried to get comfortable, but my arm was in a sling and it hurt to make the slightest move. The bandaged fingers of my left hand throbbed where the nails once were. It felt like I had golf balls for fingertips. My scraped knees stung. Shifting the weight of my arm to my chest or to the mattress caused the ball of my shoulder to adjust, and the resulting pain was instant and intense.

I fought a hard, mental battle to stay asleep, to remain protected by the cocoon of slumber, but the pain demanded my attention, poking, stabbing, and screaming at me until my eyes flashed open.

I was sweating all over and, as odd as this

might sound, it didn't smell like me. I smelled like I'd fallen into my plate at an Indian restaurant. I figured it must be the Vicodin leaking out of my pores.

The room was dark, dimly lit by the glow of the parking lot lights through the closed drapes. The bathroom door was ajar and I could see that it was empty.

Where had Monk gone?

I turned my head and glanced at the clock radio. It was 7:37 p.m. An odd number. Monk wouldn't have liked that omen at all.

I'd slept through almost the entire day and for some reason that angered me. It's not like I'd slept through a busy schedule or that I'd put off necessary work. But I still wasn't happy about losing a day to a drugged stupor that left me in a curry flop-sweat. And I didn't like that I wasn't able to keep my eye on Monk, though I probably needed care more than he did.

My pills were laid out on a napkin on the nightstand alongside a bottle of Summit Creek water, a box of Wheat Thins, and a handwritten note from Monk.

The note looked as if it had come out of a laser printer. It had probably taken Monk hours to write.

Natalie,

I am sorry I couldn't be here when you awoke, but I had a train robbery and three murders to solve.

Here is your medication. Follow the directions on the bottle and take the pills with twenty Wheat Thins. Drink lots of liquids and get plenty of rest.

I will see you in the morning and tell you all about how the cases were solved.

Yours truly,
Adrian Monk

P.S. I have locked the movie channels as a precaution against you accidentally incurring extra charges in a drug-induced delirium. I recommend the wholesome and thrilling programming on the Weather Channel and the Game Show Network.

I took the pills, washed them down with water, and ate some Wheat Thins while I pondered the situation and waited for the Vicodin to kick in.

What was Monk thinking going off on his own? Didn't he realize how dangerous that was? What was the hurry? Why couldn't he wait until morning to wrap things up?

My last memory before falling asleep that afternoon was the satisfied look on Monk's face after he'd read to me from Abigail Guthrie's journal.

He'd solved Manny Feikema's murder, Clifford Adams' murder, and the robbery of the Golden Rail Express. But he was too damn egotistical and stubborn to just call Chief Kelton or Captain Stottlemeyer and let them handle it.

Then again, maybe I was wrong about that.

I snatched my cell phone off the nightstand and scrolled through the list of calls. Monk had made several outgoing calls while I was napping and Captain Stottlemeyer was one of them. That was a good sign. He'd made two other calls that, judging by the area code, were to people in Trouble.

It wasn't easy holding the phone with one hand and also pressing the keys with my bandaged fingertips. I dropped the phone a couple of times trying to key in the phone numbers and almost threw it against the wall in frustration.

I started by calling Stottlemeyer's office, but his phone was answered by a detective I didn't know who said that the captain was out. I asked for Lieutenant Disher and was told that he was out, too.

I tried to reach them both on their cell phones and got bumped to their voice mail each time. They were probably at a crime scene or shadowing some suspect.

That left the two local numbers. I dialed the first one and got the voice mail of the Trouble historical society. I didn't know why Monk had called Doris Thurlo, but I guessed that perhaps it was to double-check some facts about the Golden Rail Express robbery or even to learn more about Artemis Monk.

The other number connected me to the voice mail at the Gold Rush Museum. Now *that* was a disturbing development. Bob Gorman worked at the museum. He'd lied when he told us that Gator Dunsen came to town looking for Manny Fcikcma.

Did that mean Gorman was involved in the murders? Or did someone bribe him to lead us astray?

I didn't know the answers, but I hoped that Monk hadn't gone alone to the museum to ask Gorman those questions. But I didn't see any calls to Chief Kelton in my cell phone log and that made me very nervous.

I swung myself to the edge of the bed and stood up. I immediately wished that I hadn't. The swift movement must have sent a whole bunch of blood rushing to my arm. It hurt so bad that I sat right back down and cried.

I couldn't imagine what it must have felt like for Kelton after he'd dislocated his shoulder twice in one day. Was the pain he'd felt the same as mine? Or was it doubled? If so, no wonder the guy drank.

The pain ebbed and I stood up tentatively, but it didn't hurt so badly this time.

I went to my purse, retrieved Kelton's business card, and went back to the bed to give his office a call.

The dispatcher told me that he'd gone out for dinner. She asked if I wanted to leave a message but I figured a face-to-face meeting was probably better.

I was still wearing the surgical scrubs and didn't want to go through the trouble of getting dressed with one arm in a sling and one hand with bandaged fingertips. So I got my jacket, put my good arm through the sleeve, and then draped the rest over my other shoulder. I didn't even try to zip it up.

I slipped my purse strap over my head and draped my bag under my good arm. The strap served a double purpose — it also helped keep the right side of my jacket from slipping off my bad shoulder.

I'd kicked off my running shoes without untying them before getting onto the bed.

So I jammed my feet back inside them and managed, after some squirming, to get them on comfortably.

By the time I was done with all that, I was sweating all over. I won't tell you how bad I smelled.

I grabbed my room key and walked out.

The Vicodin was kicking in and the pain in my arm was morphing from a hot poker jammed in my armpit into the dull ache of a badly pulled muscle.

And even though I was being strangled by the two straps around my neck, one for the sling and the other for the purse, the pills seemed to take the edge off of that, too.

Ah, the wonders of modern pharmaceuticals.

I saw Kelton through the front window of the Chuckwagon. He was sitting with his back to me at the counter. I could see four other customers in the place.

The chief was talking to Crystal DeRosso, who looked at me as I came in like I was covered in vomit. It didn't make me feel very welcome but, in her defense, I must have been a horrifying sight in my sweat-stained scrubs with my pillow-pressed hair, bloodshot eyes, my arm in a sling, and bandages on my fingertips. And that's not even factoring in my lovely scent.

My breath probably smelled like a mountain goat's butt, too.

There was no mystery as to what drove Monk out of the motel room to solve the mystery right away.

It was me.

Kelton turned around to see what Crystal was staring at and seemed startled to see me standing in the doorway. I noticed that he was wearing his gun. That was good. He might need it tonight.

"Natalie, what are you doing out of bed?"

"I'm looking for Monk," I said. "Have you seen him?"

"No, I haven't. He isn't with you?"

"If he was, do you think I'd be here asking you where the hell he is?"

"You're right, that was a dumb question." He got off the stool and motioned to one of the empty booths. "Sit down and let me get you some coffee."

I didn't sit down. "Have you talked to him?"

"No, I haven't," he said. "Calm down, take a seat, and tell me what's got you so upset."

"Oh, I don't know, maybe it was being in a bloody shoot-out yesterday, or maybe it was having my fingernails ripped off and my arm yanked out of its socket while pulling Mr. Monk out of a pit, or maybe it was seeing a couple of vultures eat Clifford Adams for breakfast. It's really hard to say, Chief. So why don't you pick one for me?"

Everyone was staring at me now. The chief's face hardened and he opened the door.

"Let's have this conversation outside," he said. It wasn't a suggestion.

I walked past him into the parking lot. I glanced back and saw Crystal and the customers still watching us. I was tempted to flip them off, but I'm too ladylike for that.

"Okay, so Monk left the motel," Kelton said. "I'm sure it's no big deal. He probably just went out for a walk or to grab a bite to eat."

I would have shaken my head but the two straps lashed around my neck made it difficult to do without strangling myself.

"You're wrong," I said. "He's solved the Golden Rail Express robbery and Manny Feikema's murder and I think he's gone after the killer."

His eyebrows shot up so high they nearly went into earth orbit.

"Who is it?" he asked.

"I don't know," I said.

"Where's the stolen gold?"

"I don't know that, either."

"Then how do you know that Monk solved those crimes?"

"Because he told me he did, right before the drugs knocked me out," I said. "When I woke up, he was gone and he'd left me a note saying that he'd see me in the morning when it was all over. I'm afraid the over part could include his life."

The chief frowned and rubbed his chin. "Don't get melodramatic. Assuming you're right, and he has solved those cases, what makes you think he's in any danger?"

"He hasn't called you, which means he's going after Gorman alone."

"Gorman?" Kelton said. "What does Bob have to do with this?"

"He lied to us about Gator Dunsen coming to Trouble," I said.

"How do you know that?"

"Because there were no butterflies in the grill of Gator's car and the photos of the museum that were found in his house were taken *after* the murder," I said. "The prospector's pick wasn't in the shots of the diorama."

Kelton grimaced. "Why the hell didn't Monk tell me that yesterday at the crime scene?"

"He didn't want to embarrass you and get you into any more trouble than you were already in."

"I've had worse embarrassments on the job," he said. "The damn fool."

"What do we do now?"

"I don't know where Monk is, but I know where to find Bob," Kelton said. "I'll go talk with him. You go back to the motel and wait for me."

"The hell I will," I said.

"You're in no condition to go anywhere," Kelton said.

"I am not going back without Mr. Monk," I said and started walking purposefully towards the museum. "Let's go."

# Chapter Eighteen: Mr. Monk at the Museum

The clip-clop of our footfalls on the plank sidewalk underscored the emptiness of Trouble's dusty streets. With each step, I felt like I was traveling backward in time to the 1850s. I wouldn't have been surprised to bump into Artemis Monk and Abigail Guthrie, our historical doppelgangers, in the darkness.

It must have been the drugs working on my brain.

"What else do you know?" Kelton asked, walking at my side. I glanced at him and, for just a moment, I could see Sheriff Wheeler and his raccoon-sized mustache.

"That's it," I said.

"There's got to be more. I can't solve either crime based on what you've just told me and what we already know."

"Me neither," I said. "That's what makes Mr. Monk a genius. He sees things that we can't. What happened to Clifford Adams?"

"Someone clubbed him with a blunt object and dragged him out to those boulders. He'd been dead since about midnight."

"So Mr. Monk was right. The killer called me to lure us out there and used Adams as bait to get us to step on one of his booby traps."

"It certainly looks that way," Kelton said. "There were several pits out there covered with plywood and dirt. In fact, if you'd walked another few feet, you would have fallen in a pit yourself."

"Someone was afraid we knew who killed Manny Feikema or that we were close to figuring it out."

"It had to be Gorman," Kelton said. "He was the one who lied to us and sent us after Gator Dunsen."

"Not only that," I said. "Adams was at the museum last night."

"He was?"

"We saw him leave right before Gorman arrived. But Gorman saw him go, too. He was standing on this corner," I said as we rounded it and headed up Second Street. "Maybe Adams knew Gorman's motive for killing Manny and went there to confront him."

"You think that's what got Adams killed?"

"I hope not, because if it was, it doesn't

bode well for Mr. Monk."

But then it occurred to me that Bob Gorman couldn't have killed Clifford Adams. Gorman worked nights at the museum and had to log in with several sensors around the property to prove he was doing his rounds on time. Adams lived too far outside of town for Gorman to have gone out there and back without missing one of his rounds.

Gorman must have had an accomplice.

Or Gorman had nothing to do with the murders and had simply been paid to throw us off the trail by the killer.

Either way, there had to be another person in the mix. But who?

Crystal DeRosso immediately came to mind, mostly because her father may have been a train robber and Gorman was in her restaurant when he told us that whopper about Gator Dunsen.

Why would either Gorman or Crystal want Manny Feikema dead? What did Adams know that got him killed?

Just as I was pondering those questions, we reached the Gold Rush Museum. Kelton took a shiny new key from his pocket and unlocked the door.

"You have a key to the museum?" I asked.

"I'm the chief of police," he said with a smile. Then he opened the door and waved me inside. "After you."

I stepped into the dark museum. I could hear a strange, metallic scraping sound from somewhere in the shadows.

Kelton took one of those powerful little Maglites from his pocket, turned it on, and swept the area with the beam, briefly illuminating the rockers and sluices, the stagecoaches and carriages. The flashlight beam reflected off of the silver daguerreotypes on the wall and created ghostly faces that flashed in the darkness. It was creepy.

I followed Kelton as he weaved through the displays towards the Golden Rail Express. I was surprised that Gorman hadn't noticed our presence yet. He wasn't much of a security guard.

The closer we got to the train, the louder the scraping sound became, though it had an odd, echoish quality to it. It was like someone scratching a nail on the inside of a church bell.

Kelton stopped in front of the train. A light glowed inside.

"Bob," Kelton said. "I need to talk to you."

A moment later, Gorman emerged from the engine of the train. He was wearing a mechanic's jumpsuit, a miner's hat with a light in the center, and there was black schmutz on his cheek and hands.

Why wasn't he in his uniform? What was he doing mucking around in the train in that getup?

"What the hell is going on?" Gorman said.

Kelton drew his gun. "We're looking for Adrian Monk."

"He ain't here," Gorman said.

"I think you're wrong about that, Bob," Kelton said, then raised his voice. "Monk, this is Chief Kelton. I've got Natalie here with me. Come on out."

I heard some rustling behind us. Kelton aimed his flashlight at the prospecting diorama.

Monk emerged from the faux log cabin. He'd been hiding in there just like Manny's killer did. He was wearing his signature outfit and made his way around the mannequin miners and stuffed donkeys and over to us.

"I'm glad you're okay," I said.

"You look awful," Monk said. "You should have stayed in bed."

"You shouldn't have left me," I said. "I was worried about you and it turns out I was right to be. What were you hiding in here for?"

"I wanted to catch Gorman in the act."

"Of doing what?"

"Robbing the Golden Rail Express of its gold," Monk said.

I looked back at Gorman and then at the train. What Monk was suggesting didn't seem possible.

"It's *still* on the train?"

Monk nodded. "Slocum told us the truth. The third man was DeRosso. But what Slocum didn't know was that the boiler man and engineer were in on the robbery, too. DeRosso fell off the train after delivering the bags of cash and gold to Leonard McElroy and Clifford Adams in the engine."

"What did they do with it?" I asked.

"They threw it in the furnace, of course," Monk said. "That's why the bags were burlap, so they'd burn quickly."

I looked at Kelton, but he didn't seem shocked by Monk's explanation at all.

"It's really not as crazy as it sounds," Kelton said.

"Yes, it is," I said. "Throwing the bags in the furnace would have burned up all the money, too."

"They didn't care about the cash," Kelton said. "It was the gold that they wanted."

"How did they get the gold by throwing it in a furnace?"

"They melted the gold and lined the furnace with it, then hid it under a layer of black soot," Monk said. "But it wasn't necessary. It never occurred to anybody that the robbers would incinerate the loot."

"Until now," Kelton said.

"It wasn't until I read about how Artemis Monk, Trouble's legendary assayer back in the 1860s, solved another robbery on the Golden Rail Express that it all came together for me," Monk said. "In that case, the robbers hammered the gold coins into dust in a scheme to salt a mine. The plan got me thinking about Clifford Adams, his poorly performing mine, and something he said about how malleable gold is."

"Maybe it's the drugs I'm on," I said. "But I still don't understand why they burned the bags and melted the gold."

"The train was supposed to be scrapped after that last run. They were planning to recover the furnace afterwards, scrape the gold out, and make it appear as if it came from Clifford Adams' mine," Monk said. "Nobody would have known that the gold actually came from the train robbery."

I could see now why reading Abigail Guthrie's journal made everything fall into place for Monk. And it was happening in my mind, too. All the pieces of the puzzle fit together. I could almost hear them snapping into place.

"Their plan might have worked except for one unforeseeable twist of fate," I said. "The robbery made the Golden Rail Express famous, and instead of being decommissioned, the train continued in operation for another twenty years. They couldn't get the gold off the train."

"They were screwed," Kelton said, nodding in agreement. "But they weren't going to give up. They had the gold. They just had to wait things out. So they kept on working. McElroy shoveled coal into that golden furnace year after year until the soot finally killed the poor bastard."

"But there was still one more cruel twist left," I said. "All those years of protecting their treasure and waiting were for nothing. When the train was finally scrapped, the museum snapped up the engine and there was no way that Adams could ever recover his gold."

"What a bunch of losers," Gorman said.

I'd almost forgotten that Gorman was still standing there. Monk pointed at him.

"You killed Manny Feikema so you could get his job and spend your nights scraping the gold out of the furnace," Monk said. "But there was only one way I could prove it."

I glanced at Gorman's dirty hands and

remembered him washing the soot off at the restaurant. The answer had been right in front of us all along.

Then again, it usually was.

I never would have guessed that Gorman was smart enough to solve the Golden Rail Express mystery. Monk had taken a huge, and very stupid, risk setting his trap.

"If you wanted to catch Gorman in the act," I said to Monk, "why did you come alone? Why didn't you bring Chief Kelton with you?"

I glanced back at Kelton. And that's when I noticed that the gun that he held wasn't actually aimed at Gorman.

It was aimed at me.

# CHAPTER NINETEEN: MR. MONK AND THE SURPRISE

I felt shocked, betrayed, stupid, and angry all at once.

*"You?"* I said to him.

"Sorry to disappoint you," Kelton said. "If it's any consolation, I'm not too proud of myself, either. I never anticipated things spiraling out of control like this."

"Then how did it happen at all?"

"I had a lot of time on my hands when I got to this hellhole. At first, I was just trying to find a way out of the boredom that didn't involve looking at the bottom of an empty bottle of Scotch. So I started investigating the robbery. I'm a pretty good detective when I'm sober."

"You had some help from my distant relative," Monk said. "I talked to Doris Thurlo today. She told me that you'd read Abigail Guthrie's journal a few weeks ago."

"I did. And it wasn't long after I read it that I figured out what happened to the

331

gold," Kelton said. "But if I told the museum about it, I wouldn't get to keep any of it. I didn't think that was very fair. So I thought of a way to get the gold without the museum knowing that it had ever been there."

"Did you go to Manny first with your scheme?" I asked.

"There was no point," Kelton said. "I knew Manny well enough to know that he'd never go for it. That's a shame, because if he wasn't going to help me, that didn't leave me much choice."

"You could have given up the idea of keeping the gold for yourself," I said.

"Yeah, right," Gorman said. "Are you on drugs?"

"As a matter of fact," I said, "I am."

It was probably the only reason I wasn't terrified, even though the homicidal chief of police was holding a gun on me.

"So you went forward with it," Monk said to Kelton. "But since you couldn't get the gold yourself, you had to draft an accomplice for the grunt work."

"I resent that," Gorman said. "I'm nobody's grunt. This is a full partnership."

"That's true," Monk said. "You are both murderers. You killed Manny Feikema and the chief killed Clifford Adams."

"How did you make that leap?" Kelton said.

"I found this on the road to Clifford Adams' place." Monk reached into his jacket pocket and came out with a piece of white, decorative rock pinched between his thumb and index finger. "You parked behind Gator's car in the gravel driveway and got this stuck in one of your tire treads. It was knocked loose when you hit that pothole on your way to kill Clifford Adams."

I felt my face getting hot as the full implications of Monk's words sunk in. I glared at him, hoping he could feel the full heat of my fury from the look in my eyes.

"You knew that Kelton was the killer since this morning and you didn't say anything to me?"

"I've actually known he was guilty of at least one murder since yesterday at Gator Dunsen's house," Monk said. "But I couldn't prove it."

"That makes it even worse!" I yelled.

Kelton stuck his gun in my back. "Quiet down."

"You didn't just keep me in the dark," I said in the loudest, angriest whisper I could manage. "You lied to me."

Gorman grinned at Kelton. "Can you believe these two?"

"I knew you were attracted to him," Monk said. "And I couldn't risk you inadvertently tipping him off about my suspicions during one of your intimate dinners."

"Intimate!" My face was so hot with anger that it was a wonder that I didn't spontaneously combust. "We had a cheeseburger at the Chuckwagon. There wasn't anything remotely intimate about our dinner and I sure as hell wasn't the least bit interested in him."

"Yes, you were," Kelton said.

I whirled around to face him. "You wish."

Kelton smiled. "Then why did you feel so betrayed when Monk told you I was behind this?"

"Because I trusted you," I said.

"Because you wanted me," Kelton said. "I knew it, Monk knew it —"

"I knew it," Gorman added. "Crystal knew it."

"The burros on the street knew it," Kelton said.

The infuriating thing was that he was right. I was attracted to him, damn it. Not that I would have acted on it. But even so, it was pretty humiliating to have been interested in a killer and then to have him mock me.

I looked down at the gun he was pointing

at my abdomen and it focused me back to what mattered. I was standing with a killer who probably had no intention of letting us walk out of this museum alive.

Our best chance to survive was to keep him talking until Monk or I figured out a way to escape. We couldn't really hope that the police would come to our rescue, not with the corrupt police chief holding a gun on us. Maybe there was a superhero in the neighborhood who would realize our deadly predicament and come crashing through the ceiling at the right moment.

There wasn't much hope for us, but I was going to stall anyway.

"Why did you kill Adams?" I asked.

"After you two talked to him, he got suspicious," Kelton said. "So Adams came to the museum to stick his head in the furnace and check on his gold. He saw that somebody had started scraping out the gold and he put the whole thing together. At least, that's what I think happened. When Bob saw him leaving the museum last night, I had to assume the worst and stop the old fool from doing something stupid."

"It wasn't hard for the chief to kill Clifford Adams," Monk said. "He was an experienced murderer by then. He'd just killed Gator Dunsen and tried to frame him for

Manny Feikema's murder."

"It would have worked." Kelton glanced at Gorman. "If somebody hadn't screwed up the pictures and left the pick out of the diorama."

"Oh," Gorman said, realizing his mistake. "Well, you're the detective. You should have noticed that the pick wasn't there when you reviewed the photos. It's your fault, not mine."

For an instant, it looked like Kelton might shoot Gorman instead of me and all of this stalling would have paid off. But the moment passed.

"It doesn't matter now," Kelton said. "Nobody but Monk caught the mistake and he's not going to be around to tell anybody about it."

"How did you plant the file of photos in Gator's house?" I asked.

"He didn't," Monk said. "Gorman did. He was already in the house when we arrived."

"He was?" I said.

"He'd been there for a while," Monk said. "My guess is that Gorman forced Gator at gunpoint to drink himself into a stupor and then bound him with duct tape. It was Gorman who shot up the front door. Once we took cover, and Kelton was in the house, all the gunshots we heard, except the one that killed Gator, were for show. They used the time to stage the scene, take the duct tape off of Gator, and cover Gorman's escape out the back door."

"Gator's bleeding lips," I said. "That's how you knew his mouth had been taped."

Monk nodded. "He had chapped lips. When they ripped the tape off his mouth, it tore off the dry skin."

"There, now you have closure," Kelton said. "That's one less thing for you to worry about in your final moments, which will be coming shortly."

"You're going to shoot us right here?" I said. "You'll have a hard time explaining that away."

Kelton shook his head. "You're going to die in a terrible car accident tonight on your way back to San Francisco. You never should have let Monk drive, Natalie. At least, that's what everybody will be saying at the funeral. But I'll speak up for you and remind everyone what terrible shape you were in, physically and mentally."

"How considerate," I said.

"Don't worry, Natalie," Monk said. "We aren't going to be hurt."

"How do you figure that?" Gorman said.

"Because the moment Chief Kelton

stepped into the museum, a special weapons and tactical unit from the California State Police moved into position," Monk said. "They've got the building surrounded."

Kelton grinned. "Are you sure it's just the California State Police? Maybe the FBI and National Guard came, too."

"They couldn't make it," a familiar voice said, filling me with relief. "But the San Francisco Police showed up."

The lights came on in the museum and I saw Captain Stottlemeyer inside the stage-coach behind Kelton and aiming his gun at the chief.

"And we've got everything on tape," Lieutenant Randy Disher said, bursting out of the back office with Detective Lydia Wilder and several California State Police officers. All of them had their weapons out and trained on Kelton and Gorman.

Of course, that left Monk and me in the cross fire, but I didn't think too much about that. In the tense moment that followed, I thought about those calls Monk made from my cell phone to the museum and Captain Stottlemeyer. Now I knew what they were about and why I couldn't reach the captain when I tried to call him — he was busy hiding out in the museum with Monk.

I should have known that Monk would

never have tried to take on Gorman alone. I blamed the painkillers for impairing my ordinarily sound judgment.

Kelton dropped his gun and put his hands on his head. Gorman raised his hands, too. Stottlemeyer climbed out of the stagecoach and took out his handcuffs.

"You're both under arrest for the murders of Manny Feikema, Gator Dunsen, and Clifford Adams," the captain said.

"I want to make a deal," Gorman said.

Kelton chuckled ruefully. "That's got to be a new speed record for one crook selling out another."

"I'll be sure to notify the Guinness people," Stottlemeyer said and handcuffed Chief Kelton.

# CHAPTER TWENTY: MR. MONK GETS IN TROUBLE IN TROUBLE

An hour or so later, Monk and I were sitting in a booth in Dorothy's Chuckwagon. I was having a cheeseburger, French fries, and a milk shake. He was having toast.

Stottlemeyer and Disher were still busy with Detective Wilder and the state police. But I knew that they planned on spending the night at our motel and that Disher would drive Monk and me back to San Francisco in my car in the morning.

The two of us sat in an uncomfortable silence while we ate. At least I hope it was uncomfortable for Monk. I wasn't very happy with him and I wanted to be sure that he knew it.

Crystal DeRosso came over to our table and set an entire uncut apple pie down between us.

"It's on the house," she said. "It's a small token of my thanks for solving the Golden Rail Express robbery, though I can't say I'm thrilled to find out that my father was a crook after all."

"You have nothing to be ashamed of," Monk said. "You had nothing to do with his crimes."

"But I feel stupid having defended him all these years," she said.

"You were his daughter," I said. "You loved him. Of course you defended him."

"So did the town," she said. "I feel bad for them, too."

"You shouldn't," I said. "Once the news gets out about the discovery of the gold, business here is going to boom. I'm sure that every major network will have a news crew here by this time tomorrow. Trouble will become a tourist destination again."

"If you're right, that will be the second time the robbery of that train has rejuvenated this town," she said. "It's kind of sad."

Her comment reminded me that we had to call Jake Slocum and tell him how it all turned out. Once word got out about the discovery of the gold, and that one of the original robbers was still alive, he was likely to become a minor celebrity. He might enjoy that.

"You'll just have to find a way to rob that train every fifty years," I said.

"Don't give them any ideas," Monk said.

"Now that there's a fortune in gold on the train, the museum is going to have to make a significant investment in security measures. The gold is going to become an attractive target for thieves."

"How could anybody steal the furnace out of that train?" Crystal asked. "It must weigh a ton."

Monk shrugged. "Never underestimate the cleverness of the criminal mind."

"You're right," I said. "Maybe in fifty years they can beam it out."

"Beam it out?" Monk said. "What's that mean?"

"You know, like 'Beam me up, Scotty'?" I said. "The transporter beam?"

Monk stared at me blankly.

"It's from *Star Trek,*" Crystal said.

Monk stared at her blankly.

"You ought to join our culture, Mr. Monk," I said. "It's fun."

Crystal smiled and went to wait on other customers, leaving Monk and me alone. I nibbled on my French fries.

"It was nice of her not to cut the pie," Monk said. "But now we're in a fix. I'm not sure how we're going to do it accurately. I hope this will teach you to never leave the house without a compass, string, a T square, and a level."

"Me?" I said.

"Yes, you."

"Why me?"

"Because it's your job as my trusty assistant to help me be prepared for any situation."

"Trusty?" I set down my fry and pinned him with a look so cold that it made him lean back. "If you trust me so much, you wouldn't have withheld information and lied to me."

"We've been over that already," Monk said. "At gunpoint."

"Not everything," I said. "I'm not so drugged up that I didn't notice how you used me."

"You're paid for that," Monk said.

"Not to be used like this," I said. "You knew I'd go looking for you and bring Kelton with me."

"Why do you say that?"

"Because otherwise you would have arrested Gorman as soon as he started scraping the gold off that furnace," I said. "But you didn't. You were waiting for Kelton and me to show up."

Monk couldn't even look at me. "I don't know where you got that idea."

"You told me in the museum. You said the police surrounded the building after Kelton came in," I said. "They wouldn't have waited for him to enter unless they'd been expecting him all along."

"Oh," Monk said. "That's where you got the idea."

"You took advantage of my concern for you to lure Kelton into a trap."

"And your attraction to him," Monk said.

"I was *not* attracted to him," I said, but my protest sounded hollow. "Don't you dare try to change the subject by putting me on the defensive. You're the one who has some explaining to do."

"You were never in danger," Monk said. "The state police had you under surveillance from the moment you left the motel."

"That's not the point, Mr. Monk. You tricked me, lied to me, and used me. Is that your idea of trust?"

"Chief Kelton murdered three people," Monk said. "I had to stop him, for the greater good and to make things right, even if that meant irritating you a little bit."

"Look at me, Mr. Monk. I dislocated my shoulder, tore off my fingernails, and scratched up my knees saving your life today. But none of that hurts me as much as your betrayal of *my* trust in you."

Monk reached into his pocket and set a Wet Ones packet on the table.

"That's not going to help," I said.

"What do you want from me?"

"What do you think?"

"I can't afford a raise," he said.

I threw a French fry in his face. I don't think I could have startled him more if I'd poured a bucket of ice water over his head.

"What was that for?" he said.

I threw another French fry in his face.

"How many of those pills did you take?" he exclaimed.

I threw two French fries at him this time so he couldn't avoid getting smacked with one even if he dodged the other.

"Okay, okay." He held up his hands in surrender. "I'm sorry. I shouldn't have used you like that."

I picked up another French fry and prepared to toss it.

"And I promise I'll never do it again," Monk said. "I was wrong — very, very wrong."

I set the French fry down. Monk sighed with relief.

"That's a start," I said.

Stottlemeyer and Disher came in and approached our table.

"Did I just see you throwing French fries at Monk?" Stottlemeyer said.

"Yes, you did," I said.

"What for?" Disher asked.

"Some consideration," I said.

"Seeing you do that was worth the drive out here all by itself," Stottlemeyer said.

Monk slid out of the booth. "Excuse me, I have to go."

"Why?" Disher said.

"Look at me, I am soaked in grease," Monk said. "Are you blind? What kind of detective are you?"

He marched off in a huff. Stottlemeyer and Disher watched him go, then they both slid onto the bench that he'd vacated across from me.

"Feeling better?" Stottlemeyer asked me.

"I'm getting there," I said. "It's going to take a little while."

"When Monk called today and told me his plan, I warned him that you'd be pissed," Stottlemeyer said. "But he felt that catching Kelton was more important than your feelings."

"What did you say?" I asked.

"I told Monk that I completely understood how he felt," Stottlemeyer said. "And that's probably why my wife left me and I haven't had a single successful relationship with a woman since then."

"There was that real estate agent, Linda Fusco," Disher said, eating one of the

French fries off the table. "Things were going great with her."

"Until she was arrested for murder," Stottlemeyer said.

"That wasn't your fault," Disher said. "You held up your end of the relationship."

"So I may have some problems in my relationships with women," Stottlemeyer said, "but at least I've done all right dating murderers."

Disher nodded. "You've got to keep a positive outlook. That's key."

"Thanks, Randy, for that helpful insight," Stottlemeyer said.

"No problem," Disher said and looked at me as he tipped his head towards the pie. "Are you going to eat all of that?"

"I was planning to share it with some friends," I said with a smile. "And they just got here."

Monk would have been shocked watching us eat that pie. We didn't bother to cut out individual pieces. We dug into it with our forks, devouring it. He would have found it uncivilized, unsanitary, unbalanced, and probably immoral.

While we ate, I told Stottlemeyer and Disher about our adventures in Trouble and how they dovetailed with the experiences of Artemis Monk, which led to Adrian Monk solving a fifty-year-old robbery and three murders.

"It's like there's two Monks," Disher said. "Our Monk and his identical twin in an alternate, Western universe."

"It's not like that at all," Stottlemeyer said. "Artemis Monk really existed one hundred fifty years ago."

"But what if past and present don't come one before the other," Disher said. "What if they co-exist?"

"They don't," Stottlemeyer said. "The present wouldn't exist without the past. The present is the result of past events."

"But what if you're wrong?" Disher said.

"I'm not," Stottlemeyer said.

This was like a conversation I might have had while I was high on pot in college. We weren't on dope, but we were definitely on a sugar high.

"What if this town sits on the precipice between two dimensions, like Sunnydale is with Hellmouth."

"Where is Sunnydale?" Stottlemeyer asked.

The three of us were crossing our forks like swords in a fencing patch as we scrounged for the last bits of tasty crust and the few remaining drops of the sugary filling in the pan.

"It's the California town where Buffy the Vampire Slayer lives," Disher said. "Trouble could be Monk's Hellmouth."

"Everywhere is Monk's Hellmouth," I said.

"So whatever happened to Artemis Monk and his assistant?" Stottlemeyer asked me.

"I don't know," I replied.

"If I were you, I wouldn't leave town until I found out," Stottlemeyer said.

"We're leaving tomorrow morning, no matter what," I said, sitting back and dropping my fork. I was done and the pan was empty.

"Don't you have to return that book first?" Disher said, picking up the pan to retrieve the last few crumbs with a moist fingertip.

"Yes," I said. "I was just going to drop it off and run."

"You aren't in any shape to run," Disher said.

"Your talk with the local historian should be interesting," Stottlemeyer said.

"Who said we were going to have a talk?"

"Maybe I'll tag along," he said.

"Me, too," Disher said, setting down the pan.

"You have to," I said. "You're driving."

"That reminds me," Stottlemeyer said.

"The story of how you pulled Monk out of that pit, and what you did to yourself doing it, is pretty amazing. You're one tough lady."

"I don't feel so tough."

"You look it," Disher said.

"I'll take that as a compliment," I said.

"I've got one question, though," Disher said. "How did you get your pants back on with a torn-up hand and a dislocated shoulder?"

"Let's not go into that," I said.

"I don't know if I can get the picture out of my head of you lying out there in your underwear," Disher said.

I picked up my glass of ice water and hurled the contents in his face. "Does that help?"

Crystal looked at me sternly from behind the counter. I was throwing more food and drinks than a three-year-old having a tantrum and I looked like a homeless drunkard. I doubted I'd be welcomed back into the Chuckwagon again anytime soon, no matter how grateful she was to Monk for solving the mystery of the Golden Rail Express.

"Yes," Disher said, dabbing his soaked face with a napkin. "Thanks."

Stottlemeyer grinned. "I am so glad that I came to Trouble."

# CHAPTER
# TWENTY-ONE:
# MR. MONK SETS THE
# WORLD RIGHT

I went back to my own motel room for the night, which Monk had thoughtfully cleaned for me while I was at dinner.

I'm sure that he did it in an attempt to make amends, but he still had a long way to go as far as I was concerned.

I climbed into bed without bothering to change out of my stinking scrubs and fell fast asleep.

But I slept fitfully, tortured by my various injuries, and awoke at seven a.m. stiff, in pain, and with a pounding headache from a sugar hangover.

I quickly took my pills and washed them down with some Summit Creek water and a handful of Wheat Thins to deaden the pain and quell my headache.

That's when I noticed how much I reeked and how sticky my skin was. I desperately needed a shower, but I wasn't looking forward to the struggle and the pain that would be involved in pulling that off.

But there was no way around it. You wouldn't have to be as sensitive as Monk to find me repulsive to see and to smell.

I couldn't even stand to be around myself.

So I girded myself for the ordeal to come, sat up slowly, and I went to the bathroom to do what had to be done.

I won't bore you with the details, but let's just say that showering and dressing involved all kinds of obstacles, physical contortions, extreme discomfort, and loud, vulgar profanity.

When I finally emerged from my motel room at nine thirty, I found Monk, Stottlemeyer, and Disher waiting patiently for me in the front lobby. Disher was even kind enough to go back to my room, get my suitcase, and put it in the trunk of my car. I guess he was trying to make amends for his bad behavior, too.

We decided as a group to skip breakfast in favor of catching an early lunch on the road. The sooner we got out of Trouble, the better, as far as Monk and I were concerned.

I got into my car with Disher. Monk insisted on riding with Stottlemeyer for safety reasons. He thought it would be dangerous to have three people in one car and that it would be much better to have two in each.

I was expecting that, but I think Monk was also afraid that I might give him another lashing on the road if he rode with me.

On the way out of town, we stopped at the historical society to drop off Abigail Guthrie's journal.

Doris Thurlo was very pleased to see the four of us. She'd heard all about what happened the previous night, of course. The parallels between the crimes Monk solved and Artemis Monk's cases weren't lost on her. Nor were the similarities between me, Stottlemeyer, and Disher to the people in Artemis Monk's life.

"It's like a balance has been created between past and present," Doris said. "It's an almost perfect symmetry."

"I like that idea," Monk said. "It feels right."

"There's a surprise," Stottlemeyer said.

"Some would call it destiny," Doris said.

"Do you know what happened to Artemis Monk and Abigail Guthrie?" Stottlemeyer asked, studying the daguerreotype of Artemis Monk on the wall.

"Throughout the rest of the 1850s and well into the 1860s, yes. There are several more journals from Abigail Guthrie that recount their adventures during that period," Doris said. "But not surprisingly, it ends abruptly after that."

"Why is that not a surprise?" Disher asked.

"The Gold Rush had ended and most of the prospectors and miners moved on to strikes in other places, like Nevada and Alaska," she said. "And the gold that was left was increasingly difficult and expensive to get to. Most Gold Rush towns withered and died, and Trouble nearly joined them. So there wasn't much assaying for Monk to do, and that was how he made his living. Investigating crimes was more of a hobby."

"Well, that was very interesting and informative. Good day," Monk said and headed for the door.

"So they moved to San Francisco after they got married," Doris said.

Monk stopped dead in his tracks.

"Monk married his assistant?" Disher said, clearly amused. So was Stottlemeyer. I wasn't.

"That's what they say," Doris said.

"Do they?" Stottlemeyer said with a grin.

"I don't have a marriage certificate or anything like that to confirm it," Doris said. "But it's pretty common knowledge. I believe there are some references to his assistant, Mrs. Monk, in other accounts from that period."

Stottlemeyer turned to Monk, who appeared mortified. I could sympathize.

"If you really want to maintain the crucial balance between past and present, you know what you have to do," the captain said.

I wished I had a French fry or a glass of water or a big cream pie to throw at Stottlemeyer. But I didn't. All I could do was give him the nastiest look I could muster, which I'm sure made me appear constipated on top of everything else, and that only seemed to amuse him even more.

Even Doris was grinning like an idiot.

"That's totally outside the realm of possibility," Monk said.

"I agree," I said.

"I'm sure Abigail Guthrie thought the same thing," Doris said. "But love finds a way."

"It will have to find another way," I said and headed for the door, which Monk opened for me.

"I agree," he said.

And we walked out.

"The past is the past," I said. "It has nothing to do with us."

"Besides, there's no evidence that Artemis Monk and his assistant got married," Monk said. "It's just scandalous hearsay."

"Because it didn't happen," I said.

"It couldn't have," Monk said.

"Why not?"

"Because it would upset the perfect balance."

"What perfect balance?"

"The one that they had," he said. "And that we have. I wouldn't do anything to upset that."

I stopped at my car. "Why is that, Mr. Monk?"

"Because it means too much to me."

With my good arm I reached out and gave him a hug. To my surprise, he didn't stiffen up or resist. He even gently patted my back.

That's when Stottlemeyer and Disher came out of the historical society. Disher started humming "Here Comes the Bride." I promised myself that I'd make him pay for that. I didn't know how yet, but I would find a way.

"Did Monk already pop the question?" Stottlemeyer asked me.

"You keep this up and I'm going to pop you," I said and then turned back to Monk. "You're forgiven."

"Thank you, Natalie," he said, obviously very relieved.

"But I'm taking the rest of the week off," I said. "Maybe next week, too."

"Why?" Monk asked.

"Because I've got a dislocated shoulder and a bad left hand," I said, trying not to get annoyed and ruin the sweet moment we'd just had. "I need to recuperate."

"You can recuperate with me," he said. "You'll need someone to take care of you."

I was touched. "You'd do that?"

"To a degree," he said.

"What's that mean?" I asked.

"Whatever you can't do for me I'll do for myself."

"And what about the things that I can't do for *my*self?"

"Don't do them," he said. "Problem solved."

"I don't think that's going to work," I said.

Stottlemeyer turned to Disher. "Listen to them. They sound like an old married couple already."

"They always have," Disher said, walking around to the driver's side of my car. "I'll take the lead. You can follow us."

"No," Stottlemeyer said, walking to the driver's side of his car. "I think it's better if you follow my car."

"Why?" Disher said.

"Because I'm in an official police vehicle and you're not," Stottlemeyer said. "If I speed a bit, you can, too."

"Wouldn't it work the same way if you were behind me while I was speeding?"

"No," Stottlemeyer said.

"Why not?" Disher said.

"Because I say so!" Stottlemeyer said, getting into the car and slamming the door.

"We'll see about that!" Disher said, getting into my car and slamming the door.

"Those two are always arguing," Monk said, shaking his head with disapproval. "They could learn a thing or two about cooperation and mutual respect from us."

"Like what?" I said.

"That I'm right all of the time," Monk said. "And you're right the rest."

"You're probably right," I said.

"I know I am," he said and got into the car, obviously pleased with himself and certain that the universe was in balance once again.

Maybe he was right about that, too.

# ABOUT THE AUTHOR

**Lee Goldberg** has written episodes for the USA Network television series *Monk,* as well as many other programs. He is a two-time Edgar® Award nominee and the author of the acclaimed *Diagnosis Murder* novels, based on the TV series for which he was a writer and executive producer. His previous *Monk* novels are available in paperback, including *Mr. Monk and the Two Assistants,* which won the Scribe Award for Best Novel from the International Association of Media Tie-In Writers.